SHARON
SALA

GOING
GONE

Recycling programs
for this product may
not exist in your area.

ISBN-13: 978-0-7783-1659-6

Going Gone

H HARLEQUIN®
™ www.Harlequin.com

Printed in U.S.A.

Praise for the novels of

SHARON
SALA

"Vivid, gripping...this thriller keeps the pages turning."
—*Library Journal* on *Torn Apart*

"Sala's characters are vivid and engaging."
—*Publishers Weekly* on *Cut Throat*

"Sharon Sala is not only a top romance novelist,
she is an inspiration for people everywhere
who wish to live their dreams."
—John St. Augustine, host,
Power!Talk Radio WDBC-AM, Michigan

"Veteran romance writer Sala lives up to her reputation
with this well-crafted thriller."
—*Publishers Weekly* on *Remember Me*

"[A] well-written, fast-paced ride."
—*Publishers Weekly* on *Nine Lives*

"Perfect entertainment for those looking for
a suspense novel with emotional intensity."
—*Publishers Weekly* on *Out of the Dark*

Also by Sharon Sala

Forces of Nature

GOING TWICE
GOING ONCE

The Rebel Ridge novels

'TIL DEATH
DON'T CRY FOR ME
NEXT OF KIN

The Searchers series

BLOOD TRAILS
BLOOD STAINS
BLOOD TIES

The Storm Front trilogy

SWEPT ASIDE
TORN APART
BLOWN AWAY

THE WARRIOR
BAD PENNY
THE HEALER
CUT THROAT
NINE LIVES
THE CHOSEN
MISSING
WHIPPOORWILL
ON THE EDGE
   "Capsized"
DARK WATER
OUT OF THE DARK
SNOWFALL
BUTTERFLY
REMEMBER ME
REUNION
SWEET BABY

Originally published as Dinah McCall

THE RETURN

When you live life on the edge and in constant pursuit of one goal, you are missing what matters most. Once time is spent, it's not the pot of gold you found at rainbow's end that you will remember. It's the people you met and the life you lived along the way.

Time is precious, going once through childhood; going twice as fast as your teenage years fly by. And once you walk into the world of an adult, life flies by before you know it; going once, going twice, going gone.

I dedicate this book to dreamers like me, the ones who remember the trip better than the destination.

GOING
GONE

One

The climax slammed into Laura Doyle so fast that she lost her mind. She heard Cameron groan as he let go and went with her, riding the bliss of pure lust. She threw her head back and laughed as the last shudder rolled through her. Making love to him was the most wonderful thing that had ever happened to her, and she didn't ever want it to stop.

"That, my love, was amazing," she said as she locked her fingers around his neck.

"Am I really your love?"

"Yes, yes, a thousand times yes...forever and ever," she said as she pulled him down for one last kiss.

It was the scream of someone shouting Laura's name that woke her, but within seconds she'd gone from the afterglow of a sexy dream to heart-pounding fear as she scrambled to tighten her seat belt. The private jet she'd boarded in Los Angeles was in trouble.

An alarm was sounding inside the cockpit, and the pilot, Ken Price, was shouting at everyone to buckle up.

God in heaven, they were going down!

Marcy, her friend and coworker, who was sitting across the aisle, was crying as she tried to text someone on her cell phone. Laura thought of her sister, Sarah, and then of Cameron, but there was no time for goodbyes. She could hear someone praying, and the nose of the plane was no longer level with the horizon.

Marcy gave her a frantic look and tossed her a folded blanket. Laura caught it in midair and put it in her lap only seconds before she assumed the crash position. Her last conscious thought was that the blanket smelled like mouthwash, and then—*impact!*

It was pain, rolling, stabbing, unbelievable misery like nothing Laura ever felt, that woke her next. Something wet was running down the side of her face, and she couldn't figure out why the house was so dark. She reached for the bedside table to turn on the light, felt hair and then the side of someone's face, and imagined an intruder had broken into her house, and screamed until the back of her throat closed up from the panic.

The moan that followed was not her own, and that was when she remembered the plane crash. The fact that she was not about to be murdered in bed was a relief, but that she might die in this wreckage after living through the crash was not. The scent of an electrical short was strong, although she couldn't see any flames. She heard another moan, followed by a short, choking gasp.

"Marcy, is that you? Dan? Ken? Anyone?"

No one answered.

"Please, God, don't let this be happening," she whispered, and then realized she was shaking, but not from shock.

It was cold-to-the-bone freezing inside the cabin. She didn't know where they'd crashed, but it was February, and if they had gone down in the Rockies, her troubles had just grown exponentially.

She began fumbling at her waist, trying to undo her seat belt and find the blanket that had been in her lap. In moments she discovered she was flat on her back on the floor between the seats, which meant it was probably Marcy on the floor beside her. She shook her friend's shoulder, trying to get her to wake up.

"Marcy! Where are the blankets? We need the blankets. Can you find yours?"

Marcy didn't say anything, and Laura felt the first symptoms of hypothermia setting in.

"I did not survive this plane crash just to freeze to death," she mumbled, and tried to get up, but her leg was caught, and it was too dark to see how to free herself. Moments later something shifted above her, and she threw her arms up in defensive mode just as a duffel bag fell out of an overhead compartment and onto her chest. The sudden impact sent a pain through her body that was so strong she passed out. When she woke up again, the bag was still on her chest and she was struggling to breathe. If her ribs hadn't been injured in the crash, they were now. Every breath she took hurt, and she was getting light-headed from the pain. She had to find something to keep her warm, or next time she passed out, she might never wake up.

After a few moments of fumbling, she managed to unzip the bag and then began digging among the items until she found what seemed to be a heavy bath towel. When she felt an insignia embroidered in the terry cloth, she guessed this was the complimentary bathrobe that had been on the hook inside each hotel bathroom. This must be Dan's bag. He was notorious for taking things from hotels and then wondering why his credit card bill was higher than everyone else's.

Her hands were trembling as she covered herself with the robe. After that she began piling the rest of the garments from inside the bag on top of the robe, layer after layer. The scent of Dan's aftershave was the last thing she smelled as she passed out again.

The next time she woke up it was morning, and Marcy had rolled away and was lying on her side just out of Laura's reach.

"Marcy! Marcy! Can you hear me?"

Marcy didn't answer.

Laura pushed aside the covers to look at herself and then gasped. Her arms and hands were covered in dried blood, and her fingers were trembling as she began a self-examination.

Her chest hurt—a lot. The blood on her forehead was dried, and her leg was still trapped and aching terribly. When she heard something scratching at the outside of the plane her heart soared. Surely that was their rescuers, already on scene.

"Help! Help! We're in here!" she cried, but no one answered, and the scratching stopped.

When she realized it wasn't people making that noise and they were not being rescued, she broke down in tears, sobbing from pain and disappointment. It took her a few minutes to get her emotions under control and focus on getting free. Now that it was daylight, she could see how to remove the debris under which she'd been trapped.

She sat up slowly, moaning as pain rolled through her midsection, then, one at a time, began moving things aside until she was finally free.

Her leg was throbbing with every heartbeat. She reached down to pull up her pant leg and check it out, then nearly passed out from the pain and stopped. Okay, bending over was a bad idea, but at least when she stood up, her aching leg held her weight.

But her relief was short-lived when she heard a snarl, and then a low, throaty growl from outside the plane and remembered the scratching from before. At that point she panicked again. The thought of falling victim to wild animals was horrifying, but a quick glance about the cabin told her it was still intact.

The good news was that no animals could get to her. The bad news was that Marcy was apparently dead. She began to cry as she set about looking for Dan, and quickly found his body crumpled up in a corner near the door to the pilot's cabin. Her fingers were trembling as she felt for a pulse at the base of his neck. His skin was as cold as the air around them, and there were no signs of life. They had been more than coworkers with the Red Cross. They were her friends, and they were dead. Then she remembered the pilot, Ken Price. He had to be alive. She couldn't do this by herself.

The door leading into the cockpit was ajar. She stepped inside, then slapped a hand over her mouth to keep from screaming. Ken's eyes were wide-open in a death stare that gave her the chills. All the rest of his facial features had been completely obliterated by the impact.

All of a sudden the walls began to spin around her. She staggered out of the cockpit and slid down the wall into a sitting position, quickly putting her head between her knees to keep from passing out. As the wave of nausea passed, she began to think what to do next, and talking aloud seemed to help her focus.

"I need my coat, and I need to radio for help."

But that meant going back into the cockpit. She forced herself to go, and sobbed all the way through the ordeal of trying to make Ken's radio work, but to no avail.

She didn't know if private jets like this one were equipped with locator beacons, but she was determined not to lose hope. After one brief moment of panic, thinking she might never see Sarah or Cameron again, she had to believe she'd lived through this for a reason. It was time to get practical. She moved back into the cabin, putting on as many pieces of Dan's clothing as she could wear. When she finally found her coat, she threw it over her arm and began searching through the debris for cell phones.

Cameron Winger was on his way out of the Federal Building, buttoning up his coat as he went. He ducked his head against the blast of winter wind as the door swung shut behind him. Tiny flakes of snow lit on his hair like bits of white lace on black satin. He was a tall man with features more refined than his attitude. He didn't like the word *no* and had no tolerance for ineptitude. He squinted when he was deliberating a decision until his green eyes were barely visible, and there was just the tiniest hint of a dimple in his right cheek. He'd been with the FBI since college and never once regretted the decision.

He was on his way to his car when his cell phone rang. He glanced at caller ID and frowned. Why was Laura's sister, Sarah, calling him?

"Hello?"

"Cameron! Thank God you answered!"

His gut knotted when he heard the panic in her voice.

"What's wrong?"

"Laura's plane never landed. It went off radar late yesterday evening."

The world stopped. Cameron felt the bitter bite of winter on his face as he turned away and closed his eyes. This couldn't be happening. Laura was everything to him. Then he took a deep breath and made himself focus.

"She was coming back from that convention in L.A., right?"

"Yes."

"Do they know where it went down?"

"All I know is they're setting up search and rescue somewhere around Denver. Can you go? I'm in Canada. Someone needs to be there for her, and I can't get there fast enough to do any good."

"Absolutely."

"Keep me informed?" she begged.

"Of course," he said, and made a U-turn on the sidewalk, resisting the urge to run as he headed back into the Federal Building.

It took over an hour, but Laura finally found all four cell phones, then, one by one, her hopes were dashed as she failed to get a signal.

"Can you believe it?" she muttered, talking to Marcy as if she could still hear. "Four phones and not a single signal from any of them."

Marcy had nothing to say.

At least during the search for the phones she'd found a first-aid kit, some snacks and two bottles of water. She put the food and water in the farthest corner of the plane, away from the bodies, then made her way to the tiny bathroom. There was no getting around bodily functions, but she had to leave the door open for light so she could see.

When she caught a glimpse of herself in the mirror, she stifled a horrified gasp. When she sat down on the commode, she groaned from the pain, and when she got up, she groaned again.

The cut in her hairline had bled into her scalp while she was passed out, leaving her white-blond hair with garish streaks of red. Now it was freeze-dried to her skin and nothing short of multiple scrubbings was going to take it out.

Her face was normally heart-shaped but was swollen on one side more than the other, and her lower lip was puffy and bruised. Her eyes, normally blue, reflected the pain she was suffering to the point that they were almost gray. She was dressed like a scarecrow with all the layers of clothing, but considering the danger of her circumstances, her appearance wasn't worth further consideration.

She stumbled as she came out of the bathroom, grabbed at a seat to keep from falling and then winced from the pain of the added jolt. After a thorough search through the first-aid kit, she found a few butterfly bandages and used them on the cut in her scalp. She chewed and swallowed three extremely bitter aspirin, hoping they were enough to offset the steady throb between her eyes. Used one wet wipe to clean some of the blood from her face and hands, then managed to open one of the bottles of water and took a drink.

It hurt terribly to inhale, and she was guessing her

ribs were either broken or severely bruised. She dug farther into the kit and found a couple of ACE bandages. Reluctantly, she removed enough clothing to wrap up her rib cage. It hurt like hell in the process and as soon as she was done, she dressed hastily, shivering from the encroaching cold.

Her next problem was finding a way to get warm. There were three other suitcases that had been tossed about the cabin, and she went through them one by one, digging out the contents and tossing anything usable toward the tail section. Once the suitcases were empty, she began arranging the clothing until she had made a nest for herself within the pile.

Exhausted and reeling from so many aches she could hardly breathe, she crawled into the middle of all that fabric, then pulled the coats and the blankets she'd found around her. Secure within her makeshift bed, she tried the phones again, praying to get a signal. Tears welled as she finally accepted it was a lost cause.

It was quiet outside now, and she thought about the animals, hoping they were gone. The wind rose in an eerie wail that mirrored her despair. She was staring at one of the tiny windows, telling herself that any moment the face of a rescuer would appear and look inside, and she would be saved.

When it began to snow, it added another dimension to the danger she was in. This would slow down search planes, and if the snow was too heavy, the planes would never be able to find the wreckage of a white, snow-covered plane from the air.

Sometime later the animals came back, once again scratching at the outside of the fuselage. Listening to them snarling and yipping as they tried to dig their way inside, she guessed they were wolves. Despite the fact that the extreme cold had all but stopped decomposition of the bodies, she was sure the pack could smell them.

Wanting to see what she was facing, she got up, moving quietly through the cabin toward the cockpit to look out. Just as she reached the doorway, two huge wolves suddenly leaped up onto the nose of the plane and begin digging at the cracked windshield, trying to get to the pilot's body. The sight was so startling that she screamed.

The unexpected sound took the wolves by surprise, and they spun about and leaped out of sight. Though she knew they would be back, it was the first visual she had of how truly trapped she was. Even if she wanted to try to walk out, she would never be able to outrun them.

In a panic, she slammed the cockpit door shut. She couldn't make the wolves go away, but she didn't have to see them again. As she turned to walk away, she heard a click and turned around just as the door swung open on its own. Once again she was faced with a new fear.

Logically, she didn't think they could break through the windshield, but just in case, she needed to know there was a boundary between them and her that they couldn't breach. She tried to push some of the loose debris in front of the door to hold it shut, but it wasn't substantial enough, and the seats, which *were* heavy enough, were bolted to the floor.

When the two wolves jumped back up on the nose of the plane and began digging at the windshield again, she screamed and slammed the door, then used her body weight to keep it closed.

"Oh, God, oh, God, please! Don't let this be the way I die," she cried, sobbing hysterically.

Her fingers were so cold she could barely feel them as she buried her face in her hands. Her sister slid through her mind as she choked on a sob. What if she never saw Sarah again?

And Cameron—there was no way she could describe what he meant to her. She'd been enchanted with him almost from their first meeting, and as the months went by, she'd begun dreaming of a happily ever after with him. Now she didn't know if she would see tomorrow.

She could hear the wolves still outside the cockpit and more that were surrounding the plane, digging and yipping and whining. She grabbed a piece of metal and began beating it against the inside wall.

"Stop! Get away! Get lost! Leave me alone!" she screamed.

The noise silenced them again, but she knew it wouldn't last. She was looking around for an answer to her latest dilemma when her gaze fell on Dan's body.

He was a big man and less than three feet away from the door. *He,* or at least his body, could hold the door shut. At first she hesitated, uncertain how to go about it and leave him any dignity, then realized that couldn't matter, not when her life depended on it. Without looking at his face, she grabbed him by the arms and began dragging his body backward toward the door. Pain racked her chest and legs as she strained against his weight, while the wolves continued to circle the plane, howling and growling.

Finally it was done.

Exhausted and so shaky she thought she would faint, she turned around and went for Marcy, dragging her body up beside Dan's. When she was done, she fell to her knees beside them. Her chest was on fire, and there wasn't a place on her body that didn't hurt, but the deed was done. The door was shut and wasn't about to come open.

"I'm sorry! I'm so sorry!" she sobbed, as she patted Marcy's arm, then picked up Dan's hand and laid it across his chest. "Please, forgive me. Just know that your last physical act on this earth will be protecting me, and for that I thank you from the bottom of my heart."

She scuttled backward like a crab, and as she did, she realized the wind was rising. Just as she stood, a gust buffeted the plane, strong enough to actually rock it.

She grabbed hold of a seat to steady herself while it dawned on her that in fact she had no concept of how precarious her situation really was. If they hadn't landed in a fairly level area, and if the wind got too strong, it could dislodge the plane, which would slide off the mountain with her trapped inside.

The notion gave her pause, and for the first time, she realized it might be to her advantage to limit her movements. She gave her coworkers one last look and then made her way to the back of the plane to the minuscule bathroom.

When she came out, she cleaned her hands on another wet wipe, ate half an energy bar, washed it down with two small sips of water, crawled back into her nest, pulled up her makeshift covers and cried herself to sleep.

Moonlight came through the cabin windows, bathing the bare skin of the two lovers caught up in the simple act of love. That the joining of one body to another could cause such an intense, physical reaction was understood, but at the same time, for them it was a new and wonderful thing. When Laura began to climax, the satisfaction on Cameron's face was nothing short of bliss. She was still riding the high of her own pleasure when she slid her hands between their bodies. Moments later he was spiraling out of control. Her heart was still hammering from the aftershocks when he brushed his mouth across her lips.

"I love you most, Laura Doyle...so, so much."

Laura woke up with a gasp, then grabbed her chest and tried to stop the shock wave of pain that ripped through her. It was getting dark inside the cabin. Had she been asleep that long? She glanced toward the windows. They were nearly covered with snow.

Oh, dear Lord, not that, too. "Stop the snow. Please, stop the snow."

She crawled out of her makeshift bed, but her leg buckled when she tried to stand. Something was very wrong. The more time passed, the stiffer her whole body became, but the pain in her leg was different. She leaned against a seat and slowly pulled up her pant leg, then moaned when she saw the size of the gash.

It was about a half inch deep, running from just below her knee to her ankle, and the only reason she hadn't found it sooner was that the extreme cold had been as successful as cauterization, and what blood there was had soaked into her black slacks unnoticed, and then into her shoe.

She fumbled around in the first-aid kit for the bottle of disinfectant and poured it into the gash. The burn was intense, but it was better than getting infection and having gangrene set in. Once the burn began to fade, she got a couple more pain pills and chewed them up, then washed them down with another sip of water.

Her belly growled, but putting food in her mouth was more than she could handle. She crawled back into her bed and began to pray. She didn't want to die, but unless a miracle occurred, it would happen.

When she closed her eyes, she thought of Cameron. He belonged to the FBI. They found bad guys who murdered people, and good people who were kidnapped. Surely they could find this plane.

"Please, find me," she whispered as she started to shake.

She pulled the covers up over her head.

The wolves were still circling. She could hear their whining and digging, and every so often the sounds of a quarrel as one trespassed on another's space. The first time she heard one on top of the fuselage, she realized they were getting braver. Would this nightmare never end?

Once Cameron had given the director a quick explanation of what had happened, he headed home. After packing for cold weather, he caught a ride on a government jet flying a team of forensic specialists to the West Coast after the pilot agreed to drop him in Denver on the way. After takeoff, there was nothing to distract him from the fact that the woman he loved might be dead. The passengers he was traveling with were otherwise occupied, which suited him fine. He wasn't in the mood for conversation.

It was late afternoon and only hours away from nightfall when they landed. He had a text from the assistant director giving him the location of where search and rescue had set up, and after renting a car, he wasted no time getting there.

The search-and-rescue station was in a small community center in a suburb on the outskirts of Denver. When he pulled up and began looking for a place to park, a local police officer flagged him down.

"I'm sorry, sir. This area is closed to the public."

Cameron flashed his badge. "Special Agent Winger, FBI. Who's in charge here?"

The officer immediately relaxed.

"That would be Lieutenant Clark. You can park in that lot just ahead. The lieutenant should be in that long building behind it."

"Thank you," Cameron said, and a few moments later he parked and killed the engine.

The sudden silence inside the vehicle made him shudder. Then his phone rang. It was his friend and fellow agent Tate Benton.

"Hello."

"Cameron…I just heard about Laura. Do you know anything yet? Have they located the plane?"

"I don't know. I just arrived at the main search-and-rescue site."

"Is there anything the rest of us can do?" Tate asked.

It was the sympathy in his friend's voice that did him in. Breath caught in the back of Cameron's throat as he swallowed a couple of times to keep from crying.

"I've got to go," he said quickly. "If I learn anything, I'll let you know."

"Will do," Tate said.

Cameron pocketed his phone and got out. He had a large duffel bag over one shoulder and a hiker's backpack on the other as he headed for the building.

Inside, the place was a hive of activity. Maps of the mountainous area around Denver were taped to the walls and marked up with search grids. Radio communication was at the other end of the room, and, from the static and squawks of intermittent traffic, it was obvious that they were already in search mode.

He stopped a young woman hurrying past him.

"Is Lieutenant Clark in here?"

She pointed at a tall, stoop-shouldered man with graying hair near the com center.

"That's him on the phone."

"Thank you," Cameron said, dropped his gear against a wall and quickly moved in that direction. Once the lieutenant hung up the phone, Cameron flashed his badge as he introduced himself.

Clark frowned. "What interest does the FBI have in this?"

Cameron pocketed his badge. "It's strictly personal, sir. I'm involved with Laura Doyle, one of the passengers."

Clark's expression cleared. "Ah. Sorry."

"Is there any news?" Cameron asked.

Clark's shoulders slumped a little more, as if weighed down by his responsibilities.

"Not really. We have a general idea of where the plane most likely went down, but it's snowing heavily up in the mountains today, so the search planes are grounded."

Cameron's heart sank. "I want to help. Assign me to a search team. I have all the necessary training."

"I don't—"

"Please," Cameron added. "I can't just sit by and wait when I have the skills to help."

Clark eyed Cameron, who knew what the lieutenant was seeing: a big man, twenty-eight or twenty-nine, and obviously fit. He wasn't the type to slow anybody down.

"I brought clothes and equipment," Cameron added.

Clark relented. "Very well. We have cots set up in the adjoining room and a temporary kitchen beyond that. Find a place to bunk. You can go out in the morning."

Cameron groaned inwardly. So close and still he had to wait.

"Yes, sir, thank you," Cameron said, grabbing his gear.

Two

The snow stopped at midnight, but Laura continued to slip in and out of consciousness, unaware of her surroundings, alternately freezing and burning up with fever. Once when she woke up, she saw wolves standing in the doorway, snarling. Before she could panic, she passed out again. The next time she woke up, her sister was peering in through one of the small windows.

"Wolves, Sarah. Run," she mumbled, then slipped back into her mental abyss.

The next time she came to, it was pitch-black, and her tongue was sticking to the roof of her mouth.

"Water," she muttered, and felt around in her bed until she found her stash, knowing she had to hydrate so her internal organs would not shut down.

Her hands were shaking so hard she could barely hold the bottle, but she drank until it was gone.

Easy, honey. Too much, too fast.

She tried to sit up, but didn't have the strength.

"Cameron? Is that you?" When no one answered, she dropped her head and closed her eyes.

"I'm lost, Cameron. I'm so lost. Please, find me."

She passed out with the empty water bottle still in her hand.

Cameron was up and dressed for the task ahead long before daybreak. When he went to the kitchen in search of coffee, the first thing he heard from the even earlier risers was that it had stopped snowing in the mountains. That meant the search would move into the air as well, which was a positive. Now they just needed to find the wreckage. He picked up a sweet roll and a cup of coffee, and sat down at an empty table to eat.

Lieutenant Clark walked in and spotted him. He, too, got a sweet roll and a cup of coffee, then walked over.

"Good morning, Agent Winger. I see you're ready."

Cameron wiped his mouth as he stood.

"Yes, sir."

"I have planes about ready to go up. You can go with the air search, or with a ground crew. It's your choice."

"I choose ground."

Clark nodded. "As soon as you've finished, I'll—"

Cameron interrupted. "I'm ready now. Let me get my gear."

Once Cameron returned, Clark headed for the back door.

"Follow me," he said, and took a big bite of his sweet roll on the way out.

Large four-wheel-drive vehicles were coming into the parking lot every few minutes to unload cold, weary searchers who'd been out since the day before. Two big trucks were loading up on fuel, while other vehicles were waiting to take new crews of searchers out.

Clark flagged down one of the drivers, who was standing beside an older-model Suburban.

"Hey, Wilson, got room in there for one more?"

The driver, a heavyset woman with a shock of crimson-red hair, turned around. She eyed Cameron's gear and backpack, and then nodded.

"Get in, but you may have to sit on that pack."

"I don't mind," Cameron said, and climbed in.

The men inside shifted enough to give him legroom as he shoved the backpack in a corner, and then sat down in front of it, using it for a backrest. A few minutes later the doors slammed shut, and the vehicle began to move.

Cameron nodded cordially at the men but had no desire to visit. Still, one of them was more curious than the others and took away his decision to remain under the radar. The man leaned over, his hand extended in welcome.

"Reno Brown," he said as he shook Cameron's hand.

"Cameron Winger."

"You're not a local," Reno said.

Cameron shook his head. "No, I'm from D.C."

The other men in the vehicle eyed him curiously, but it was Reno who asked the pertinent question.

"That's a far piece to come to look for a downed plane."

Cameron nodded, but Reno wasn't satisfied.

"Do you work for the FAA or something?"

"No," Cameron said.

Reno waited for more, but when he figured out he wasn't going to get it voluntarily, he smiled, shrugged and shut up.

Cameron shifted focus to a large clod of dirt beneath a seat that was turning into mud from the snowmelt next to it. They rode for almost an hour before the vehicle began slowing down.

"I guess we're there," Reno said.

A few moments later the doors opened.

"Leave your sleeping gear in the big tent, and if we're lucky, you won't need it," Wilson said as the searchers began getting out.

"From your lips to God's ears," Reno said, and strode toward the waiting snowmobiles.

Cameron was right behind him.

"We ride in pairs," Reno said. "The driver makes sure we don't fall off the mountain. The rider looks for wreckage."

Cameron stopped. He was anxious to search but didn't want to waste time watching where they were going. He wanted to watch for signs.

"I know the area. Want to ride with me?" Reno asked.

Cameron nodded as he followed the men inside.

The on-site quarters consisted of a very large tent with at least three dozen cots set up. Another radio operator was on-site to monitor updates from the air searchers and pass info on to the ground crew. Extra food and fuel were stacked in any available free space.

The terrain was heavily wooded, with at least four, maybe five, inches of fresh snow, and it all looked alike. He left his gear beneath one of the cots and was second-guessing his decision to go with the ground search when Reno arrived carrying a handheld GPS.

"I've got our search coordinates entered in here. They said the temps went down to five below last night. If we don't find the wreckage today, we'll go from rescue to retrieval."

"Shut the hell up," Cameron said shortly.

Reno blinked and then gave Cameron a closer look. "Sorry, man."

Cameron sighed. "No, I'm sorry. Look, this is personal. My girlfriend is one of the missing passengers."

Reno frowned. "Well, hell, I'm sorry all over again. So let's get going. We've got a long day ahead of us."

Cameron held out his hand. "Can we start over?"

Reno smiled. "I'm Reno Brown."

"Cameron Winger."

"Nice to meet you, Cameron. You know what to look for out there?"

"Yes."

Reno handed Cameron a helmet.

"Then off we go," he said.

They put on the helmets as they moved toward the parked snowmobiles, and one by one, the searchers took off, moving toward the new grid pattern. Once the official search began, Reno Brown's affable manner disappeared. He all business as he wove through the thick growth of trees with steady skill.

Their arctic gear was welcome protection against the high-altitude cold, but it also made Cameron conscious of what the passengers in the downed plane would be enduring. He kept his gaze focused on the trees, looking for signs of broken treetops or a snow-covered shape that did not fit in to the surroundings.

The noise of so many engines startled an elk, and it bolted out of hiding and across a small meadow. Cameron watched it bound through the snow then disappear back into the forest.

The sun was bright, which made looking at the vast expanse of snow painful. The dark glasses they were wearing helped deflect the glare, but within a couple of hours he had a dull ache behind his eyes anyway.

The radios in their helmets made communication easier, but it was sparse and depressing. When they finished the search of their first grid, the crew stopped long enough to put new coordinates into their mobile GPS systems and discuss the situation.

As the day rolled on, Cameron's hopes began to fade. When he figured out that getting a signal for a cell phone up here was next to impossible, it alleviated one fear he'd had: that the reason no one had called for help was because they were all dead.

They stopped just after three to refuel. Reno was eating an energy bar and Cameron was relieving his thirst when they received word from air search of a possible crash site a couple of miles north of their present location.

The urgency of the situation had just risen.

Reno thumped him on the shoulder as he headed for their ride.

"Let's go get this done," he said.

Moments later, the snowmobiles and their riders were speeding off in a new direction, desperate to reach the target location before dark.

Laura was alive between one world and the next, waiting to see who came for her first. Once she saw her mother standing beneath a snow-covered tree, but when she suddenly disappeared, Laura felt abandoned. Then she saw Dan and Marcy in the distance and called out, wanting them to wait, but they were too far away and didn't hear her. She didn't understand why everyone was leaving her behind. She was cold and hurt. Why wouldn't they help? Why wouldn't they take her with them?

Twice she thought she heard voices and pushed the covers aside each time, crying out in relief.

"Here! I'm here!"

But no one came to help, and the wolves were back. She could hear them digging and yipping, trying to get in.

"Go away," she mumbled, and then started to cry. "Cameron, please find me. Why can't you find me?"

A wolf howled.

She pulled the coats back up over her head as her fever pulled her under.

The vista spread out before them as Reno topped a small rise. From this angle Cameron could see the downward slope of the land, as well as a startling anomaly. Despite the snowfall, there was a very visible and distinct path of broken treetops below.

He thumped Reno on the shoulder and pointed.

"There! Look there!"

Reno nodded, then swung the snowmobile to the left and accelerated, using the radio in his helmet to alert the others to their find.

Cameron's heart was hammering.

We're coming, Laura. We're coming, baby. Don't give up on us yet.

When they began to see debris, Cameron felt sick. The worse the destruction had been to the plane, the less protection they would have had from the elements. There was a piece of a wingtip caught in a large stand of pines, and an entire wing lay on the ground a few yards farther on. Despite the snow, the heavy tree growth had partially protected it, leaving most of it visible, but they still hadn't found the plane.

Cameron's heart was pounding as Reno began confirming their find. All of a sudden the radio traffic that had been almost nonexistent was loud and rapid in his ears.

When they came up on the main crash site and saw the plane, the sound of their engine sent a pack of wolves running.

Cameron groaned. As if the crash itself wasn't enough to weather.

Between the wind and the wolves, enough snow had been dug or blown away from the fuselage for him to see that it was intact.

Reno wheeled the snowmobile into a vacant space between some trees and killed the engine. He was on the radio, alerting headquarters that they'd found the wreckage, but Cameron had abandoned his helmet and was already off and running.

The doors were half-buried in snow, and no matter how hard he pulled, he couldn't get them open. He began circling the plane, and as he rounded the nose and saw the dead pilot through the shattered windshield, his legs went weak.

Reno ran up behind him with a crowbar in his hands.

"The doors are jammed," Cameron said, then crawled up on the nose section of the plane. "Throw me the crowbar!"

Reno gave it a toss.

Cameron caught it in midair and then used it to hammer at the shattered windshield until it gave way, exploding inward into thousands of tiny pellet-like pieces.

Reno saw the pilot as he crawled up beside him.

"Oh, hell," he said softly.

Cameron handed off the crowbar and then climbed inside, but when he tried to open the door to get into the cabin, it wouldn't budge.

"What's wrong?" Reno said as he climbed inside with him, the crowbar still in his hand.

"Something's up against the door," Cameron said. "Probably debris."

"Here, let me help," Reno said, and together they threw their weight against it until it began to give.

That was when they realized it wasn't debris blocking the door. It was bodies. Cameron saw a man's leg and shoe first and kept pushing, but as the door opened farther and he saw a woman's ankle and shoe, his heart sank.

God, please, God, no.

One more push and all of a sudden they were in.

Once Cameron stepped over the bodies and into the main cabin, he went weak with relief when he realized the deceased woman was a brunette. Laura was blonde.

Reno felt for a pulse, then shook his head. "They're both gone. Is this your girl?"

"No," Cameron said, and then looked through the debris toward the back of the plane. "Someone has cleared a path through here."

The sound of approaching snowmobiles became apparent.

"The others are arriving. I'm going to try to open a door from the inside," Reno said, and took the crowbar toward an exit door as Cameron began wending his way toward the tail section.

It wasn't far. There weren't that many seats in the private jet. He should have been able to see her, but he couldn't.

"Laura, where are you?" he yelled, and began turning over boxes and suitcases as he went.

It took him a few moments to realize that all the suitcases were empty, but there weren't any pieces of clothing strewn about, and that was when it hit him. Someone had emptied the contents to stay warm, which had to mean Laura had survived the crash! When he saw the big pile of clothes, he leaped toward it, frantically calling her name.

Laura was standing in a sunlit meadow, waiting. All she knew was that someone was coming to get her and she had to be ready. The breeze was warm on her face. The air smelled rain-fresh clean, and when someone began calling her name, she stepped forward. He was here! She didn't know where they were going, but she was ready to leave.

The voice was nearer. *Laura. Laura.*

"I'm here!" she cried, and then all of a sudden the sun went behind a cloud and the wind grew cold. She cried out, "Help me!" and then felt a touch on her face, then at her neck. "I'm ready," she said, and let go.

"Is that your girl?" Reno asked, as Cameron was feeling for broken bones.

"Yes, this is my girl, and she's alive," Cameron said, unashamed of the tears on his face.

Suddenly the plane was filled with searchers.

"Radio for a medevac! We have a live one!" Reno shouted while Cameron continued to assess her injuries.

She was burning up with fever, which meant infection and possibly internal injuries. He found the first-aid kit beside her, and when he began examining her body, discovered the ACE bandages she'd wrapped around her rib cage, the gash in her head and the wound on her leg. She'd tried to doctor herself, but it was obvious she was in dire need of more extensive care.

"A chopper's already in the area. They'll be here within minutes," Reno said as he dropped to his knees beside Cameron. "Looks like she was trying to patch herself up."

"She works for the Red Cross," Cameron said, remembering all the times he'd seen her working tirelessly, helping others in times of disaster. This time *she* was the one in need.

Reno eyed the nest she'd made of all the clothes, and the little food and water stash beside her.

"Looks like she's quite a survivor," he said.

Laura moaned.

Cameron cupped her cheek. His voice was steady, but his hands were trembling.

"Help is coming, baby. Hang on."

Her lips were cracked and bleeding from the cold,

and her long blond hair was bloody and matted, but she'd never looked as beautiful to him as she did right now.

"Help?"

When he heard her voice, he reached for her hand. "Yes, Laura, help is here, baby. We found you."

Her eyelids began to flutter, and then she opened her eyes.

"Cameron?"

"Yes, honey, it's me."

A frown rippled across her forehead.

"Are you real?"

He gave her hand a slight squeeze.

"I'm real, and we're here to take you home."

Tears slipped from the corners of her eyes.

"They're dead. They left without me."

He leaned down and kissed the side of her cheek, so overcome with emotion his voice was shaking.

"I'm really glad you waited for me to find you."

She blinked so slowly that he thought she was passing out again, and then all of a sudden her eyelids flew open.

"The wolves...have to hide."

"No, baby, they're gone," Cameron said.

She clutched his arm in sudden panic. "No. They dig. They'll find me."

Cameron looked over his shoulder, then shouted at Reno, "Where's that chopper?"

"On approach," Reno said.

Cameron cupped Laura's cheek. "The medics are here. They're going to take you to the hospital."

A visible surge of panic swept through her as she clutched his sleeve tighter.

"Might die. Need to tell you—"

Cameron's stomach rolled. "You are not going to die, do you hear me, Laura?"

"—to tell you I love you."

He swallowed past the lump in his throat, then leaned down and whispered in her ear, "I love you most."

The familiar words brought tears, and then her eyes rolled back in her head.

"They're here!" Reno called, eyeing a pair of medics as they came through the trees carrying a backboard and a stretcher.

Cameron patted her arm and then began looking through the stuff she'd gathered around her. He saw her purse and put it beside her so the medics would take it. Laura knew her job well and always traveled with a copy of her medical history and prescriptions. When he moved it, he saw four cell phones lying beneath it and groaned, imagining her panic and frustration at having so much technology in her hand and none of it working. He tossed her cell phone in her purse and left the others behind.

Then all at once the medical team was there. He moved aside, watching as they stabilized her neck, started an IV to push fluids and then rolled her onto the backboard, taking precautions even though it was obvious she had been mobile. After Cameron's insistence and a brief explanation, they strapped her purse on with her.

"Where are you taking her?" Cameron asked as they headed out the door.

"University of Colorado Hospital in Aurora," an EMT said.

Cameron followed them out. Unwilling to let her go, he helped carry her through the snow to the open meadow where the chopper had landed. He wanted to go with her, but once he saw how small the chopper was, he didn't even ask.

She was still unconscious when they strapped the stretcher down inside the chopper. As they began lifting off, the air filled with wasplike shards of icy snow. Cameron turned away to protect his eyes, and when he looked back again, they had gained enough altitude that they were already heading back.

He watched until the chopper was little more than a speck, and then ran to catch up with the others. The search teams were in the process of leaving. The bodies and the wreckage belonged to another kind of team. Armed guards were standing by until the authorities came to remove the bodies. Then the NTSB would show up to recover the plane.

He looked around for Reno, saw him standing near their snowmobile and moved as fast as he could to get there. "Are you getting ready to leave?" he asked.

"Yeah. We need to hurry. Night's coming, and we don't want to be out here on snowmobiles after dark."

"When we get back to camp, will anyone be going back down the mountain?"

Reno shrugged. "They may wait until morning to break camp, but we can ask."

One thing at a time, Cameron thought, and climbed on.

Three

It was after dark when Cameron caught a ride with a van load of searchers on their way back to Denver. The ride down from the mountain staging area was even more treacherous at night, but about halfway down he got a cell signal and was finally able to send Sarah a text. Ever conscious of losing the signal, he kept details brief.

Laura alive. En route to University of Colorado Hospital in Aurora.

Her answer to him was just as abbreviated.

On my way. Between planes at airport. Thank you forever for giving Laura back to me.

He wouldn't begin to take credit, but he understood what she meant.

When they finally saw the lights of Denver in the distance, everyone breathed a little easier. By the time the van reached the community center where the initial search and rescue had been set up, it was almost eight o'clock.

Cameron unloaded his gear with the others and headed into the community center to change back into street clothes and get the rest of his belongings.

He came out a short while later, his stride long and hurried as he crossed the parking lot. It felt like snow, but so far the overcast sky was holding whatever it carried. He tossed his bags in the trunk of his rental, entered the hospital address into the car's GPS and took off through the city.

His belly growled as he pulled up at a stoplight, a reminder that he hadn't eaten since the sweet roll this morning. After all that had happened today, that felt like a lifetime ago.

When the light turned green he accelerated through the intersection, then swung into the first fast-food drive-through he came to and ordered. He ate as he drove, washing his meal down with a cold Pepsi and wishing he'd asked for coffee instead. But he had to admit it was a smart move, because he felt less shaky, which was good. And once he got there, he wasn't leaving Laura's side.

Still, the closer he got to the hospital, the more anxious he became. By the time he pulled into the parking lot, a sense of finality was setting in. He'd done all he could have done by helping find her, and whatever was happening now was out of his hands. He had to trust she hadn't survived all that horror for nothing.

As he headed toward the entrance, he felt a raindrop, then another, but before he got into the building it had turned into snow. He lengthened his stride.

Learning she was in Intensive Care wasn't surprising, but it amped up his concern. Visiting hours in ICU were on the hour, every hour, and brief. He glanced at his watch and headed for the elevator. It was almost nine.

Laura moaned as pain pulled her out of her semiconscious state. Something was beeping. The plane! The alarm! The plane was going down.

I don't want to die.

Tears rolled out from beneath her eyelids as she waited for impact. Instead, she heard the muffled sound of soft voices, a faint cry of pain and then a woman's soft, reassuring voice. But it wasn't until she homed in on the sharp click of footsteps coming toward her that she tried to open her eyes, because she recognized the stride.

Cameron.

Something brushed against the side of her cheek, followed by the warmth of a breath and the sweet sound of a familiar voice near her ear.

"Hey, baby," Cameron said softly, and leaned over the bed just long enough to kiss her forehead and slip his hand in hers.

It is *Cameron! He found me.*

"You're in a hospital, honey. Your plane crashed. Do you remember?"

Images flashed behind her eyelids. The pilot's face obliterated. Marcy's eyes frozen open in death. Dragging Dan's body across the door to keep it closed. Her fingers curled around his hand, his presence anchoring her to reality. "They died." The tone of her voice reflected her horror. His grip tightened.

"I know," he said softly.

Panic shifted within her. It was hard to accept she'd been saved.

"I prayed for you to find me," she whispered, then licked her lower lip where it had cracked from the cold.

"And we did. Lots of people were looking for you," he said.

She finally managed to open her eyes. Cameron's face was blurry, as if it was melting. It took her a few moments to realize she was still crying.

"I hurt."

"I know, darlin', with good reason. You have a concussion, three broken ribs, a buttload of stitches on your leg and you're fighting pneumonia."

"Am I dying?" she asked, then watched his eyes darken and a frown spread across his forehead as he leaned closer.

"No. You're getting well and coming back to D.C. with me to live happily ever after."

Breath caught in the back of her throat.

"With you?"

He ran a finger lightly down the side of her cheek.

"I had planned to say all this on Valentine's Day, which happens to be next week, but sometimes plans change. I love you, Laura, more than I thought it was possible to love anyone, and almost losing you just made me more certain of that fact. You have to hang in there, baby."

The room was spinning, or maybe it was all in Laura's head. She grabbed hold of his wrist, trying to stop the motion so she could focus on his voice, but things were turning faster and faster, sucking her down with them.

"I'm going to pass out," she mumbled, and proceeded to do exactly that.

"Sir, visiting hours are over," a nurse said as she approached the bed.

Cameron lifted Laura's hand to his lips.

"Be strong and get well, sweetheart. I'll be back," he promised, and reluctantly walked away.

Time dragged for Cameron as he waited between visits. Exhaustion finally caught up with him as the waiting room cleared out. The quiet washed over him as he changed his chair for the sofa. The soft leather pillowed his body when he turned and stretched out. It was just for a few minutes, he told himself, grateful to be off his feet. But at six feet three inches tall, his long legs had nowhere to go except over the arm of the sofa. He fell asleep with one arm flung over his eyes to keep out the light. He'd set the alarm on his watch, though, and when it went off, his feet hit the floor before his eyes were fully open. He turned and staggered to the bathroom.

He was still wearing jeans, which had been part of his traveling clothes, but after the first hour in the waiting room he had made a trip out to his car for a fleece jacket to pull over his shirt. The waiting room, like the hospital, bordered on cold, and he was glad for the added layer. The thought of coffee was enticing, but there was no time. He wanted to see Laura again.

There were others in line with him, waiting for the doors to the ICU to open. Even though they all shared the experience of having loved ones with critical health issues, no one seemed inclined to talk, looking instead at the floors or the walls, anywhere but at each other.

Cameron was worried. The last time he'd seen her they had put her on oxygen, and she'd slept all the way through his visit. He knew she needed rest to heal, but seeing her motionless and so vulnerable scared him. He needed to reconnect, to hear her voice and see recognition in her eyes, to know she wasn't getting worse.

There was a nurse beside her bed when he walked up.

"Everything okay?" he asked softly.

The nurse recognized him from prior visits.

"She's been crying out in her sleep," she said, and injected the contents of a syringe into the IV port.

"What's that for?" Cameron asked.

"Antibiotic. Her fever is still high."

He frowned. "The wound on her leg was bad. Is it infected?"

The nurse hesitated. "Doctor Rector usually begins rounds about 7:00 a.m. He'll be able to answer your questions then."

Cameron didn't push the issue. He knew nurses weren't free to share medical information about their patients. As soon as the nurse left, he moved closer to the bed.

Laura moaned as he touched her forehead. Her skin was hot and dry.

"Shh, shh," he said softly. "You're safe, baby, you're safe."

Her lips were moving.

He leaned closer, caught just enough of what she was saying and sighed. She was still talking about wolves.

"They're gone, Laura, they're gone."

She grabbed his arm. "Cameron?"

He took her hand. She still knew him. Thank God.

"Yes, it's me."

"Found me?"

"Yes, we found you. You're in a hospital in Denver. You are safe, and you *will* get well."

"Stay."

"I can't stay, baby. You're in ICU. But I'm right outside the door, and I'll be back when they let me."

Her eyes opened. "Cameron?"

"At your service," he said.

"Sarah?"

"She's on her way."

"Love you," she said, then closed her eyes.

She was already out when he answered, but it didn't matter. He said for himself as much as for her, "I love you, too."

The time went all too quickly, and soon he followed the other visitors out. But as they headed for the elevator, he went back to the waiting room alone. He was too wired to go back to sleep, and after digging through his wallet for some singles, he headed for the snack machines.

Sarah Doyle was holding Cameron's last text close to her heart, counting on its truth.

Laura in ICU. I spoke to her. She knew me. Injuries severe, not life threatening. Worried about pneumonia. I'm in ICU waiting room.

Laura was all the family she had, and if she lost her, she would be as alone in the world as a person could be.

By the time her plane landed in Denver it was well past midnight, and the ground was dusted with snow. She caught a cab to the hospital and then texted Cameron to let him know she was on the ground, but he didn't answer. She glanced at the time. One in the morning. He was probably in the ICU with Laura.

Her eyes burned from the bouts of crying she

couldn't seem to stop, and she caught a glimpse of herself in the cab window as they passed through the city.

Both sisters were blondes, and while the family resemblance was noticeable in their features, she was older and taller. Laura's chosen path in life had gone nonprofit and led her to the Red Cross, while Sarah had gone the corporate route. And oddly enough, as Laura's personal life had heated up, so had Sarah's career; something she had yet to share.

The ride to the hospital was long, and the heater blasting in the front of the cab never quite raised the temperature in the backseat high enough to keep her comfortable. Even though the cranberry wool slacks and gray sweater she was wearing were warm, and her winter coat was good protection from the cold, she was shaking.

She paid the driver upon arrival, grabbed her bag and got out on the run.

Cameron was kicked back on the sofa checking his messages. The pretzels he was eating were all he'd had since dinner, along with the can of Pepsi at his elbow. Wade and his wife, Jo, had sent a text earlier wishing Laura well. He smiled, thankful for good friends. He was still scanning messages when he got a text from Tate. It was after three in the morning in D.C. That guy kept seriously late hours. He began to read.

How's Laura?

Cameron popped another pretzel in his mouth and then answered.

Fighting infection and pneumonia.

So sorry. Nola sends her love. Keep us in the loop.

Will do and thanks.

He left the other messages for later, finished off the pretzels and washed them down with the last of the Pepsi. He was tossing away the trash when Sarah Doyle walked in.

The moment she saw him, she dropped her bag and started crying. Seconds later she was in his arms.

Cameron patted her on the back as he gave her a hug.

"It's going to be okay, honey. She's alive, and that's a damn miracle in itself."

Sarah grabbed his wrist. "Is it bad? Tell me the truth. Did she get worse? I've been scared through this whole freaking trip, afraid I wouldn't get here in time, and at the same time, afraid to get here and learn the whole truth."

"Come sit," Cameron said, and filled her in on the extent of Laura's injuries, then glanced at the clock. "The next visitation is at 2:00 a.m. You take it."

When he suggested visiting Laura, she almost panicked, afraid of what she would see.

"We can't go in together?"

"They do allow two visitors at a time, but I've been in several times already. She asked about you, and her attention span is brief, so having two of us there will only be confusing. You go alone, and once you see her, you'll feel better, I promise."

Sarah smiled through tears. "You are the best thing that's ever happened to our family. I hope you plan on staying around for a very long time."

Cameron managed a lopsided grin. "It's definitely my plan, but Laura has the last word on that, doesn't she?"

"You're a shoo-in," Sarah said.

"Want some coffee, or something to eat?" Cameron asked, using the mundane question to hide how moved he was by her words.

"Coffee would be wonderful."

"Black, right?"

"Yes, please."

He got up for another trip to the snack machines, and came back with coffee and a bag of M&M's.

"I seem to remember this is a favorite in the candy dishes at your house," he said.

"Thank you so much," she said, took a quick sip of the coffee and then tore into the candy and popped a couple in her mouth.

Cameron answered a new text, giving Sarah some space while she ate.

When the candy was gone, she settled back with the coffee, holding it between her palms as welcome warmth.

"Cameron?"

He dropped the phone in his pocket and looked up.

"Was it bad at the crash site?" she asked.

He grimaced. "Yes, and you need to know two things. There were wolves trying to get into the wreckage, probably from day one. She's still dreaming about them."

Sarah clasped a hand over her mouth, too horrified to speak.

"The other thing is that she saved her own life. She managed to tend to her injuries with next to no supplies and kept herself warm enough not to succumb to hypothermia. She is one tough, amazing woman, and I am in awe."

Sarah was crying all over again. "I don't know what to say."

"There's nothing *to* say, but you needed to understand what she's been through before you go in there. Her two coworkers died, as did the pilot."

Sarah nodded. "Yes, I know and I agree. I'm just overwhelmed by everything."

"Believe me, I understand," Cameron said.

"I need to go wash off the tears and fix my face before I go in. Excuse me for a few minutes."

"Good plan," he said, and settled back onto the sofa.

When it was time, he walked Sarah to the area where she needed to wait.

"I'll be in the waiting room when you come back."

"Thanks," she said, and went inside with the others as he walked away.

Sarah paused at the nurses' desk for her sister's location before moving past the other patients. She kept her eyes on the floor in front of her without looking at the people within.

She was scared; this holding area between life and death impacted so many others besides the patients themselves. Sooner or later they would leave, some breathing and some not, the latter leaving their families behind to deal with their grief. The common thread among all of them was the number of machines keeping them alive.

When she finally saw Laura she stumbled, then caught herself and kept walking until she was at the bed, pausing a moment to look her fill.

The dried blood staining the bandage on Laura's scalp was a macabre reminder of what she had endured. The bruises on her face and neck were in coordinating shades of red and purple, and her raspy breathing under the oxygen mask made Sarah anxious. That would be from the pneumonia.

She knew about the stitches in Laura's leg and the broken ribs, but after learning what her sister had gone through, she wondered if the scars that would last the longest would be the ones that remained unseen.

Aware that her time would be brief, she touched her sister first, then leaned closer and lowered her voice.

"Laura? Honey? It's me, Sarah. Can you hear me?"

Laura's eyelids fluttered.

Sarah spoke again.

"I'm here, Laura. Cameron is in the waiting room."

It seemed *Cameron* was the magic word. Laura's eyelids fluttered again, and then she opened them and saw her sister's face.

"Sarah."

Sarah cupped Laura's cheek, then leaned down and kissed her.

"Yes, little sister, I'm here. Are you in pain?"

Laura sighed, winced, then blinked.

"Hurts."

"I'm so sorry, honey, but you're going to be okay."

Laura fumbled for her sister's hand, needing the contact to give her strength.

"Oh, Sarah, they died…they all died," she whispered, and then choked on a sob.

"I know, honey, but that's not your fault."

Laura's eyelids felt too heavy to keep open. She let them drop, then suddenly she remembered old horror and they flew open. Her gaze locked on Sarah's face.

"There were wolves."

Sarah tightened her hold on her sister's hand, trying to find a way to ground her in the reality of the present, instead of the past.

"I know, honey. Cameron told me."

Laura looked toward the exit.

"Cameron?"

"He's still here. He's in the waiting room."

"Love him," Laura whispered.

"I know you do, sweetheart. He loves you, too."

"I want to go home," Laura said.

Sarah smiled. "And you will, when you're well."

"Thought I'd never see you again," Laura said.

In spite of Sarah's determination not to cry, tears filled her eyes.

"Yes, well, I had the same fear when I first heard the news, but we've been blessed."

"Best sister ever," Laura said softly. Her eyelids drooped and then closed.

Sarah's heart was full. She let Laura sleep, knowing rest was the thing she needed most. She said a brief prayer for her healing and left the ICU with the other visitors when time was up.

This time when she walked into the waiting room, there was purpose in her step. She was thankful for Cameron's presence.

"She looked better than I expected. She knew me and talked to me. It was such a relief."

Cameron relaxed, glad to know Laura hadn't taken a turn for the worse.

"I know what you mean."

"I have something to tell you," she said. "It's about the reason I was in Canada. I was interviewing for a new opening in my company."

"Oh, yeah? How did it go?" he asked.

"I got the job."

Cameron grinned. "That's great news, Sarah. What will you be doing that's different from what you do now?"

"For starters, I'll be director of operations and living in London. I'm supposed to be in residence within

the month. I already told them I'd do it before I found
out about the crash. Now I don't—"

Cameron held up a hand. "Stop right there. You
have to know I'm going to be there for Laura in every
way. This sounds like the job of a lifetime. Don't let
misplaced guilt sideline you, okay?"

She got teary all over again, but she was smiling.

"You are seriously the best thing that's ever happened to Laura. I hope you know that."

"It works both ways," he said, and then looked away
so she wouldn't see his tears.

The next time visiting hour rolled around, they
went in together, but as time passed, the stress of travel
and worry finally pulled Sarah under, and now she was
asleep on the sofa, leaving Cameron back in a chair.
People came and went inside the waiting room, but he
paid them no mind. He slept sitting up, and by seven
in the morning, they were both awake and waiting for
Laura's doctor to make rounds.

Lake Chapala, Mexico

Hot pink jacaranda blooms in the courtyard between the retirement condos drooped in the hot afternoon sun. The teal-blue water in the shared pool was
motionless. A red-and-white-striped life preserver was
stalled near the middle of the pool, like an off-center
belly button. It was siesta, a time to sleep through the
hottest hours of the day, giving the aging residents a
much-needed respite.

Hershel Inman and his wife, Louise, had always planned to retire to this place. But fate had changed their plans. When Louise died, so had Hershel's dreams. In a way, he'd died, too, because when he finally moved into the retirement center, it was as retired businessman Paul Leibowitz. After years of enacting his own version of retribution, he'd finally done what he needed to and let go.

He liked condo living and puttering about in the little courtyard just outside his breakfast room. He liked the huge jacaranda blossoms and often floated one in a crystal bowl on his dining room table. He liked to think it gave his condo a feminine touch, something sadly lacking in his life.

He continued the slow process of having scar tissue removed, scheduling yet another surgery in Guadalajara only after he'd sufficiently healed from the previous one.

The elderly couple who lived across the courtyard had become his friends. He had eaten dinner at their home more than once in the past few months, and while he wasn't much of a cook, he knew he needed to return the favor. He didn't cook, but he'd acquired quite a taste for the local food and ate out more than in to satisfy his hunger for the spicy dishes.

Hershel rarely thought about the past other than with a sense of satisfaction. He had served his own brand of justice to the powers that be, and that knowledge gave him the ease he needed to get on with his life, and it had obviously given his deceased Louise spiritual rest, since she didn't talk to him anymore.

It was only at night, when the world was quiet, that his life came back to haunt him. Most of the images were of Hurricane Katrina, of him and Louise clinging to the roof of their house as the floodwaters rose. In the dreams, Louise was in his arms crying for her insulin, begging to be rescued. And the dream always turned into a nightmare, just as life had, with him watching as she slowly slipped into a diabetic coma and died.

Every time he woke up, he was so angry he couldn't take a breath without thinking he was going to puke. He got out of bed and prowled the house in bare feet, waiting for daybreak by drinking coffee and watching television, doing whatever it took to rebury the memories. By sunrise, copious amounts of caffeine had usually dulled his emotions.

At that point it was Paul who would begin his day with a long walk that always ended up at a local café for breakfast.

Sarah had stayed for five days and now had been gone for five more. She'd gone back to her job and the chaos of making a move to a foreign country, but it wasn't until Laura had been moved from the ICU to a private room that she told her sister about the job promotion. To her relief, Laura seemed happy for her, which made everything easier.

In reality, Laura was proud of Sarah but at the same

time a little sad she would be living so far away. But as each day passed, Laura grew stronger. Her ribs were healing, the stitches had come out of her leg and her lungs were clear.

She'd heard nurses talking about her imminent dismissal, and was anxious to be home. But the problem now was how to get there. She hadn't mentioned it to the doctor or said anything to Cameron, but there was an issue that was going to hinder her homecoming. Denver was a long way from Washington, D.C., and she was afraid to get back on a plane, and yet it was something she knew she was going to have to face.

Cameron came into the hospital room carrying several shopping bags and smiling from ear to ear.

"What's all this?" Laura asked, as he laid them on her lap and then gave her a quick kiss.

"Clothes. You can't go home in a hospital gown, and the doctor said tomorrow is the day."

"You bought me clothes? Ooh, I hope they fit."

"Oh, they fit. I asked Sarah your sizes. She bought you underwear before she left, and I did the rest."

"I can't believe it!" Laura said, and began looking through the bags. "I love this sweater. It's so soft, and it's pink—one of my favorite colors. It will look great with these gray slacks. Oh, Cameron, you even got shoes and socks. These half boots will be perfect. Is there still snow?"

"Not here, but there is back home," he said as he pulled the last two items out of a larger sack.

One was a winter coat made of soft gray wool, the other a small duffel bag to pack her things. The smile on her face warmed his heart.

"Cameron, I adore you! You're the best. You thought of everything."

He grinned. "I have us booked on a 2:00 p.m. flight tomorrow afternoon. It's a nonstop straight into D.C. We'll be home in time for dinner."

When the smile froze on her face, he knew something was wrong.

"What is it, honey?"

She clutched his hand, her voice trembling.

"I'm scared to death to get back on a plane."

He groaned inwardly. How stupid of him not to realize.

"I didn't think. I'm sorry. I can rent a car and drive you back, but it will be a rough trip, and it will take days. Some of the roads are snow packed."

"No, no car. I'll get on the plane, but I need you to know I might freak out."

He frowned. "The doctor can prescribe something for you to take. It will be okay. I'll be right beside you all the way."

She nodded, her eyes tearing again. "I know, and I'm sorry. But it is what it is."

"You do not need to apologize. Anyone in their right mind would feel the same. Don't worry, okay? I'll take care of the meds and everything else."

"Okay," she said, and then made herself change the

subject. "What's in that one?" she asked, pointing to a bag at the foot of her bed.

He handed it to her. "It's another pair of pants and a heavy sweater. I wanted you to have choices."

All of a sudden her eyes were swimming with tears.

"What, honey? What's wrong? Are you in pain?"

"I was just thinking about Marcy and Dan, and the pilot. I get to go home, and they're dead and buried."

He dropped the sack and took her in his arms. Her hair, still damp from her morning shower, clung to his cheek as he held her. She was trembling and weepy, and he wished this could be fixed with a kiss and a hug, but it couldn't. After a few moments he leaned back and tilted her chin up to meet his gaze.

"I'm very sorry about your friends, but I'm grateful beyond words that you survived. You have no idea how frightened Sarah and I were when we got the news."

Laura leaned into his embrace.

"I can imagine. I am so tired of crying, and I'm very thankful that I'm still here, too, but some days it still overwhelms me."

"How do you feel about Sarah moving to London?" he asked.

She shrugged. "Happy for her. This is what she's been working toward."

"You've still got me," he said.

A crooked smile shifted the somber expression off her face. "I'm not about to forget that."

"Good, because when we get home, there's something I want to discuss with you."

"What?" she asked.

He grinned. "Not until we get home."

Her eyes widened. "Is it a secret?"

"It won't be after we have that discussion."

She groaned. "Seriously, Cameron, you can't just drop such a loaded comment and then make me wait to find out what it is."

He grinned again.

When she realized he wasn't going to budge, she shrugged.

"At least I'll have another reason to want to get on that plane tomorrow. The sooner we get back, the sooner I find out the big secret."

Cameron was thinking about that engagement ring in his safe at home and the Valentine dinner that never happened. Sarah was moving out. Maybe it was time for him to move in.

Four

An airport attendant pushed Laura and her wheel-chair through the airport, with Cameron about a step and a half ahead, parting the crowd for them to pass.

They'd checked their luggage at curbside and were traveling light on their way to the boarding gate. Laura's new coat and purse were in her lap, giving her something stable to hold on to, pushing her fear of the flight down to a level just below screaming. As they approached yet another shop on the concourse, Cameron slowed down.

"Hey, honey, it's almost an hour until takeoff. Do you want something to read, or some snacks to take with us?"

Laura's stomach was rolling. The thought of food made her want to throw up.

"No. Better not," she said. "I feel kind of queasy already."

"I have the meds your doctor gave you for traveling. You're going to be fine." He stopped the attendant. "Please, wait here a second. I'm going to get her some pretzels. Something salty might help."

The attendant wheeled up to the storefront, then parked her out of the line of traffic as Cameron went inside the store.

Laura watched, noting his confident stride and the way he had of slipping in and out of the moving crowd, grabbing snacks, magazines and a couple of bottles of water. When he turned around to look at her and caught her watching, he winked, which made her smile. Just for a moment, the fear within her settled. She didn't have words for how much she loved him.

A few minutes later he was back, and then they were off, negotiating the crowds, the rise and fall of conversations as they passed different gates, the continual announcements of arrivals and departures.

Anxiety returned with a vengeance. God, oh, God, she couldn't believe she was about to do this.

All of a sudden Cameron's hand was on her shoulder, as if he'd sensed she was already freaking out.

"Get out the meds the doctor gave you," he said, and she did. He handed her a bottle of water as she popped them in her mouth and washed them down, then packed it back up. "Just breathe easy," he said softly.

She closed her eyes and nodded, but it was easier said than done. Minutes later they were at the gate. Before she could wrap her head around their imminent departure, early boarding for those needing extra time was announced.

Cameron caught the frantic look on her face and took her hand.

"Laura, sweetheart, just close your eyes and picture home."

And so she did, flooding her mind with images of the way sunlight came through the front window of her house in the afternoon and through the blue glass dish that had belonged to her great-grandmother Jewel. She thought of how the hardwood floors took on an amber gleam just after they were cleaned, and how the chime of the grandfather clock at the end of the hall reminded her of her childhood, counting off the hours until bedtime.

Her eyes were still closed when they handed the attendant their boarding passes. As they entered the jet bridge, fear of what she was about to do made her lose the connection to home. The inside of the covered walkway smelled of plane fuel and cold air. When the ramp began to slope downward, she felt the slight pull of gravity and panicked. It felt just like the plane had when it began to go down. She whimpered slightly and leaned forward, bracing herself for impact.

Cameron frowned. He didn't know what was going through her mind, but he could tell it was bad. Her knuckles were white and her body was shaking.

"You're okay, baby. You're okay."

She could hear voices. People were talking and laughing, nothing like what she'd heard before. No praying. No crying. She took a breath and finally looked. There was a family of three in front of them: a man, a woman and a small child in a stroller. It cleared the emotional confusion but not the fear.

The closer they got to the plane, the colder the air became. When they reached the end of the ramp, she had to stand up. The attendant stood aside with the wheelchair while the family in front of them folded up the stroller and tagged it for baggage. These were all simple ordinary tasks. She could do this.

And then she glanced toward the plane, saw tiny flakes of snow blowing in through a small gap by the open door and grabbed Cameron's arm, her voice mirroring the panic she felt as she said, "It's snowing."

Cameron nodded. "Just tiny little flakes. Look, there's nothing on the ground. It's okay, honey. Just take my hand."

"You go first," she begged.

He stepped into the plane and paused, waiting for her to step across. He could see the horror in her eyes as she looked down.

"Look at me, honey. Don't look down. Look at me."

Their gazes locked, and she stepped in.

"Is everything all right?" a flight attendant asked, eyeing Laura.

"It will be," Cameron said.

He'd gotten tickets in first class, knowing she was going to need all the pampering and room she could handle just to make the trip, then led her a few steps to their seats.

The flight attendant took their coats as Cameron got Laura settled in the window seat and buckled her up.

"You've already taken your pills, so you'll feel easier soon," he said, then gave her a brief kiss of reassurance as he settled into the seat beside her.

His lips were warm and gentle. He was familiar. She was safe. It was going to be all right.

She glanced out the window at the ground crew loading luggage and remembered opening all the suitcases inside their plane and using the clothes she found to stay warm. If it happened again, she wouldn't be able to get to the luggage this time, because it was in the belly of the plane. Maybe there would be enough clothing in the carry-on bags. And then she caught herself.

What was she doing? The plane wasn't going to crash. She had already had her plane crash and lived through it. Surely God didn't let things like that happen twice.

A flight attendant stopped by their seats.

"Can I get either of you something to drink?" she asked.

Startled, Laura almost jumped, then focused on the question.

"Coffee? Could I have coffee? I can't seem to stay warm today."

"Certainly," the attendant said, then looked at Cameron. "How about you, sir? Anything to drink?"

"Coffee is fine," he said, and then turned his attention to Laura again as the attendant walked away. "It will be a while till they finish boarding and we pull away from the gate, but the meds will kick in before then. Do you want to go to the bathroom before we take off?"

She nodded and unbuckled her seat belt.

Cameron stood up, then helped her back up the aisle.

"She needs the restroom," he said.

As Laura went in and locked the door, the flight attendant glanced at the bathroom, and then at him.

"Is she okay? Is she not feeling well?"

He flashed his FBI badge and then dropped it back in his pocket.

"She's not sick. She's scared."

The attendant acknowledged the badge as she smiled sympathetically.

"Ah, is this her first flight?"

"No, but this is her first flight since a crash."

The pilot was standing in the doorway to the cockpit, listening. When he heard that, he frowned.

"What crash was that?" he asked.

"Two weeks ago. A private jet went down in the mountains outside of Denver," Cameron said softly.

"Ah, damn, I heard about the crash and that there was a survivor."

"She's the one," Cameron said.

The bathroom door opened. Laura came out, then paused, a little startled by the people grouped in the aisle.

The attendant's smile was just a little wider, and the pilot nodded his head.

"Welcome aboard, ma'am."

Laura blinked, then glanced at Cameron. He pointed up the boarding ramp.

"Here come the regular passengers. We'd better get back in our seats."

Immediately after they were seated, the attendant had coffee on their trays and was back at the doorway, welcoming passengers aboard.

Laura took a quick sip and then glanced at Cameron.

"You told them, didn't you?"

He shrugged.

She sighed. "It's okay. If I freak out later, maybe they won't throw me off the plane."

"If you get scared, just grab my hand. If that doesn't help, maybe we can make out a little to keep you otherwise occupied."

She laughed, picturing that happening in full view of a planeload of strangers.

He grinned. The foolishness of the remark did the trick. Now having sex with him was on her mind instead of flying.

The passengers filed past, some looking longingly at the first-class seats, others just anxious to get in and get settled. And then fate played a cruel joke.

The boarding line stalled, and people standing in line were getting impatient while a flight attendant tried to iron out a conflict back in coach between two people claiming the same seat. Voices were raised, and everyone was craning their necks, trying to see what was going on.

Cameron was sending a text, and Laura was looking at a magazine when she heard someone say her name.

"Laura? Laura Doyle? Is that you?"

Cameron looked up and then quickly glanced at Laura. She looked rattled, and his first instinct was to intervene; then Laura laid down her magazine and gave the middle-aged brunette a quick glance.

"Oh, hello, Tessa. Small world."

"Oh, my God! I never imagined I would see you here. I can't believe you've got the guts to fly again after what happened to you, what with everyone dying and all."

Every passenger within hearing distance turned around to look.

A muscle jerked near Laura's right eye. "Technically, everyone didn't die, Tessa, because I'm still here."

Cameron's seat belt clicked, then slipped to the side as he stood up, which instantly removed Laura from the woman's line of vision. His voice was soft, but his intent was firm, and there was no mistaking how pissed he was.

"Excuse me, ma'am, but that was an insensitive remark and best left unspoken, if you get my drift."

Tessa frowned as she lifted her chin, challenging his disapproval.

"I'm sorry. I don't know who you are, but she's my friend. We were at a conference together a few weeks ago. We were all horrified when we heard about the crash, and I wanted to wish her well."

He smiled, but it never reached his eyes.

"I don't know *you,* either, but just for the record, I'm the man who rocks her world, and I did not hear you wish her well. What I heard coming out of your mouth was morbid curiosity."

Someone snickered at the back of the line.

Tessa glared.

Cameron didn't budge.

The line began to move.

Cameron continued to stand, smiling politely until Tessa finally gave in, and the situation was resolved. Only then did he sit back down.

Laura was pale and teary as he reached for her hand. He grinned wryly, trying to ease the shock.

"We should have bought a lottery ticket today. Wonder what the odds were of something like that happening?"

She sighed. "Thank you."

He lifted her hand to his lips and kissed the knuckles, then winked and leaned close to her ear.

"Ready for that make-out session yet?" he whispered.

She rolled her eyes but smiled, which was his intent.

I love you, she mouthed silently.

He kissed the side of her face. "I love you most,"

he whispered, then leaned back, turned off his phone and buckled up. "Is your phone off?" he asked.

"It's dead," she said, and then looked horrified at what she'd just said. "I mean, it needs to be recharged."

He frowned. "Look, honey, that word doesn't hold any special power. It does not have to be purged from your vocabulary."

Her eyes narrowed angrily. "I hate this. I hate what happened. I hate that my friends are gone. I hate being afraid."

"I know, and I hate it for you, but nothing can change what happened."

She looked out the window without answering, then angrily pulled the shade down.

He let her be. It wasn't enough that she'd been rattled by the flight, but the universe had thrown in a brainless "friend" to boot.

Then all of a sudden they were backing away from the gate, and Laura's focus shattered. She clutched the armrests so tightly that her knuckles whitened.

Cameron grabbed her hand.

"Laura, look at me."

She turned her head.

"Lean back, take a deep breath and hold on to me. It's going to be okay. I promise."

She did as he asked without arguing, but she knew better. It wasn't possible to make promises like that. Not when fate was in charge.

The plane began to taxi. She moaned beneath her breath and closed her eyes, focusing on the strength of Cameron's grasp. By the time the plane was cleared for takeoff she was crying without making a sound.

Cameron was sick at heart for what she was going through, but he had no way to make it better. It was a blessing when the pills finally took effect and she fell asleep.

They served food an hour into the flight, but Laura was still sleeping. Cameron ate lightly, paying more attention to her than his tray, and was glad when the attendant took it away.

He got up once to go to the bathroom and asked the attendant to stand watch until he returned. He was on his way back when the plane hit rough air. The flight attendant headed for the intercom as the seat belt sign came back on. Just as he got to his seat and buckled in, the ride became rougher.

Laura woke up with a gasp, the sensation of déjà vu so horrifying, she turned to look for Marcy. Instead, she saw Cameron reaching for her.

"What's happening?" she gasped.

"Just rough air, baby. No big deal. It's happened plenty of times before, right?"

She heard his voice but couldn't focus enough to understand the words. She covered her face and bent forward, ready for impact.

Cameron knew she was only seconds away from screaming when he unlocked their seat belts and pulled her into his lap.

The passengers around them looked sympathetic.

They'd heard enough during boarding to understand what was happening, but the moment she was in his lap the flight attendant was on her feet.

Cameron had his arms wrapped around her so tightly that she couldn't move, her head tucked beneath his chin. He kept his voice low, but the urgent cadence in his voice was obvious.

"Laura, listen to my voice. We're not going to crash. The plane is safe. You're safe. Open your eyes. Look at where you are."

She couldn't hear him.

"No, no, the wolves will come. Watch out for the wolves."

Cameron grabbed her face and made her look at him.

"Look at me, baby. Look at me. There are no wolves here. They're gone."

Laura blinked, saw her own reflection in Cameron's eyes and then hid her face against his chest. She was shaking so hard she could barely breathe, but Cameron had arrested her free fall, and the scream in the back of her throat dwindled to a moan.

The flight attendant was beside them now, frowning, but Cameron couldn't have cared less.

"Sir, I'm sorry, but she can't sit in your lap. You have—"

Cameron interrupted. "Either you find a belt extender and buckle us up together, or she has an emotional meltdown and starts screaming. It's not going to help in this rough weather for everyone on this plane to hear a bloodcurdling scream and you know it."

The flight attendant spun and dashed toward the galley. She came back moments later with two belt extenders, fastened them together and then belted both of them in.

Cameron nodded. "Thank you. If I can have some water, I'll get her to take some more meds. As soon as she's calm, I'll buckle her back into her own seat. I promise."

Once again the attendant headed back to the galley while Cameron managed to slip his hand into his pants pocket. Laura had wrapped her arms around his neck so tightly it was hard to breathe, but he wouldn't have pushed her away, even if it meant giving up his last breath. The moment he got the pill bottle out of his pocket, it slipped out of his hand and rolled backward down the aisle and into coach seating.

"Damn it," he muttered.

"I've got it," he heard someone say, and moments later footsteps came up behind him. "Here you go."

Cameron looked up into the bluest eyes he'd ever seen set in a face wreathed with wrinkles and framed with short curly hair in flyaway gray.

"Thank you so much, ma'am," he said.

"You're welcome," the little woman said, then patted Laura on the shoulder. "Sugar, the only thing you have to fear sitting in this pretty man's lap is that he might put you down. If I was thirty years younger, I'd give you a run for your money."

Cameron chuckled, and Laura felt the rumble beneath her ear. That was a happy sound. No one would be happy if they were going to crash.

Cameron shook two pills out into his hand just as the attendant came back with the water, and set it in the cup holder near his elbow.

"Please, get her back in her seat as soon as possible," the attendant said.

Cameron understood she was doing her job, but so, by God, was he.

"Laura, honey...look at me. You need to take your pills."

Laura shuddered, so afraid that, if she opened her eyes, she would wake up back in that plane in her nest and hear wolves digging outside in the snow.

"Are you sure the wolves aren't here?" she whispered.

Cameron sighed. "No, honey. No wolves."

The woman across the aisle from them was purposefully staring at the magazine in her lap, but it was obvious from the tears rolling down her cheeks that she was locked in to their ongoing drama.

The man in the seat in front of them turned around and gave Cameron a quick sympathetic look. Even the flight attendant came back with a different attitude as she put a blanket across Laura's shoulders.

"I'm so sorry," she said as she tucked it around her and then moved down the aisle, checking to make sure the other passengers had fastened their seat belts.

It was the warmth of the blanket and Cameron's

reassuring voice that finally pulled Laura back into reality.

"I did it, didn't I? I freaked. Oh, my God, I am so sorry."

Cameron shook his head. "No apology needed, darlin'. Just take these pills for me, okay?"

She put them in her mouth and took a big drink before leaning back in his arms. She didn't talk. There wasn't anything she could say that would make this choking horror go away.

He pulled the blanket closer around her and then rested his chin on the top of her head, waiting for the moment when the tension left her body. By the time her panic had disappeared, the flight had also smoothed out.

He gave her a quick hug. "You ready to get back in your seat?"

"After I go to the washroom," she whispered.

"Absolutely," he said, and undid the seat belt.

She slid off his lap, then stepped over his legs and limped up the aisle with her head down, too embarrassed to look up.

Cameron tucked the belt extenders into the seat pocket in front of him and waited for her to come back.

The door to the bathroom opened, and when Laura emerged he could tell she'd been crying and was heartsick for how hard this was for her.

But then something happened as she started up the aisle.

The woman across the aisle began to clap her hands.

"Bravo to you, honey," she said.

Then the man in front of them joined in, and then the couple behind them, and by the time Laura got back to her seat the whole front of the plane had joined in the applause.

Cameron stood up and then slipped into the aisle to give her room to get in. Instead, she walked into his arms and hugged him.

"Once again you came to my rescue when I needed you most. Thank you forever," she said.

He hugged her back and then scooted her in.

"Buckle up before we both get in trouble all over again," he said.

"We got in trouble?"

He grinned. "It's a long story best told over a bottle of wine."

"And in front of a fire, please. I don't think I'll ever be warm again."

Cameron leaned over and kissed Laura squarely on the lips.

"You are the best," he whispered.

"My mouth feels weird. I could barely feel that kiss," she said.

He cupped her cheek. "It's the pills. Go to sleep, baby. I'll wake you up when we land."

She pulled the blanket up over her shoulders, reclined her seat and passed out.

The next thing she knew they were landing.

Five

The sun was only an hour or so from setting when their plane landed, and it was almost dark by the time the cab finally reached Laura's house. The tires made crunching noises as they rolled through the crust on the snow-packed driveway.

The driver jumped out and quickly carried the suitcases to the porch while Cameron carried Laura through the snow. There were dark shadows beneath her eyes and a slight muscle tic near her left eye. The journey had exhausted her, both physically and mentally.

"Easy does it, honey," he said as he set her down on the covered porch.

She smiled. "I'm okay."

But he could see she wasn't. Cameron turned to pay the driver as Laura unlocked the door and then held it open as he carried the suitcases into the house.

The cab driver backed out of the drive and took

off down the street as Laura closed the door behind them. Her voice was shaking as she reached for Cameron's hand.

"I didn't think I would ever see this again."

He wrapped his arms around her. "I have no words for what you've endured. I'm just so grateful that you're here. Welcome home, honey. Welcome home."

Laura closed her eyes for the kiss, waiting for the wave of love to wash through her, and it did.

Cameron smiled as he let go, but his gaze was focused on her pallor.

"I'm going to take the suitcases into the bedroom," he said.

She nodded absently as she absorbed the familiar surroundings of the home in which she'd grown up. Her sister had been careful to leave the heat on so that pipes wouldn't freeze in their absence, but it smelled a little stuffy. Still, she was at peace. This was her refuge.

Her leg was hurting, probably from too much sitting, and she needed something to flush the drugged feeling out of her system. She limped her way into the kitchen, taking joy in the simple act of being able to make a pot of coffee. She measured out hazelnut crème, which was her favorite grind, but noticed her hands were shaking as she poured the water into the reservoir. She had just turned on the machine when she heard Cameron's footsteps. From the look on his face, he was worried about her, so she pushed past the exhaustion and made herself smile.

"I thought some coffee might help me shake the effects of those pills. I don't know what was in them, but once they kicked in, I was gone."

"I'm seriously glad we had them," he said.

"I can only imagine what a scene I made. I'm grateful I only remember bits and pieces of that."

He smiled. "On a good note, I just got a text from Tate and Nola asking if we were home. I told them we'd just arrived. They sent their love and a heads-up that they ordered take-out dinner for us. We should expect a delivery of Chinese food within the hour."

Her shoulders slumped as she leaned against the cabinet.

"Oh, wow. I just love them. That's the best gift they could have sent, considering there's nothing in the refrigerator and a good two feet of snow on the ground."

The thought of gifts made him remember the engagement ring back in his apartment. He reached for her, pulling her close.

"I'm so glad you're safe. If I had my way, I would never let you out of my sight again."

"I feel just the same," she said, and closed her eyes, anchored by the warmth of his embrace.

At his urging, Laura settled down in the living room under an afghan until the house warmed up a bit more. By the time dinner arrived, she was so tired she could barely eat. She picked at it for a few minutes, then finally gave up.

"The food is good, but I'm too tired to enjoy it,"

she said as she stirred her fork through a helping of fried rice.

Cameron saw the dark shadows under her eyes and frowned.

"I'll clean up. Why don't you get in bed?"

She laid the fork on her plate.

"I think I'm going to have to. I feel like I'm about to drop."

"I'll be there shortly. You're not too shaky to do this on your own, are you?"

"No, I'll be okay," she said, and got up from the table and left the room.

He began putting away leftovers, then put their dishes and cups in the dishwasher. He emptied the coffeepot, then cleaned it and got it ready for tomorrow, stopping a few moments longer to send a message to Tate and his wife, Nola.

Food delicious. Laura exhausted. Going to help her get ready for bed.

He hit Send, then made the rounds through the house, making sure everything was locked up, the security system was set and the lights were turned off before going to check on her.

Laura was just getting out of the shower when he walked into the bedroom. She was so out of it she hadn't even bothered to close the bathroom door. He quickly turned back the bed, found a nightgown in the dresser and took it to her.

"Is this okay?" he asked.

"It's fine," she said, then dropped the towel and held out her arms.

He pulled the nightgown over her head. When she reached for a hairbrush, he took it from her hand and gently smoothed the tangles out of her hair.

She brushed her teeth as Cameron began digging through his suitcase for some of his things, and when he turned around, she was headed for the bed.

He caught her just as she stumbled, and then carried her the rest of the way. Her eyes were closed before her head hit the pillow, and by the time he came out of the shower she was fast asleep.

It wasn't the first time they'd slept together, but it *was* the first time they'd slept together in her house. As soon as he turned out the last light and crawled into bed, the unfamiliarity was gone. It wouldn't matter where they were, because as long as Laura was in his arms, he would always be home.

As night fell on the East Coast of the United States, the social butterflies of the retirement community at Lake Chapala, Mexico, were getting ready for a birthday party.

Hershel had quickly learned after he moved in that it didn't take much of an excuse for someone to throw a party here. Considering the ages of the residents, it could just as likely have been a wake, though, so birthdays were even better. There was a no-gift rule. The food was always cake and punch, and the entertainment was the movie of the night, chosen by the birthday honoree, and shown in the private screening room at the complex. The room seated fifty, and the comfy leather recliners meant someone was always falling asleep before the movie was over.

Some of the residents had been decorating since morning, hanging paper lanterns, arranging floral decorations for the tables, and someone was just now hanging an oversize piñata above the arched entrance.

Hershel was walking home after an early dinner when he saw the group of ladies through an open doorway.

One of them, a lady named Barb Wentworth, saw him and called out.

"Hey, Paul…Paul Leibowitz! Don't forget Patsy's party tonight. It's at 7:00 p.m."

"At seven," he echoed, and waved.

Sometimes Hershel went. Sometimes he didn't. But now that they'd seen him and issued a concrete invitation, he wouldn't ignore it. Part of his cover was living the lifestyle of a retired businessman with a healthy outlook on social activities.

The birthday girl, eighty-eight-year-old Patsy Lincoln, had a reputation as something of a matchmaker. She made Hershel nervous, always trying to pair up the singles in the neighboring condos, which made him a prime target of interest. He didn't want another woman and had managed to evade her suggestions. He wondered absently what it would be like to be eighty-eight years old, then shrugged it off. Without

Louise, it didn't really matter anymore. He was here until he was not.

By the time he reached his condo, he was uncomfortably warm. The air-conditioning was a welcome relief as he locked the door behind him, then turned on the television before going to wash up.

Once inside the bathroom, he paused, eyeing himself in the mirror, and then leaned toward it for a closer look. His mustache was in need of a trim and a fresh dye job, and he needed to run the electric razor over his head. Opting for completely bald had been part of the new look, and he didn't regret it.

He felt his face to check for whiskers. It needed a bit of a shave as well, but that wouldn't take long. Even though the plastic surgeon had done wonders at minimizing the burn scars on his face from the boat explosion in Louisiana two years earlier and the other scars left from the injuries he'd suffered in the Missouri tornado last year, only a portion of his face grew whiskers. The need for revenge that had turned him into a killer had also done a number on his appearance. Once he'd used disguises to hide his identity; now he hardly recognized himself. But the need for killing was in the past. He had purposefully avenged his wife's death in brutal fashion. The authorities who'd ignored him and Louise before would, by God, not forget them again.

He backtracked into his bedroom, took off his sweaty clothes and then went to shave and shower. He would tend to the dye job tomorrow.

He emerged a short while later in search of something appropriate to wear. After a quick scan of the closet, he opted for a short-sleeve, button-up shirt with a straight tail. Wearing untucked shirts was common here, and he liked it. He chose a pair of cotton slacks in cinnamon-brown, which coordinated nicely with the pale yellow color of his shirt, and opted for a pair of brown loafers, always striving for lightweight. After the burns he'd suffered, he could no longer tolerate heat, and even though the winter temperatures in this area stayed in the high seventies to low eighties, it didn't take much for him to feel uncomfortable.

Once he was dressed, he grabbed his keys and headed for the community center. The security lights at every corner marked the distance as he walked, and since the sun was down, the night was already cooler, which was a relief. He could hear the celebration in full swing even before he saw the building, and when he arrived, both doors were wide-open.

He walked in unobserved, grabbed a glass of punch and a piece of cake and then found an empty chair at the far end of one table. One of the residents saw him, waved a hello and then resumed his conversation with the people beside him.

Hershel smiled and nodded, then took a bite of cake. He always thought of Louise when he came to the events. She would have loved every minute of the social life here, right down to the birthday cake. She would have cheated a little on her diabetic regimen just to have the sweets and added more insulin later.

Louise always had been one to push a boundary. He took a second bite of cake, washed it down with a sip of punch and made himself quit thinking about Louise. She'd been Hershel's wife—not Paul's.

Within a few minutes he got caught up in the party to the point that he went looking for the birthday girl. He wished her a happy eighty-eight years and eighty-eight more, which made her giggle.

When it came time to break the piñata, everyone laughed at her feeble attempts. Finally she handed the stick off to one of the men, who broke it for her. The goodies inside were always something of a joke. This time they'd added individually wrapped condoms along with the pieces of candy, and when they hit the floor, the partygoers erupted in laughter.

A few minutes later they began heading toward the screening room to watch the film. Hershel thought about skipping out but had waited too late to decide. Instead, he got caught up in the moving crowd and soon found himself seated between two couples. He knew them well enough to settle comfortably and leaned back, absently gauging the distance to the screen.

"What's the movie we're going to see?" he asked.

One of the ladies leaned forward. "I heard it was *Titanic*. Patsy always wants to watch it because she claims she had a relative who survived the real *Titanic*."

Hershel flinched. The skin crawled on the back of his neck as the food in his belly rolled a warning.

He'd never seen that movie, but he knew how it ended and had no desire to watch people drown. He stood abruptly, trying to keep a calm expression on his face.

"I'm afraid I'm going to beg off, then. I had a family member drown. Not a story I want to see repeated," he said. "Have a nice night, and I'll see you around."

He got up while they were all making sympathetic noises, and kept smiling and nodding as he made his way up the aisle and out the door. His stomach was still gurgling, and his legs were shaking as he walked back through the room where the party had been held. He made it all the way to the courtyard just outside his front door before he got sick and threw up.

When the nausea finally passed, he staggered to his condo, relieved to finally be inside. He went straight to the refrigerator for a bottle of beer, popped the top and took a big drink.

"Son of a bitch," he muttered as he staggered back into the living room and dropped into his favorite chair.

He emptied the beer, went back for another and proceeded to drink himself to sleep.

In his dreams he was standing in a funeral parlor, looking across the room at an open casket. He couldn't see who was in it and moved closer, then closer still, until he realized the casket was empty. He turned around, and to his horror, someone had filled the room behind him with caskets, all of them empty. When he realized he was trapped, he panicked.

Help! Help! I can't get out.

In the dream, a woman came to the door. *The only way out of this room is in one of those,* she said, pointing to the caskets.

He woke up with a gasp. The sun was just coming over the horizon. He had dried vomit on his shoes, a headache of massive proportions and he needed to pee.

Cameron woke just before daylight to find Laura curled up behind him, molded to the shape of his body like one puzzle piece fitted into another. Her arm was around his waist, and he knew her nose was buried against his back because he could feel the soft warmth of her breath against his spine.

God, what an amazing way to wake up.

And if he had anything to say about it, he was going to wake up that way every morning from now on.

On the heels of that thought there came another. Before this day was over, he would be engaged to Laura Doyle.

He glanced at the clock. It was just after six. He was going to have to check in with work today and let them know when he would be coming back. Laura was capable of being on her own now, but he wanted to make sure she had everything she needed beforehand.

He was still planning the day when he realized she was beginning to wake up. He eased out from under her grasp and turned to face her just as she opened her eyes.

"Good morning, sunshine," he said softly.

She smiled. "If this is a dream, I don't want to wake up."

"It's real, and so am I."

She eyed his sleepy look and the tousled strands of dark hair across his forehead, then reached for his hand.

"I like waking up to see your face."

Cameron's pulse was racing, but to no avail. He threaded his fingers through her hand and lifted it to his lips.

"There is nothing I want more than to make love to you right now. But you, my love, still have a lot of healing to do, and I have no intention of making things worse."

"You wouldn't ma—"

He put a finger on her lips before she could finish.

"Yes, I would. Not on purpose, but it would hurt you, and abstinence won't hurt me. So I'm going to get dressed and make coffee. Go back to sleep if you want."

"No. I'm so grateful to be home, I just want to walk through the house and center my world, you know?"

"Yes, I know," he said, and then kissed her.

Her lips were warm and soft, and when she cupped the back of his neck and pulled him closer, he groaned.

"We're so not going there," he said, then kissed her again to underscore the warning. "Since you are getting up, make a list of things you need, including groceries. I'll get everything before I come back."

"Okay," she said, and then smiled to herself as she

watched him walk into the bathroom. He was naked except for a pair of gym shorts, and she did love to look at those long legs and broad back.

Cameron had already shopped for groceries and dropped them off at Laura's house before stopping by FBI headquarters to check in. After a short visit with his boss and an update on Laura, it was decided he would report for work in two days. He was more than ready to resume a regular routine.

It was just after ten in the morning when he reached his apartment building. There were no surprises as he entered the apartment. It wasn't any cleaner than it had been when he left. When he got to the bedroom, the clothes he'd tossed aside were still on the unmade bed and the light was still on in the bathroom.

He'd been so scared while packing to go search for the downed plane, praying Laura had survived, that neat and clean had been the last things on his mind.

Whatever.

He refolded, then put away the clothes he'd left behind, took the dirty ones out of his suitcase and repacked it with clean things, ready to stay over again tonight and, he hoped, forever.

He stepped inside his closet to open his private safe and took out the small black-velvet box sitting on top of his passport. He dropped it in his pocket, then took it right back out and opened it, imagining how it was going to look on Laura's hand.

Two carats of square-cut diamond winked as it

caught light from above. He shut the box and dropped the ring back in his pocket, took the suitcase into the living room and added his unopened mail and his laptop before heading out.

As he got in the car and drove away, it began to snow.

Laura was going through mail and paying bills when she came upon a letter from two sisters who had worked as on-site volunteers with her in Louisiana, where she'd first met Cameron when he and his partners had arrived on the trail of a serial killer known as the Stormchaser. She smiled, remembering how funny Peg and Mary were together, like a comedy duo. One played the straight man, and the other always followed up with the funny remarks. They'd been in charge of cooking for the displaced residents. She remembered Peg was taller and Mary was the redhead.

When she opened the letter, some snapshots fell out. She let them lie in her lap as she read the letter.

Laura, we heard about the plane crash. Very sorry for your coworkers, but we were thrilled to learn you had survived. Always thought there was a tough cookie beneath that pretty face and blond hair. Peg sends her love, and I'm sending love and pictures. We took them at the gym when we were helping out. Get well soon.
Love, Mary

She smiled, then picked up the pictures and turned them to the light for a closer look. Some of the names she remembered, some she didn't, but the faces were all familiar. She often formed special bonds with volunteers while working together during disasters—some, like Cameron, were more special than others.

When she got to the last picture, she gasped. Of all things, there was a picture of the man she'd known as Bill Carter, who'd turned out to be Hershel Inman, aka the Stormchaser.

It was strange that her memory of him was of a hard worker with a ready smile. She searched his expression for clues to the cunning and madness that lurked behind his smile, but she saw nothing that would have given him away. He'd had the perfect cover, helping those displaced by disaster, to keep him in close proximity to people in need of rescue, the same people who had become his victims.

His complete lack of compassion was horrifying. And from the way the picture had been taken, it was as if he was looking straight at her. She knew he'd been off the FBI radar since last year in St. Louis, and no further deaths had been attributed to him. Someone had made the suggestion he might have died at last, after cheating death more than once by living through an explosion and a tornado, but until they found a body, the case would remain unsolved. She shuddered and laid the picture aside.

She was still going through mail when she heard a car slow down and then come up her driveway. Her pulse jumped when she saw it was Cameron, and she got up to let him in.

"You're back!" she said as he came up the steps, his arms loaded with groceries, and stomped snow off his shoes on the mat.

"And you're gorgeous," he said as he bent down and gave her a quick kiss.

He'd brought the scent of winter in with him, which quickly dissipated as he carried the sacks into the kitchen and shed his coat.

"You sit and tell me where stuff goes, and I'll put it away," he said, and then proceeded to empty the bags.

The ring was burning a hole in his pocket. Before, he'd planned on a romantic dinner and finding the right moment to propose, then he'd nearly lost her. Waiting for a better moment didn't seem so important anymore. As soon as everything was put up, he turned around and looked at her.

Laura smiled, but when he kept looking, she shifted nervously in the chair.

"What? Is something wrong? What aren't you telling me?" she asked.

He started to speak, then stopped to clear his throat and started over.

"Nothing is wrong."

She relaxed. "Thank goodness. For a moment there I was afraid you were about to tell me the Stormchaser was back."

He frowned. "What would make you think of him?"

"Wait until you see what came in the mail," she

said, and went back to the living room, got the pictures and quickly returned.

"Remember Peg and Mary…the two sisters who cooked at the shelter we set up in Louisiana?"

"Yes, they were great ladies."

"So they heard about the crash and sent me a nice little letter, and included some pictures that had been taken there. Look at this one. Who do you see?"

It was the first face he focused on.

"I'll be damned. Hershel Inman."

"Who I knew as Bill Carter, and honestly, the picture gave me the creeps. We still don't know what happened to him, do we?"

Cameron frowned. "No."

"Do you think he's dead?"

He sighed. "There's no way in hell to know that unless a body turns up."

When she frowned and looked away, he hesitated. This had turned awkward really fast. Not the most perfect moment to propose.

Then Laura looked up. "I just remembered something!"

"What?" he asked.

"You said we had something to talk about and you told me we'd talk about it once we got home, right?"

He grinned. *Yes. There is a God!*

"Why, yes, I believe I did say that."

She put her hands in her lap and looked up.

"Am I going to like it, or is it going to piss me off?"

He laughed. "Why do you think I would ever discuss anything with you that would piss you off? I live to see a smile on your face, not a frown."

She shrugged. "I don't know. It's just not like you to be so secretive, and the past two weeks of my life have already left me in something of a pissy mood."

He took the box out of his pocket and dropped to one knee.

Her eyes widened. Her mouth made a perfect little O.

He struck while she was still in shock.

"I had plans to do this on Valentine's Day at your favorite restaurant. What happened to you changed my view on making plans. Now I'm more of a 'there's no time like the present' kind of guy, and I'm counting on you to agree."

He opened the box and watched her expression go from shock to awe.

"Cameron! Oh, my Lord!"

He took the ring out of the box.

"Laura Doyle, the luckiest day of my life was walking into that high school gym and seeing you behind the desk. You have become the most important thing in my life, and I want to spend the rest of it with you. I love you most. I love you madly. Will you marry me?"

"Yes, yes, a thousand times, yes!" she said.

He slipped the ring on her finger, then stood up and pulled her into his arms.

"Right now, I am one seriously happy man," he said, and kissed her senseless.

Laura's head was spinning, her heart pounding, when he finally pulled away.

She stopped him. "Now I have something I want to discuss with you."

He smiled. "I can assure you the answer is yes."

She put a hand on his chest. "Don't say that until you hear me out. I don't want to push you into something you're not ready to do."

He frowned. "If it involves you, I'm ready."

She rolled her eyes. "At least let me ask."

His smile widened. "Sorry. I'm listening."

"This house belongs to Sarah and me, but I know she's never moving back here again, so how would you feel about moving in with me? It's not because I'm afraid or anything, so if you aren't comfortable making such a big change so quickly, please, don't say yes just because you think I need to be taken care of or something."

He laughed.

"What?" she asked.

"My suitcase is in the car."

She threw her arms around his neck.

"Oh, Cameron! This is the best day of my life."

He slid his hands beneath her hair and cupped the back of her neck.

"This is the *second* best day of *my* life."

She frowned. "What could be better than this?"

The smile died in his eyes. "The day I found you alive in that plane."

Laura's vision blurred as she buried her face in the

curve of his neck. When she started to cry, his eyes filled with tears.

"Love you, baby," he said softly.

Her shoulders were still shaking.

"I love you, too."

Six

Lake Chapala, Mexico

Hershel had settled in quite nicely, and once he'd had his last surgery, finished his weight loss project and had the excess skin removed, he was a completely different man. In fact, he'd gotten so immersed in his new identity that there were days when the bad parts of his past seemed as if they had happened to someone else.

But there was an anniversary coming up that meant a brief return to the States. Louise had died on August 31, and he hadn't missed a year since of putting flowers on her grave. Despite his reluctance to return to United States soil, he felt it would be bad luck to miss what had become a tradition.

So two days before the date, he packed his little carry-on with a change of clothes, loaded it into his Volkswagen and drove into nearby Guadalajara to spend the night. He caught an early flight north to New Orleans, which was just a direct hop across the Gulf of Mexico, and got a room for the night in one of the local hotels.

Within hours of his arrival, the familiar sounds of the city drew him outside. The scent of pralines cooking in a shop down the street in the French Quarter and the aromas of Cajun cooking wafting out of the nearby restaurants made him homesick. He continued walking down the street until he came to a restaurant that looked appealing and went inside.

He ordered gumbo and rice, with a crème brûlée for dessert, and then settled down to wait for his food to arrive. As he waited, he started to panic when he saw a couple walk in whom he actually knew. What were the odds of that happening? He shifted nervously in his seat and wished he had a newspaper to hide behind. If they recognized him, what should he do?

But the question became moot. They looked at him as they passed by, just as they would have any stranger, and kept going without a glimmer of recognition. He was safe.

His food came soon afterward and he ate slowly, savoring the tastes of home.

Later, he walked back to the hotel, then, rather than go to his room, sat in the bar for a while absently watching the television as he nursed an after-dinner drink.

He thought of tomorrow and another visit to the cemetery and sighed. He'd lived all these years without

Louise, but he was only sixty-two. His father had lived well into his eighties, his mother into her nineties. He wasn't sure he wanted to hang around another thirty or so years. By the time he quit the bar and went to bed, his steps were dragging from dejection. Coming back here had only put him in a bad mood. He should have stayed in Mexico and left Hershel Inman buried, too.

Later, after he finally fell asleep, he began to dream and tossed fitfully, wanting out of the horror in which he'd been caught.

Hershel was walking naked down the aisle of the church he and Louise had always attended. The pews were packed. The choir was singing, and he was in a panic. He wanted to turn around and run out, but his feet would only move forward, as if being pulled by an unseen force. And the farther down the aisle he went, the more humiliated he became. Any minute now they would see him, and the proverbial shit would hit the fan. Some would laugh. Others would be shocked and horrified at his lack of decorum. Louise would never speak to him again.

And then he saw a casket at the front of the church. He broke out in a sweat as his heart began to hammer. He didn't want to go any farther, but he couldn't stop his feet from moving. Closer and closer he walked, until he was standing at the casket. The lid was open. When he saw his wife's battered body, he threw his head back to scream, but no sound came out. He turned to face the congregation and admit

his shame, that he'd come naked to his wife's funeral,
then realized they couldn't see him.

He woke with a start, momentarily confused by
where he was, and then took a deep breath and relaxed, thinking back to the crazy dream. It took him
a few moments to realize what it meant, and then he
relaxed when he finally got it.

The mourners hadn't seen him or his naked body
because that man no longer existed. He could walk
among anyone today without fear of recognition.

Relieved, he rolled over onto his side and went back
to sleep. The next time he woke it was almost one in
the afternoon.

He'd slept almost half the day away.

He dressed in a pair of pale blue slacks and a blue-
and-white floral shirt. After a cup of coffee from the
coffee shop downstairs, he walked out of the hotel
and down the street until he came to a florist. He was
inside the store before he realized he'd been in here
numerous times when Louise was still alive. Once
again, he was anxious.

The clerk greeted him cheerfully but without recognition, and as soon as he was satisfied she didn't
see through his disguise, he shifted focus.

"I need a dozen red roses, please."

"Yes, sir. Do you want them arranged in a vase or
boxed?"

"In a vase, please, but none of that extra stuff, just
the roses with their own leaves."

"I'll get right on it," she said. "If you'll follow me up to the counter, you can sign a card to go with them while you wait."

Hershel followed, eyed the cards and then chose one with flowers on one corner. Louise loved her flowers.

Without thinking, he started to write his name and then stopped. Instead, he wrote "Love you," then slipped the card into a small envelope, wrote "Louise Inman" on the outside, then sealed it.

The woman was at a worktable a few feet beyond the counter, snipping stems and poking them into a vase. She glanced up, saw him watching and smiled.

"These are really nice ones. Just got them in this morning," she said.

"They look fine," he said.

She smiled again and kept working. A few minutes later she carried the vase to the counter.

"How does this look?" she asked.

"It looks good. Thank you. How much?"

"Seventy-five dollars."

He handed her cash, poked the envelope in between the stems, walked out and hailed a cab.

"Where to, sir?" the driver asked.

"Greenwood Cemetery."

The driver nodded and drove off. A short while later they were driving through the gates.

Hershel leaned forward to speak to the driver.

"Take that road," he said, pointing, "and then take the third right. After that, I'll tell you where to stop."

"Yes, sir," the driver said, and drove slowly past the tombstones, crypts and mausoleums.

Within a couple of minutes, Hershel leaned forward again.

"Stop at this corner. I'll walk from here."

The driver stopped. "I'll be waiting right here for you, sir, when you're ready to leave."

Hershel got out with the flowers and started walking, and was immediately enveloped in the heat and humidity. Once he bent his head to sniff the roses and frowned that they had no scent. How could something so beautiful be so lacking? Then he remembered she couldn't smell them anyway, decided it wouldn't matter and kept moving. The grounds were unusually silent, save for the birds chirping from nearby trees, oblivious to the fact that they were singing to the dead.

The farther he walked from the cab, the more anxious he became. He kept looking over his shoulder, half expecting to see the police coming at him with guns drawn. By the time he found Louise's grave site, he was shaking. He'd taken a risk coming here, even in this disguise, and was banking his freedom on the fact that, even if someone was watching, they would never recognize him.

He paused to check out the area. There was one mourner about twenty yards away, and a couple at the far end of the row murmuring to each other. He could hear their voices, but not what was being said.

I almost didn't recognize you.

Hershel stumbled, then looked around nervously as he spoke in a low tone.

"Louise?

Who else did you think it would be? Of course it's me.

"What are you doing here? I thought you were gone," he said.

I was thinking the same exact thing of you. You shouldn't be here. You need to go back to Lake Chapala.

"I will, as soon as I put these flowers on your grave."

He quickly put the vase down in front of the aboveground tomb. The card fell out, and when he realized the name of the florist shop was stamped on the outside of the envelope, he frowned. Worst-case scenario: that could lead the authorities to him again. He took the card out of the envelope and poked it into the flowers alone, pocketing the envelope to throw away later.

I remember flowers. I wish I could smell stuff down here again.

He frowned. "Don't worry. They don't have a scent."

It doesn't matter. Go home, Hershel. Go home... home...home.

Her demand sounded anxious. Maybe she knew something he didn't. He turned around and headed back to the cab. The closer he got, the faster he went. By the time he got inside, he was breathless.

"Take me to the Marriott, please."

"Yes, sir. Right away, sir," the driver said.

Hershel kept an anxious eye out for police, but the ones he did see on the way back were on their way to somewhere else.

Once back at the hotel, Hershel began to pack. He had an early-morning flight tomorrow and didn't want to be late.

When he went down to dinner later in the evening, instead of choosing one of the hot spots he knew so well, he ate in the hotel, picked up a half-dozen news-papers from different parts of the country and headed back to his room. It would be a treat to read a larger variety of American papers for a change.

He skimmed through a local paper and then the *New York Times,* before he picked up the *Washington Journal.* He was already yawning and about ready to call it a night when he turned a page and realized it was the society section. The photo of the little blonde looked familiar, and he stopped to read the story below it.

That was when he realized why she'd looked fa-miliar. The soon-to-be bride was Laura Doyle, the Red Cross woman he'd worked for during the floods. He kicked back to read further, but when he read the name of her fiancé, he gasped.

"What the fuck?"

Cameron Winger? The third fed. The one he'd cracked on the head when he'd kidnapped Nola Landry. He wasn't dead? Why wasn't he dead?

He sat up to read further. The notice mentioned a wedding shower being given by Jolene Luckett and Nola Landry. His heart skipped a beat. That damn female agent hadn't died, either?

"Son of a bitch," Hershel muttered, and then grabbed his iPad out of his luggage and began running a search of death certificates for Tate Benton and Wade Luckett. He couldn't find one for either one. "They're alive. They're all alive. Why didn't they die? I thought it was over. I thought I'd won."

He was sick to his stomach as he crawled into bed, and then when he finally fell asleep, his dreams were filled with horror and recriminations.

Cameron was at his desk writing up a report on a case he'd just closed when his cell phone signaled a text. When he saw it was from Laura, he stopped typing to read.

Wedding shower amazing. So many pretty gifts. Bringing you some goodies. Leaving in 15. Will text when I get home.

He frowned. The one side effect Laura still suffered from after the crash was the fear of being in trouble and no one knowing where she was. He typed in a response and hit Send.

Drive safe. I'll be home around 6. Don't cook. I'll take you out. Love you, too.

He got a happy face back for an answer and grinned, then finished up the report. Just as he was filing it, he got a phone call and noticed it was from fellow agent Tate Benton. He answered quickly.

"Hello. How goes it?"

"Hello to you, too," Tate said. "I heard from Nola. She said Laura's shower was a big success. You'll be writing thank-you cards for days."

Cameron laughed. "Yes, Laura just texted me. She sounded excited."

"How's she doing? Does she still have PTSD?" Tate asked.

"Yes, she's still afraid she'll be in trouble and lose touch with me. I'm not sure what to do to reassure her, although the promotion she got after she went back to work was huge. She doesn't have to go out to disaster sites anymore, so that's almost eliminated travel. She's seeing a counselor a couple of times a month, and I'm hoping, with time, some of this will smooth itself out."

"I had a thought," Tate said. "Remember when we were in St. Louis and the Stormchaser tried to snatch Jo? We had the CIA implant a tracking chip in her."

"Are you saying Laura should do that?"

"That, or something similar. Maybe put one inside something she always wears—a watch or something."

"That's a good idea," Cameron said. "Thanks, buddy. I'll check into it."

"Good. However, that's not why I called. There's something you need to know."

Cameron frowned. "Like what?"

"I've already told Wade, and I'm giving you a heads-up, too. Do you know what today is?"

Cameron glanced at the calendar to confirm. "The last day of August."

"It's also the day Hershel Inman's wife died."

Cameron's stomach rolled. "You still think he's alive, don't you? Even though he hasn't killed anyone since St. Louis."

"Let's just say I'm leaving nothing to chance, which is why I put in a call to the New Orleans police department today and asked them to send an officer to the Greenwood Cemetery, where she's buried."

"And?"

"And someone left a dozen red roses at her grave."

Cameron groaned. "Was there a card?"

"Yes, but no name…just 'Love you.'"

"Do they have security cameras?"

"The ones they have don't cover the grounds, and what they have aren't working anyway," Tate said.

"It could have been a friend."

"A friend wouldn't send a dozen red roses. That's from a lover or a spouse," Tate argued.

"So what do we do? Wait for the next shoe to drop?"

"Or the next storm," Tate added.

"This is why you asked about Laura, isn't it?" Cameron asked, and then heard Tate sigh.

"Look. He's really mad at us," Tate said. "Nola threw the first kink in his plan, and Jo made it worse. You're pulling Laura into the circle, and I just don't want to leave her unprotected if he decides to resurrect the Stormchaser."

Cameron felt sick. "Damn it! She's still traumatized from the plane crash. She doesn't need to be worrying about becoming a target for a serial killer."

"Better safe than sorry," Tate said. "Get a pen and paper. I'll give you the number of my CIA contact, the one who helped me with Jo's tracking chip."

Cameron picked up a pen. "I'm ready. Go ahead."

Tate gave him the name and number, then disconnected.

Cameron didn't hesitate. He made the call, anxious to get everything lined up before he went home. There was a thunderstorm predicted, and he would rest easier knowing he was doing all he could to keep Laura safe.

Laura was arranging the shower gifts on the sideboard and the dining table when she heard a car pull up in the drive. She glanced at the clock. Not quite five. It couldn't be Cameron. Then she heard a key in the door and smiled.

It *was* Cameron.

She went to meet him with a smile on her face.

"You're early!" she cried.

He planted a kiss on the side of her neck and then swept her off her feet.

"Now, this is my kind of welcome home," he said as he slid his hands beneath her hair and proceeded to kiss her until they were both lust-high and hungry for more. "Oh, baby, if we didn't have plans, I would so be taking you to bed." He kissed her one last time to emphasize the promise.

Laura smiled. "So how come you're home early? Did all the bad guys take a holiday?"

"I wish," he said, and then took a small oblong box out of his jacket pocket. "I have something for you."

"A present?"

"A very useful present," he said as he handed it to her.

Laura was still smiling as she opened the lid, and when she saw the delicate silver cross on a long woven chain, her eyes widened.

"Oh, Cameron! This is beautiful. Put it on for me, will you?"

He took the necklace out of the box and then stopped.

"There's something special about this," he said.

"You mean other than the fact that you gave it to me?" she asked.

He smiled. "The jewel in this cross isn't a diamond. It's a crystal with a tiny tracking chip embedded in it."

She gasped, and then looked up. "Tracking chip... as in 'you would always be able to find me' kind of chip?"

"Yes."

Her eyes welled with tears.

"You are forever my hero," she said as she lifted her hair and turned around.

As soon as Cameron fastened it around her neck,

she turned to face him, her gaze locked on the promise in his eyes.

"I'll never be lost again."

"That's right, honey, never again."

"This has been the best day ever," she said, fingering the cross. "Come see the amazing presents we received. We're going to be writing thank-you cards for days."

He laughed, remembering Tate saying the very same thing earlier. He followed her into the dining room to look without mentioning anything about the roses that had shown up at Louise Inman's final resting place. Right now that was the only sure thing they knew. Everything else was supposition, and he wasn't going to upset Laura based on a theory.

Later that night, the thunderstorm that had been predicted earlier moved into Reston, bringing a torrential rain. The wind that came with it blew the rain sideways, slamming into the windows of the bedroom where Cameron and Laura were sleeping.

He woke to a flash of lightning, followed by a boom of thunder. In the glow of the night-light out in the hall, he could see water pouring down the windowpanes.

Laura was snuggled in behind him, and when he moved, she woke.

"What's wrong?" she mumbled, and started to reach for the light.

"Nothing," he said softly as he grabbed her hand and put it around his neck instead.

She felt the ricochet rhythm of his pulse pounding beneath her palm, and smiled as he rolled over and parted her legs with his knee. She shifted slightly and then arched her back as he slid inside. He was hard and hot, and she was wet and aching.

"Make love to me," she whispered.

"I already am," he said as he began to move.

Once the joining happened, the storm outside was nothing to the storm they were creating. The deeper he went, the tighter she wound. Her eyes were closed, her teeth clenched against a guttural moan that slipped up her throat. It was so good it almost hurt, and yet she couldn't stop—wouldn't stop. It was all about chasing the quicksilver flutter that would make her lose her mind.

The faint whistle of wind turned into a whine as it whipped through the trees outside the house, mirroring the rush of blood through her body. The force of nature was nothing to the power of lust. When Cameron shifted into a harder, longer stroke, she rocked up to meet him.

"You like that, baby?" he whispered.

Laura moaned. The blood was pushing through her veins at breakneck speed, racing toward the pressure point of bliss. One second she was with him, and with the next breath she swallowed a scream. After that she was gone, riding the climax that exploded within her.

Cameron clenched his jaw, trying to maintain control, but her climax was his trigger and he lost it.

Hours after the storm was gone, they still slept, safely locked in each other's arms.

Seven

Tate Benton hadn't been satisfied with just knowing someone had put roses on Louise Inman's final resting place. He'd followed up by getting a couple of local FBI agents to check out florist shops in the area and see if someone remembered who'd bought the flowers. Normally the envelope from the florist would have had a name printed on it, but this envelope was missing. The only thing they had to go on was the card, which appeared generic. Still, he wasn't going to be satisfied until they'd followed up as far as they could. There was too much riding on Hershel Inman's whereabouts to ignore the significance of the flowers arriving on the anniversary of his wife's death.

While he waited to hear back from the Louisiana agents, he continued to get ready for work. No need to alert the director or his partners unless he learned something new.

* * *

Cameron rolled out of bed just before the alarm went off. He glanced back at Laura and smiled as he headed for the shower. She was still asleep. Even though she'd taken yesterday off because of the wedding shower, they both had to go into work today.

He was just getting out of the shower when she slipped into the bathroom. He smiled as she wrapped her arms around his waist and licked the water drops off his chest.

Just before he got any ideas, she pulled back with a sexy little grin.

"I made coffee. Do you have time for breakfast?"

"I'd rather make time for you," he said.

She slipped her nightgown over her head, letting it fall to the floor as she wrapped her arms around his neck.

"I had a feeling you would say that."

His heart thumped out of rhythm at the thought of a repeat of last night.

"I'm going to get you all wet," he warned.

"You always do," she said.

He laughed, swung her off her feet and carried her back to bed.

When Hershel woke the next morning, he dressed without thought for how he looked, wanting only to get home. He caught a cab to the airport and arrived in plenty of time, but as he was striding to the gate, he began seeing Louise. Everywhere he looked, she was just walking past his line of sight or disappearing into the women's bathroom or down a ramp to get on a plane.

"What's going on?" he muttered, but she didn't answer. "What does this mean? If I'm seeing you, does this mean I'm going to die?"

He sat down near his gate, his hands shaking and his heart hammering in a jerky rhythm against his rib cage. Everything had been fine until he'd come back to the States.

Go home. I told you to go home.

"Then, why am I seeing you?" he whispered.

If you don't go home, then you will *die. This is the last warning you are going to get.*

"But they aren't dead. They were supposed to be dead."

She didn't answer, and all of a sudden they were calling his flight.

He stood up, grabbed his carry-on and started walking, but instead of moving toward the gate, he was walking away, moving through the airport all the way to ground transportation, where he rented himself a car. By the time his plane was in the air, he was in a car driving north.

The logical part of him knew this was a bad idea, but the worm in his brain was already at work, telling him what to do and how to do it.

Before he left this earth, he needed at least one of those men who'd tried so hard to bring him down to know the pain of his loss. Since Nola Landry and

Jolene Luckett had already blown past his fruitless attempts to end their lives, it now appeared there was one more lady who'd moved to center stage.

Laura Doyle was set to become a bride, but not if he could help it.

Reston, Virginia—September 4

It took Hershel two days of driving to get to Virginia. Upon arrival, he turned in the rental car and purchased a used van. Then it took another day of looking for a place to live before he found what he was looking for on a sign in someone's yard.

For Rent: Garage Apartment.

He turned into the driveway, eyeing the elegant two-story brick home. It looked neat and tidy, which should bode well for the apartment. Then he saw the garage at the far end of the drive and the apartment above. He eyed the steps going up. A little steep for his knees, but he wasn't going to need it all that long. He checked out the small roofed landing at the top and decided if the place wasn't a complete dump, it would be perfect. He would have the kind of privacy he needed to come and go as he chose, but also quiet, which wasn't always possible in a hotel or motel. He got out of the van and headed for the front door.

The brass door knocker was a lion's head with a large brass ring between its teeth. Hershel grabbed the ring and banged it a couple of times, then stepped back. The door opened moments later to reveal a middle-aged woman in a maid's uniform.

"Yes?"

Hershel smiled. "I'm here about renting the garage apartment."

"Ah, yes, please come in Mr.…?"

"Leibowitz, Paul Leibowitz."

"Come this way, Mr. Leibowitz."

He followed her into a well-appointed library.

"Have a seat. Mrs. Taft will be here shortly."

He sat, curiously eyeing the room and its contents. The walls were covered with a plethora of framed certificates and degrees. But before he could get up to check them out, he heard footsteps.

He stood up as a tiny, white-haired lady dressed in a black-and-white pin-striped dress walked in. Her hair was a pale shade of lavender, and the size and number of diamonds on her fingers probably could have funded the overthrow of a small country. She walked with her head up and her arms swinging. He had the impression that if he'd remained seated, she would have booted him out the door without an introduction.

"Mr. Leibowitz, is it?"

"Yes, ma'am. Paul Leibowitz."

Her eyes narrowed as she checked him out with no apology for staring.

"I'm Lucy Taft. My deceased husband was William Harold Taft, a direct descendant of President William Howard Taft. I understand you are interested in renting the apartment."

"Yes, ma'am, but not long-term. I'm only in the area for a couple of months on business."

She frowned. "I don't like to rent by the month. Will you be staying alone?"

"Yes, and I'll gladly pay you the two months in advance, even though I doubt it will be that long. It's just that I hate hotels."

"It's fifteen hundred dollars a month, with a five-hundred-dollar deposit, including furnishings and all utilities. It has a television, and internet and Wi-Fi connections."

"Sounds great. I'd like to see it," Hershel said.

She rang for her maid.

"Mildred will show you."

"That's fine. Thank you."

The maid came into the room wearing a jacket, already aware of her duties.

"I have the keys, Mrs. Taft. Mr. Leibowitz, if you'll come with me, we'll go out the doors here in the library. It's a shorter route."

"Thank you," Hershel said, nodded politely to Lucy Taft and followed the maid out the door.

The day was sunny, even though the air was a little brisk. They crossed the lawn to the back of the property, then she went up the steps with Hershel at her heels. The door swung inward on well-oiled hinges. Mildred flipped on lights and stepped aside for him to enter.

"The furniture is clean, and the floor is hardwood.

No pets or smokers allowed, and Mrs. Taft appreciates things kept neat and tidy."

Hershel nodded.

"As you can see, the kitchen/living room is one large open space. The television has a DVD player. Every room is fully furnished. The stove is gas." She opened the refrigerator. "It's clean and already cold. We don't turn it off between renters. If you'll follow me, I'll show you the bath and bedroom."

Hershel followed.

Mildred turned on lights as she moved down the little hall.

"Bedroom on your left has a queen-size bed and matching dresser." She opened the closet. "It's a nice size with shelves in the back. The bathroom is across the hall next to a small closet with a washer and dryer inside."

"Oh, that's handy," Hershel said.

Mildred nodded. "Mrs. Taft's grandson, William Herman Taft, lived here when he was in college."

"Nice," Hershel said, imagining the privacy and convenience of being here. "I think this will work just fine."

"That's good," Mildred said. "If you'll come back to the house with me, Mrs. Taft will tend to the rest."

This was no more than Hershel expected. The little woman came across as stern bordering on bossy, which was fine. Once he paid her, he wouldn't have to interact with her again.

Mildred led him back to the library and then handed the keys to her boss.

"He approves, ma'am."

Lucy Taft had already had her say and was waiting for Hershel to speak.

"It's very nice. I'm sure I will be comfortable there for the time I need it," he said, and pulled out his wallet. He counted out thirty-five hundred dollars in one-hundred-dollar bills. "Two months in advance, plus the deposit, and I'll be sure to keep it clean."

Lucy Taft took the money and then removed one key from the ring and gave the other to him.

He noticed the fact that she kept one of the keys, a good reminder to leave nothing incriminating lying about.

"When do you plan on moving in?" she asked.

"Today, and since the refrigerator is already cold, I'll shop for groceries before I come back. If I get my business finished sooner than planned, I'll certainly let you know ahead of time and make sure to leave everything as clean and tidy as I found it."

"Agreed," Lucy Taft said.

"Then I'll be off," he said.

"Oh, Mr. Leibowitz?"

He paused. "Yes, ma'am?"

"Are you a God-fearing man?"

Just for a moment Hershel felt as if he was standing in front of Louise and she was about to read him the riot act for skipping church, and then he relaxed.

"Why, yes, I am."

She lifted her chin and then sniffed slightly, as if she could smell out a rat trying to lie.

"Good. I wouldn't want any atheists or sinners living on my property."

Hershel's smile shifted slightly.

"Ah, yes, but, Mrs. Taft, aren't we all sinners in one way or another?"

She blinked, and then her lips twitched in what he supposed passed for a smile.

"Yes, I believe my dearly departed William Harold would say that is a fair summation of the human condition." She stepped aside for Hershel to exit. "Mildred will see you to the door."

He walked out into the hall, where the maid was waiting, then followed her to the door.

"Nice to meet you," he said.

"Likewise," Mildred said, and then added, "If you have problems at the apartment, please let me know. I'll see to the proper repairmen."

"Will do," Hershel said.

He walked back to the van with a bounce in his step. He loved it when a plan came together.

By evening he was setting up shop.

His target was Laura Doyle, and in the following days he staked out her house to familiarize himself with her routine. It gave him a sense of power to know he could have taken her out any number of times and hadn't.

It wasn't just about the killing. A large part of his

satisfaction came from the game, only this time he wasn't going to contact the agents to let them know he was on the job. He hadn't known they were still alive, so he was going to repay them in kind. He had to. They had worked just as hard to take him down as he had trying to take them out. It would be a betrayal of his love for Louise if he pretended it was over, but he wasn't going to make it easy for them this time. They were going to have to figure out what was going on from the clues he laid down.

And the plan he'd come up with was actually quite simple. Their challenge in stopping him would be in seeing his plan *before* it was over, because if they waited for the final act, it would be too late.

He had a map of Reston spread out on the dining table. Working from his starting point, which was Laura Doyle's address, he measured four inches due north on the map. The person living at that address would be the first victim, but he wouldn't kill them at their home. He was going to take him down at his place of work. The second victim would be four inches due south from Laura's address, and again the victim would disappear from her place of work. The third victim would be four inches west, the fourth four inches east, and Laura Doyle, whose home was dead center at the axis of those four locations, would be the fifth and last victim.

He'd learned the hard way not to underestimate the Stormchaser team and wondered how long it would take them to figure it out. Once he had time to scope out the first victim's habits, he would waste no time carrying out the first kill.

The weatherman hadn't lied. The rain predicted for late evening arrived just before sundown, lowering the temperature into the forties and turning the September night wet and cold.

It was Patty Goss's night to close at the Chic Boutique in D.C. where she worked. The front door was locked, and she was in back counting the money from the till to put in the store safe. She never liked closing on her own, but being the manager came with responsibilities. Tomorrow was her day off. The owner would take care of the deposit in the morning, and she would be sleeping in.

She'd called her husband to let him know she was bringing home takeout for dinner. Now all she had to do was wait for the delivery. A few minutes later a knock sounded at the back door. Her delivery was here, but just to be sure she called out.

"Who's there?"

"It's me, Mrs. Goss...Charlie from Hot Wok."

She unlocked the door. The owner's son, Charlie Lee, was standing in the downpour, his delivery car idling behind him.

"Nasty night," she said.

"Yes, ma'am, that it is," he said, and handed her the bag with her food. "Sweet-and-sour chicken. Pork dumplings. Fried rice and three spring rolls...and extra duck sauce. Right?"

"Perfect," she said, and paid him.

"Have a nice night," he said, and drove off as she went back inside and locked the door.

Patty set the bag of food down on the desk and went to get her raincoat. She did a last walk-through of the boutique to make sure everything was okay, then picked up her food and opened the back door again. Her keys were in one hand and her food and umbrella in the other as she pulled the door shut behind her, then used the remote on her key ring to set the store alarm.

The rain was loud, drowning out the sound of traffic as well as the footsteps of the man who came up behind her. She felt something sharp at the back of her neck, then excruciating pain. She fell to the ground, seizing in every muscle. The horror was being able to see and hear her assailant without the ability to move or speak.

"Dinner is going to be late," Hershel muttered as he kicked the sack of takeout aside and threw her over his shoulder in a fireman's carry.

Patty Goss was finally leaving, but she wasn't going to make it home.

He got her into his van, yanked the electrodes from the Taser out of her neck and calmly strangled her. Then he drove out of D.C. with her body hidden beneath a pile of painters' drop cloths. He also had a stepladder, some empty paint cans and some used paintbrushes he had pulled out of a Dumpster as part of his cover, should he ever be stopped by the cops.

The rain was really coming down by the time he

reached his chosen dump site. It was far away from the city limits, along the banks of the Potomac River.

He wasn't a big man, but he was strong. Still, it was with no small effort that he dragged her body through the mud and grass, then rolled her into the water. Then he stayed, standing in the downpour and watching until she sank from view.

By the time he got back to his apartment, the rain was a deluge. He got out on the run and hurried up the steps as fast as his aching knees would take him, thankful for the covered overhang as he fumbled with his keys.

Once inside, he shed his wet things at the door and proceeded to turn on lights as he went through the apartment, unaware that his landlady was standing at her bedroom window, watching him in the dark.

Lucy Taft didn't trust a businessman who carried large amounts of cash and chose to stay in a secluded garage apartment rather than a posh and accommodating hotel. She didn't know what he was up to, but she didn't want to become complicit by ignorance.

After two frantic hours of no contact with his wife, Patty's husband called the D.C. police and asked them to do a welfare check at her place of business. They found her car in the back parking lot, her purse and umbrella near the back door, and what was left of the food scattered and rain soaked, but no Patty. The only security cameras were in the front of the store, so there was no way to know exactly what had happened. The

next day, her picture and the story of her disappearance were on the local news.

Cameron saw it and felt bad for the husband, thinking how he would have felt if it had been Laura.

Lucy Taft read about the abduction in the paper
and made a mental note to remind Mildred to make
sure the security system in her house was in proper
working order.

Hershel saw the broadcast. The first clue was out
there; now the rest was up to them. He was satisfied
with the way things were going and began the planning of clue number two.

Two days later the badly battered body of a woman
was pulled out of the Potomac. From the Taser marks
and the strangulation bruises around her neck, it was
obvious she'd been murdered. Despite the damage to
her face, she was positively identified as Patty Goss
by her hysterical husband, who recognized her flying-
monkey tattoo.

Now the missing person case was handed off to
Homicide, and to make the cops' job a little harder,
Patty had no known enemies and a husband with an
airtight alibi.

Hershel was watching TV and having toaster waffles and scrambled eggs when the floater in the Po-

tomac made the news. He turned up the volume and then added extra syrup to his waffles. The authorities were talking about her job, her family and how long she'd worked at the boutique. His eyes narrowed as he took another bite. The game was on.

Cameron was propped up in bed reading the morning paper and happily anticipating the breakfast in bed Laura was making when he found out about the missing woman whose body had turned up in the river. He thought briefly about the similarity to the way the Stormchaser's victims turned up and wondered if Tate knew, but for the moment he put his curiosity on the back burner. He could smell bacon and fresh coffee. Beyond that, breakfast was supposed to be a surprise.

He paused before turning the page, and not for the first time examined the bedroom décor. It pleased him to see the tiny pieces of Laura's life still hanging on the walls and sitting tucked away on the shelves among her books. He knew she had lived here all her life, sleeping in this very room throughout her childhood, her teenage years with all the drama, then coming back to visit during college, and finally moving home to care for her elderly parents after they became too old to live alone.

He was sure the decorations and colors had changed throughout the years, but her spirit had not. The loving energy within the walls of this house was powerful. He knew because he felt it every day.

Being the only child of an older couple, he'd never

really known that kind of life. His father's job as a research chemist for an oil company had them moving often, so he had no personal ties to any particular city. Both his parents had died in an accident when he was in college, and he had been without family ever since.

And now he had Laura. In just over a month they would be married, and with the words *I do* he would be gaining a wife *and* a sister. Becoming part of the Stormchaser team had also turned his partners into the brothers he'd never had. It had taken him a while, but in a roundabout way, he had family again.

The blast from a passing car horn ended his musing as he glanced back down at the paper. A few moments later, he heard footsteps coming down the hall and looked up just as Laura walked in with a cup of coffee.

"Breakfast needs about ten more minutes, but I didn't want you to have to wait for this," she said.

Cameron grinned. "This breakfast-in-bed thing could really become a habit. Am I to assume this will be a regular Saturday routine?"

She arched an eyebrow. "You are not to assume anything of the sort."

She set his coffee on the nightstand at his elbow and blew him a kiss.

"I love you most," he said as she went out the door.

"You better!" she yelled back, and kept on walking.

It made him laugh. Her sass was part of why he loved her, but it was also part of the personality that had helped keep her alive, a fact he no longer took for granted.

He took a sip of the coffee and sighed. One sugar, no cream and nearly hot enough to melt the taste buds off his tongue. Perfect, just like her.

He set the coffee aside and went back to the story on the dead Reston woman. He frowned as he continued to read. They'd found her in the river, obviously a murder victim, which didn't surprise him, considering what had been reported about her disappearance. Taser marks on the back of her neck. Autopsy pending.

His frown deepened, and the hair stood up on the back of his neck. In the grand scheme of murders, the use of a Taser wasn't that unusual, but it had been the Stormchaser's favorite method of disabling his victims.

He kept reading the article, part of which echoed what the newscaster had mentioned on the news last night, before the discovery of the body. The husband's alibi was rock solid, and robbery was not a motive. Now that the body had been found, something useful might turn up in the autopsy. For the time being, the FBI would simply follow the case's progression without intervening in police procedure. He wondered if Tate had heard anything more from the Louisiana agents. It was too early to call, but on impulse, he sent a text.

Have you seen news? Missing Reston woman found floating in Potomac w/ Taser marks on her neck. Heard anything from Louisiana?

The mere act of sending it lessened the knot in his gut. He took another drink of coffee and turned to the sports page to see which college football games were being televised, but his conscience was bugging him. He had yet to mention anything to Laura about their concern, but he would have to say something soon, just in case.

Then she walked in carrying a tray heaped with steaming-hot food and drove every other thought from his mind. She was wearing a pink bibbed apron and nothing else. The smile on her face said it all. She'd surprised him, all right.

"Even though breakfast doesn't come with dessert, I made an exception. However, you can't have it until you've eaten your meal," she said primly.

He smiled, threw the paper aside and patted the bed beside him.

"Then put that tray down and grab a fork. Either you help me eat, or some of this is going to waste."

She stifled a giggle as she set the tray down in front of him, and when he reached out to stroke the thrust of her breast beneath the bib, she slapped his hand lightly.

"Not yet, Mr. Man," she said, and made a point of sliding onto the bed sideways, so there were no sneak peeks of her bare backside.

He groaned. "Have mercy, Laura Jean. How do you expect me to eat with you sitting there like that?"

She handed him a fork. "Why…just like everyone else, lover boy. One bite at a time." She waved her hand over the tray. "Does it look good?"

"It looks amazing," he said softly.

She pointed at the food. "I meant the food."

"Dessert is my favorite."

She smiled, got up, removed the tray from the bed and untied her apron, letting it fall to the floor at her feet.

"Are you serious?" he asked.

"We'll nuke the eggs later," she drawled as she climbed back into bed.

Eight

Tate was in the shower when Nola tapped on the door. He leaned out with a smile on his face, about to invite her in, when she put a finger to her lips and held up his cell phone.

"It's Agent Delroy from Louisiana," she said, handing him a towel.

He went from play to business as he turned off the water, grabbing a towel as he stepped out.

"This is Benton."

"Good morning, Agent Benton. Sorry to call so early, but I wanted to fill you in before we left on a new case."

"I appreciate it. What did you learn?"

"That a lot of roses were sold on August thirty-first," Delroy said drily. "Over three hundred dozen in more than one hundred and fifty area florists, and that doesn't include the floral departments in supermarkets."

Tate groaned inwardly. "Really? That many?"

"Yes," Delroy said. "That many. We showed pictures of Hershel Inman's DMV photo, as well as an artist's rendering of what he might look like after his potential injuries if he survived, and not one person recognized him."

Tate sighed. "We learned early on he was a master of disguise. I should have known it wouldn't be that simple. Did you get any kind of a lead on the card?"

"No. Unfortunately the same design was in nearly every shop."

"Were they able to get DNA or a print off it?"

"There were so many prints on the card it was impossible, and the same went for DNA. Lord knows how many people handled it before someone chose it for Louise Inman's roses."

Tate sighed. "Thank you for your hard work. We had to try."

"More than happy to do what I could."

"Good luck on the case you just caught," Tate added.

"Thank you," Delroy said, and disconnected.

Tate ended the call and finished drying off. It wasn't until he picked up the phone to take it back to the bedroom that he noticed he'd missed a text from Cameron. He read it and laid the phone aside without responding. There was nothing to say. Everything in him accepted the possibility that it could be Inman, but the contact phone they had used with him for so long had been deactivated, and without a way for Inman to taunt them, there was no easy way to verify that he was still alive—which Tate was afraid he was. He hoped he was wrong about that. God in heaven, he hoped he was wrong.

Megan Oliver was twenty-seven and had been working as a court reporter for the past six years in and around D.C. When the weather was nice, as it had been for the past two days, she ate lunch outside so she could chat with her boyfriend on the phone.

She didn't pay attention to the people around her and was unaware of the man sitting nearby and listening to every word she said. She didn't see him when she walked to her car every evening or know that he followed her home.

Hershel already knew from overhearing her phone conversations that she took night classes in D.C., and that she had a business-law class tonight. He'd also heard her comment that she planned on slipping out early.

That was all the opening he needed. When she left her apartment later to go to class, he followed her. She wouldn't see him until it was too late.

Business law was boring, and when Megan's three-hour class took a break about an hour and a half in, she went to the bathroom and didn't go back. She had to be in court early in the morning and needed to get some sleep. The morning drive from Reston to D.C. was always hectic, and if the past two days were any example, court would last all day. She would be glad when this trial was over. The testimony was gruesome, the evidence was grisly and it was giving her nightmares.

She glanced over her shoulder as she hurried down the hall and then out of the building. The wind was rising. She glanced up at the sky. It was overcast. It would probably rain again before morning. She clutched her iPad and water bottle up against her chest as she hurried across the parking lot.

About halfway there she realized three of the pole lights were out and frowned. That was odd. Someone needed to take care of that. At the same time, she heard a noise beneath the car she was passing, then screamed when a yellow tomcat darted out and ran past her, yowling and hissing its discontent.

"Dear Lord, no lights, crazy cats. What next?"

She lengthened her stride, trying to find her dark car in an even darker lot. She could remember the row, but not how far down, and without the pole lights, she couldn't spot it easily. She aimed the remote on her key ring and started pressing it, then kept pressing and clicking until suddenly a set of car lights came on.

"Bingo," she muttered, and lengthened her stride.

She was almost there when she saw something dark on the hood and hoped to God it wasn't another crazy cat.

She was all the way past the bumper before she realized there was a bouquet of flowers, wrapped in tissue paper, lying on the hood.

Her first thought was that her boyfriend had done this, and then she remembered he was out of town. The next thing that occurred to her was that the guy who sat behind her in business law was finally through flirting and making a move.

"So what have we here?" she said lightly as she reached across the hood to pick up the flowers.

Hershel had followed Megan to class and then parked in the back of the lot, waiting for traffic to clear out. Once activity slowed down, he pulled out of his parking space and began cruising until he'd located her car again. Then he drove back through the lot, stopping three different times to shoot out security lights with a pellet gun before parking back behind her car. He jumped out quickly, laid a bouquet of flowers on the hood and then went back to his van and settled down to wait.

An hour passed with more people arriving and a few of them leaving, but none of them were Megan Oliver. It was well on the way into hour two when he saw movement at the front of the building again. He could tell it was a woman with short dark hair like Megan Oliver's, but from this distance he didn't know if it was her.

He rolled down the window to listen for footsteps. A couple of minutes later he heard someone coming down the row, and when a tomcat suddenly squalled and hissed, he heard a woman scream.

That was when he made his move. He slipped out of the van and ducked down to wait.

He watched her hesitate in the spotlight of her headlights, then saw the smile break across her face as she saw the flowers. When she turned sideways to reach across the hood, he stood up and fired the Taser.

Her body flailed as the electrodes hit her cheek. She fell forward onto the hood of the car, her body jerking as her brain exploded. Some of the flowers fell under her, the rest beneath their feet. From a distance, had anyone see them, it would have looked like a couple locked in an embrace as he pulled her up from the hood. But then he quickly ducked down and began dragging her backward to his van. He opened the doors and rolled her up and into the back, then climbed in and hit the lock button.

She was twitching and jerking, and he could hear a faint moan as she kept trying to scream. He got down on his knees, wrapped a length of rope around her neck and proceeded to strangle her. When it was done, he yanked the electrodes out of her face, pulled the drop cloths over her body and drove off into the night.

Halfway to the river, the first drops of rain began to fall, but he kept on driving, going back to the same distant dump site he'd used before. He needed the body to be found, but not immediately. She needed to stew in the Potomac for a while before being swept downstream toward the city. It was better to draw out the tension of her disappearance, let everyone worry like he'd worried—let everyone wonder where she was like he'd wondered about Louise's body when it had slipped into the floodwaters after Hurricane Katrina. Fair was fair.

He was tired by the time he got back to his apartment, and he still had to negotiate those damn steps. His back was hurting. It felt as if he might have pulled a muscle. He would be glad when this was all over so he could get back to Lake Chapala. Everything in his life there was on one floor.

Lucy Taft was in bed with the lights out, watching television in the dark, when she saw headlights flash across the opposite wall. This was how she used to know when her grandson came home. Now she was using it to keep tabs on her renter.

She got up to peek out the window and saw him through the rain, walking up the steps. He appeared to be wearing the same brown raincoat and hiking boots he wore every time he went out, which told her that wherever he'd been, it hadn't been at any business meeting. She watched him turning on lights inside, then marked the time down in her journal and went back to bed.

It wasn't until the next day when Megan Oliver didn't show up for court that anyone began to take notice. Then, when she didn't call in or answer her phone, her coworkers began to worry. After sending a police car to her residence, all they learned was that no one answered the door and her car was gone.

At that point her friends began to backtrack her whereabouts from the night before and found her car in the parking lot where she had class. When they found her purse beneath the car and a bouquet of bedraggled flowers scattered nearby, they called the police again.

Now she went from late for work to missing.

The story and Megan Oliver's photo made the third page of the paper the next day, along with a phone number for the Washington, D.C., police department, should anyone have information as to her whereabouts.

Lucy Taft heard the information on the news while eating her breakfast and frowned. A second woman was missing? What on earth was going on?

Laura was finishing her cereal and Cameron was making himself another piece of toast when she saw Megan Oliver's picture.

"Oh, no!" she said, and pulled the paper closer.

Cameron turned around. "What's wrong, honey?"

"I recognize her," she said, pointing at the picture. "She and Sarah were in school together."

Cameron went back to the table to read over her shoulder. When he realized another woman had gone missing, his heart sank.

"So you knew her?"

"Not like a best friend, just like someone you would see around school."

"And she's missing? Is she married?"

"I don't know. No, I guess not. At least, she still uses her maiden name."

Cameron eyed the expression on her face and then reached for her hand.

"I need to talk to you. I've been putting it off, but I can't any longer."

Laura dropped the paper and turned to face him.

"What's up?"

"This is the second woman who's gone missing in the area in the past week."

She frowned. "So what does that mean to me?"

Cameron rubbed a finger lightly across her forehead, as if trying to smooth away the frown.

"The thirty-first of August was the anniversary of Louise Inman's death. Someone left a bouquet of roses near her grave in New Orleans in her name with a card that said, 'Love you.'"

Without thinking, she grabbed the locket, tightening the chain around her neck.

When Cameron caught the move, he knew she'd connected the dots.

"We don't know anything for sure. We're just keeping track right now."

"Has he contacted Tate like he did before?"

"No, the Bureau deactivated the phone months ago."

Her fingers tightened on the necklace.

"So you can't be sure?"

"Not yet."

Her eyes welled with tears.

"Is he coming after me? Will I be next?"

Cameron felt sick. She'd already made the same connection he had.

"Why would you say that?"

"Because he went after Nola, then Jo, and I'm all that's left."

He stood up and took her into his arms, sick that he'd put fear back into her life.

"We don't know it's him, so right now let's not borrow trouble."

She could feel the thunder of his heartbeat beneath her cheek and knew he was as upset as she was. She looked up, her fingers still tight around the locket.

"You can't lose me now, remember?"

He brushed a kiss across her forehead.

"Of course I remember, and no, I won't lose you. Ever."

She was shaking from head to toe. She heard him say the words, but they both knew that when it came to the Stormchaser, there were no guarantees.

Megan Oliver had always liked long soaking baths, but thirty-six hours' worth of river water had been overkill in the worst kind of way. Unfortunately, it was a fourteen-year-old Boy Scout working on a cleanup project for a merit badge who found the body. After a frantic call to his father a short distance away, they contacted the police. They showed up within minutes, roped off the area and sent the boy and his father home. His good deed for the day had been done.

It took another twelve hours before they got a positive identification, and then the news went out. Megan Oliver was no longer missing. She had what appeared to be Taser marks on her face, and she'd been strangled the exact same way as boutique manager Patty Goss. No one at the precinct had said serial killer yet, but they were all thinking it.

When Tate Benton found out they had another murder victim, he sent a text to Wade and Cameron.

Another murder victim w/ Inman's M.O. Going to talk to director. Catch up w/ you later.

Wade was coming out of court and frowned when he saw the message. He had his own grudge against Inman and would like nothing better than to drop him out of a plane, but his job demanded capture and arrest.

Cameron was in the field office when he got the text, and his first reaction was fear. He knew in his gut that if this *was* Inman, one of their women would become a target. Two of them had already escaped his grasp, though, and Inman knew Laura well. He had worked for her, which would make it easier for him to figure out how to get to her. But she'd already survived a plane crash this year. Surely to God, fate would not put her in the path of a serial killer, too.

It was after sundown when Hershel came out of the movie theater picking popcorn from between his teeth. The popcorn had taken the edge off his appetite, but he hadn't eaten since morning. He couldn't decide whether he wanted a steak or some clam chowder. Both of them sounded good, but the chill wind whipping around the corner of the theater settled the decision.

Clam chowder it was.

He strolled across the parking lot toward his van with his hands in his pockets, thinking about the movie he'd just seen. If he had it to do all over again, he might incorporate a couple of elements from the movie into his killings—not that he was into true torture, but the thought of someone hanging themselves was intriguing.

Stand them on a rickety stool with a rope around their neck and watch to see how long they lasted before the first leg came off the stool or they slipped off from exhaustion. It might be something to think about. In the meantime, he wanted some of that hot chowder and his business finished here soon. He was more than ready to head south for the winter.

Laura had gone through her workday in a daze, trying to get a grasp on the possibility that her life was in danger, worrying until she made herself sick. She knew Cameron was concerned and probably expected her old anxieties to return. She was more than a little worried, too, and wanted to do something proactive instead of waiting for the other shoe to fall.

She'd been friends with Nola Benton and Jo Luckett for months, but they'd become even closer friends since the engagement. Now she needed something more from them than friendship. It was almost time to go home when she sat down at her desk and sent them a text.

I have a favor to ask. I want to know every chink you saw in Hershel Inman's armor. Both of you escaped him. If he comes after me, I need at least a fighting chance to survive. Girls' day out tomorrow for lunch?

Then she gathered up her things, sent a text to Cameron that she was going home and left the building.

She'd never thought much about the hours she worked until now, but now she realized how going home after dark would make it easier for someone to take her unawares. She walked with her car keys in her hand, her head up and her gaze shifting constantly to the slightest movement or hint of sound. By the time she reached her car she was running. The moment she got inside, she locked all the doors, then quickly drove away. She just wanted to be home. That was her refuge. She would be safe there.

Her cell rang, but the traffic was heavy and she didn't even look to see who was calling. Moments later her OnStar system kicked in and the car phone began to ring. She hit the button to answer.

"Hello?"

"Hey, honey, it's me, Sarah, just checking in."

She smiled in spite of herself.

"Hey, Sarah! So good to hear your voice. Are

you still loving your job? Have you made some new friends?"

Sarah laughed. Laura always did want to know everything at once.

"Yes, the job is great. My flat is amazing. I have the best view of London nightlife from my living room windows."

"I'm jealous," Laura said, trying to picture her sister's world. "What about friends? Any of them happen to be male?"

She heard her sister chuckle.

"Of course some of them are male, but none of them are special. I'm too busy getting acclimated to the job and the country for any of that. What about you? I want to hear all about the wedding shower. Was it amazing? Did you get my gift?"

"Yes! I can't believe you sent a cappuccino maker. Cameron is all excited. He said I can be in charge of the panini maker and he'll in charge of the coffee."

Sarah smiled. She could hear the joy in her sister's voice.

"So everything is perfect, right?"

Laura hesitated.

Sarah frowned. "What?"

"It may be nothing," Laura said.

"Damn it, Laura. I'm half a world away. Don't make me guess. What's wrong?"

"The Stormchaser team may be about to reactivate."

"What? No! You aren't serious?"

"It's not certain yet, but Cameron is worried. Flowers showed up on his wife's grave in New Orleans on the anniversary of her death, and now two women have been murdered. They were both Tasered and then strangled."

"Oh, my God. That's the way he killed his last victims, right? Where did this happen? Was it back in New Orleans?"

"No. It was here. D.C., to be exact. They found both bodies in the Potomac."

Sarah gasped. "I don't like this. You're connected to the team now. What if he targets you like he did the other agents' wives?"

"We have that covered. I shouldn't have mentioned it. No one is even certain it's him, so don't worry."

"Come to London. You can stay with me until they get this sorted out."

Laura frowned. "Don't be silly. I'm getting married in a month. There are too many things to do, and I'm not leaving Cameron."

"I feel sick," Sarah said softly.

Laura sighed. "I know, and don't tell Cameron, but so do I. This really put a damper on the wedding plans, but I can't think like that. Two women are dead and I'm fine. This isn't about me."

"Yet," Sarah mumbled.

Laura changed the subject.

"So talk to me. Have you done any sightseeing outside London yet? Have you been to France?"

"Yes. It's amazing, just like I always thought it

would be. You and Cameron will have to come for a visit."

"We will. We definitely will," Laura said, and then listened to her sister talk the rest of the way home.

Cameron's car in the driveway signaled his presence as she pulled in behind it, and for that she was grateful.

"Hey, Sarah. I'm home now. I'll talk to you again soon, okay?"

"Absolutely, and keep me updated on everything else."

The call ended.

The wind had come up on the drive home, and when Laura got out, it was a cold slap in the face. She didn't know what they were having for dinner, but something hot and warm sounded heavenly.

Cameron heard the key in the door, tossed the pot holder onto the counter and came out of the kitchen with a ready smile on his face. Laura was hanging her coat in the hall closet when he caught her from behind and kissed the back of her neck before spinning her around.

"What's new, pussycat?"

She threw her arms around his neck.

"I just freaking love you," she said, hugging him fiercely.

Sensing desperation in her voice, he stepped back.

"What's wrong?"

"Sarah called on the way home. I told her about the

murdered women. She freaked. A little of it rubbed off on me, but it will pass."

He could tell she didn't want to discuss it further and let it slide.

"Something smells so good. What's cooking?" she asked.

"It's gumbo and rice. I picked the fixings up on the way home, which reminds me, we need to go grocery shopping."

"Ooh, that sounds good," Laura said. "We'll start a shopping list tonight. Tomorrow is Saturday. I'll do it while you're gone."

Cameron frowned. Going to Quantico, even for the day, felt like a careless move. What if she needed him and he was too far away to help?

In her haste, Laura missed the significance of his silence. "Do I have time to change into something comfortable?"

"Sure, honey. Food's done. I'm just keeping it warm."

"I won't be long," she said, and darted down the hall.

Cameron's eyes narrowed thoughtfully as he watched her leave, and then he went back to the kitchen.

He hated this feeling of helplessness, as if they were sitting on a bomb and Hershel Inman was holding the detonator.

Nine

Hershel was heating up a can of chili and watching the evening news. He was watching the footage of the cops pulling Megan Oliver's body out of the river and waiting for someone to say *serial killer,* but it hadn't happened. He was in the backyard of the FBI, the nation's experts, and they were just as silent as the D.C. police. It ticked him off.

He took the chili from the stove and poured half of it in a dish, then carried it and a sleeve of saltine crackers to the sofa. When the news went to commercial, he let his thoughts slide to more mundane matters as he ate.

His knee-jerk decision to go to D.C. had caused all kinds of ramifications back in Mexico. The last thing he wanted was for his friends to report him missing, so he'd called the manager early this morning and told him he would be gone for a while longer, that he was taking care of a relative with failing health. He'd gotten sympathy and understanding, along with the promise to look after his mail and property until he returned.

He went back to the kitchen to put some grated cheese on his chili and refill his coffee cup. The news program resumed but without any further mention of the murders, which put him in something of a snit.

"Well, hell. What does a person have to do to get some respect around here?"

The scream in his ear was so sharp and unexpected that he actually jumped up, spilling coffee on his shirt as he turned to look behind him.

"What the—"

God has abandoned you. The angels have turned their faces away from you. Your soul is lost.

Hershel frowned as he grabbed a dishcloth and began mopping up the coffee he'd spilled.

"Damn it, Louise! What made you scream like that? Last time all you did was echo, and now this! What the hell's the matter with you? If you have something to say, just say it."

Every time you sin, it hurts. I can no longer bear the pain.

He frowned. He didn't like feeling guilty, but she was doing it to him again.

"I don't get it. You died. You can't feel pain or sadness."

I'm not talking about physical pain. You are killing people in my name.

"Oh. Shit. Well, I'm not finished with my business," he muttered.

He heard what sounded like sobbing, and then nothing.

"Louise? Louise? You still there?"

Nothing.

Both the chili and the guilt sat on his stomach like a rock.

"Still doesn't explain why you're screaming like a damn banshee," he said beneath his breath.

He carried the food to the sink and dumped it down the garbage disposal, then stomped down the hall. He took off the coffee-stained shirt, took a clean one out of the drawer and pulled it over his head as he strode back up the hall, still muttering.

"Damn it, Louise, I nearly died in that fucking flood, too. It wasn't my fault I couldn't get to your insulin. I loved you. I took good care of you when we were married. Then you died. I went crazy from grief, you know. I had myself a nervous breakdown. I've been doing what had to be done to live with myself since then, so stop screaming at me, damn it."

Louise wasn't talking, and he was in a pout. He turned off the television, went back to the kitchen and pulled out his map. The next person on his radar was the person living due west of Laura Doyle, and this time he was going to send the cops into a tailspin. It was time to up the ante and create a little confusion.

Cameron kept delaying the inevitable. He had to leave within the next ten minutes or he was going to be late. He was meeting Tate and Wade at the field office before the trip to Quantico, but thinking of the possibility that Hershel Inman was somewhere in the city, and that he was leaving Laura at that bastard's mercy, was making him crazy.

Laura knew he was nervous, and she knew why, but she was ticked that this was happening.

"Cameron, get that look off your face. I'm fine. I'm buying groceries and then having brunch in D.C. with Nola and Jo. We're going to Ghibellina's, and you're going to an all-day meeting. We'll see each other at dinner tonight. The end."

He laughed as he swept her up into his arms.

"Nothing is ending between us, damn it. On the contrary, it's just beginning. But for now, I hear and I obey. Call or text anytime you feel like it." He put the palm of his hand over the cross hanging between her breasts. "And don't forget this. I'll always have your back."

Her lips parted instinctively.

As usual, he worked his magic, driving all thought from her mind but how it felt to make love with him. When he finally stepped back, she sighed with longing.

He rubbed his thumb along the edge of her bottom lip.

"Believe me, I totally agree," he said. "See you this evening. I love you most. Lock the door behind me."

She watched until he backed out of the driveway

and drove away before getting back to business. She had groceries to buy and a date for brunch. It was time to get busy.

The weather kept getting cooler as the day progressed. By the time Laura got home from grocery shopping, the temperature had dropped dramatically. She turned up the heat before putting away the groceries, and then ran to her bedroom to change clothes. She had a little over an hour to get dressed and drive into D.C. to meet Jo and Nola at one-thirty. Brunch was served from ten to four, and she didn't want to be late.

She stripped down to her underwear and then walked into her closet. After a couple of minutes she reached for the gray slacks and pink sweater Cameron had bought for her to wear home from the hospital. She liked wearing something he'd chosen especially for her, and it was a good, warm choice. As soon as she was dressed, she dashed into the bathroom to check her hair and makeup.

She reached for her hairbrush, then paused, eyeing herself in the mirror. The cold air had put pink in her cheeks, but she didn't have time to curl her hair. She brushed out the tangles and opted for a small bedazzled headband, giving her a chic, stylish look. After a light touch of lipstick, she added pearl earrings and a pair of gray suede loafers. She stopped in the hall on her way out to get her all-weather coat. This was not a day to assume it wouldn't rain or snow.

She grabbed her shoulder bag from the hall table

on the way out of the house, and then shivered as the wind hit her face. It felt like rain again, and rain made her think of the Stormchaser, which ticked her off. It wasn't fair that one man had all this control over their lives. Even though she was nervous, she lifted her chin. Today was not for madmen. Today was for fun and friends. She got in her car and drove away.

Hershel was on stakeout at the residence of his third target. He was watching the man in question maneuver his wheelchair down the ramp to his car. He had to admit it was a testament to Charles Trent's perseverance and some high-tech engineering that he was able to live alone, practice law and drive himself around town.

It was unfortunate for Charles that the location of his home tagged him as the Stormchaser's next target, but it didn't bother Hershel. His only concern was finding the perfect location to take him out. He couldn't do it around any of the courthouses Trent frequented, because of too many people and security cameras. It would have to be in D.C. at Trent's office. The man had a habit of working late. The more Hershel thought about it, the more he knew exactly how it was going to happen.

Satisfied with the plan he'd made, he decided to grab a late lunch somewhere and then play tourist. He'd never seen the Vietnam Veterans Memorial, the Washington Monument or the Lincoln Memorial. Might as well take time to enjoy some of the sights.

* * *

It was one-thirty on the dot as Laura drove down 14th Street NW to Ghibellina's and then found a place to park. She lowered her head against the wind as she ran toward the restaurant. Once inside, she spotted Nola, who was already seated, and moved through the narrow room with a smile.

Nola stood up to greet her and gave Laura a quick hug. "This is the best idea. It's so good to see you," she said.

"I know this was short notice, but I'm really glad you could make it," Laura said as she took off her coat and sat down.

"Me, too," Nola said. "Jo texted me a few minutes ago. She's on her way. She said she had some news."

A waiter came by, took Laura's drink order, then left. Laura picked at the plate of appetizers Nola had ordered and popped a stuffed mushroom in her mouth.

"Sorry," she said. "I'm starving. I didn't eat breakfast on purpose, just so I would enjoy this."

Nola eyed Laura's expression. She was trying too hard to be happy. She started to say something more, then saw Jolene coming toward the table.

"Oh, here's Jo."

Jo slung a navy blue pea jacket across the back of her chair and sat down just ahead of the waiter, who appeared to take her drink order, as well.

"Hot tea, please," she said, then reached across the table and clasped Laura's hands. "So how's our little bride-to-be?"

"Worried I might not make it to the altar," Laura said.

Jo frowned and lowered her voice.

"Don't say that. We don't even know if Inman's alive, much less that he killed those women or that he would target you, although I know he's as loony as they come. Even if it *is* him, there's no way to predict what he'll do next."

Laura leaned forward and lowered her voice.

"I know that, but I'm not taking any chances. I asked you both to lunch because I need you to tell me everything you can think of about Inman that might help me, should the need arise."

"You first," Jo said, pointing at Nola.

Nola began to retell her story, from witnessing him murder three of her neighbors to being attacked at the Red Cross shelter, then getting thrown out of the motorboat into gator-infested waters right before the boat blew up with Inman in it.

Nola's eyes narrowed as she thought back.

"I'm thinking he's got to be in his mid-sixties by now, and he's about five-ten in height. But being shorter, his center of gravity is lower. He's also deceptively strong for his age."

Laura stared at Nola in quiet awe. She was so matter-of-fact.

"Didn't all that do a number on your head?" she finally asked.

Nola shrugged. "Well, sure, but time has a way of taking the edge off." Then she grinned. "Tate did the rest."

They looked at each other and giggled.

"You next," Nola said, looking at Jo.

Jo nodded. "My involvement was different. Nola was the witness he wanted gone. When I became a part of the team who was after him, it ticked him off. From the start, he kept saying I didn't belong. He has some kind of sick attachment to the guys because they were in on it from the beginning. After I showed up, he took it as an affront, as if an uninvited guest had shown up for his party. When he failed to kidnap me on the first attempt, he decided it was because my addition to the team had jinxed him. So he revamped his plan of attack and was successful. He's sly and smart. What you need to know is that he hears his dead wife, Louise, talking to him. For a while after he kidnapped me, he actually thought I was her. I used that to my advantage. They were faithful churchgoers before the flood, and evidently Louise chides him for the sins he's committed."

Laura was listening intently, committing everything to memory. When the waiter came back to deliver Jo's hot tea, he stopped to take their orders.

"I'd like the Napoli pizza without capers," Laura said.

Nola pointed at the menu to *pane tostato*. "This, please. French toast with all the good stuff."

The waiter smiled and then looked at Jo. "And you, ma'am?"

"I'll have the frittata, and would you please ask

the chef to add some cheese to the onion and potato that comes in it?"

"Yes, ma'am," he said, and hurried away to turn in the order.

Nola grinned. "Since when do you add ingredients? You're usually the one asking to have something left out."

Jo blinked away a film of sudden tears.

"Since I'm eating for two," she said.

Nola's mouth dropped, and Laura's eyes widened. They both knew Jo and Wade had lost a baby a few years back, so this would be a seriously emotional pregnancy for them.

"Oh, Jo! That's wonderful news!" Nola said.

Laura gave Jo's hand a quick squeeze. "Best news ever," she added. "Is Wade eating for two, as well?"

"Isn't he always?" Jo said.

The joke was not lost on any of the women. Food never went to waste around Wade Luckett. He was always hungry and frequently scavenged from someone else's plate.

By the time Hershel came out of the restaurant where he'd stopped to eat lunch, the weather had changed for the worse. He gave up the idea of checking out the monuments and decided to go home. He would rather be inside watching television where it was warm.

He had just braked for a red light when he glanced

over at the car in the lane beside him, then did a double take.

It was Laura Doyle!

The shock of seeing her so close left him stunned. She seemed focused on the light and the traffic passing in front of them, which gave him time to check her out a little more closely. She looked different, but it was clearly her.

Her hair was much longer than he remembered. It had been short when he'd worked at the Red Cross shelter there in Louisiana, and she looked thinner.

He glanced up at the light. It was still red. When he turned back, he caught her looking at him. She seemed embarrassed and quickly glanced away, but it bothered him. Now he was wondering if he seemed familiar to her in some way. What if this chance meeting alerted her to his presence? That might mean changing up the plan. Before he could come to any conclusion, the light turned green and she went straight through the intersection as he turned left.

His anxiety increased as he drove home. He had two more clues to leave before he got to her, but this chance meeting might make it necessary to accelerate the process.

Laura was thinking about what to make for dinner as she braked for a red light. A moment later she sensed that she was being watched. She looked toward the car on her left, but the driver was staring up at the light.

His profile was vaguely familiar, but on second look she decided she didn't know him. Suddenly she realized he was looking straight at her. He'd caught her staring. How embarrassing! She looked away, and when the light turned green she drove on as he turned, and by the time she got home, she'd forgotten all about it.

Brunch with the others had given her plenty to think about, and in a good way. She didn't feel as unsure of herself as she had before. She'd known the killer first as Bill Carter, a congenial, helpful volunteer. But the others had firsthand information about the man behind the alias, and now, thanks to their willingness to share the hell they'd gone through, she knew something about Hershel Inman, too.

It was a little after four when she began prepping for dinner. Cameron sent her a text telling her he would be home around seven. That gave her plenty of time to bake brownies and put on a roast. It was a big one for two people, but she'd chosen it on purpose so there would be plenty of leftovers to use later in the week. She loved nothing better on cold days than homemade soup made with leftover roast beef and fresh vegetables.

She put the brownies in to bake and then got the roast ready to go in when they were done. The aroma coming from the kitchen began to permeate the house.

As the day turned to night, the gaslight in the front yard came on, a beacon for Cameron as he turned the corner and drove down the street. The lights behind the windows welcomed him as he parked. He paused long enough to gather up his briefcase, then headed inside, glad to be home.

Laura heard the key in the door and went to meet him. The cold air blew in behind him as he entered.

"Welcome home," she said as she wrapped her arms around his neck. His face was cold, but his lips were warm.

"Mmm, you taste good, and the house smells amazing!" he said. "Do I have time to change?"

"Yes. Get comfortable, honey. I'm still finishing up."

He cupped the back of her neck and pulled her to him again, like an addict needing one more fix. Her lips were soft and yielding, but when she leaned into him, he felt the demand for more.

"My sweet Laura, I do so love you," he said softly, as he finally pulled away.

"Love you most," she said,

He grinned. That was his line. "Back in a few."

She paused to watch him go, admiring the slight swagger of a man comfortable in his own skin, and then allowed herself a delicious little shiver before returning to the kitchen to finish the meal.

They were down to coffee and brownies à la mode when he said, "Hey, honey, I haven't asked, but did you have a good time with Jo and Nola today?"

She nodded. "I did. We had the best food. I ordered pizza."

"Oh, yeah, that's the place that serves it whole at the table and you cut it with shears rather than a knife, right?"

"Yes. The crust stays much crispier that way. It's pretty much spoiled me for eating pizza anywhere else."

He liked seeing that light in her eyes. He didn't know what else they'd talked about, but whatever it was, it had done her good.

Laura didn't mention the fact that she'd grilled them about Inman. It would serve no purpose to introduce his name to a very nearly perfect meal.

They finished in near silence, and then she laid down her spoon and leaned back.

He caught her watching him and smiled.

"What? Do I have ice cream on my chin?"

"I have a favor to ask."

"Yes," he said.

She grinned. "You don't even know what it is yet."

He shrugged. "Doesn't matter. You know whatever it is, I'll do it."

"I want you to teach me some basic self-defense moves."

The smile froze on his face.

"Don't be upset," she said. "This is me being assertive, Cameron, not afraid."

He sighed. "Yes, I can see that."

"So? Will you?"

He nodded. "Of course, but, please, not tonight. I'm so full that the kid down the street could take me down with one well-placed blow to my belly."

She laughed.

"I'll take you to our gym so we'll have some padded mats to work out on," he said.

She arched an eyebrow. "Great. I wouldn't want to hurt you."

He laughed out loud.

She frowned. "And because you laughed, you get to help me do dishes."

The mood seemed lighter as they began to clear the table, but the challenge had been issued, and it was a hard one to ignore.

Lucy Taft was at the dinner table when she heard a car drive past the house.

"Home early tonight," she muttered as she sliced herself a bite of prime rib and glanced up at the clock, making a mental note of the time so she could record it later.

"I'm sorry, ma'am. Did you say you wanted the horseradish sauce?" Mildred asked.

Lucy looked up. "Splendid idea, Mildred. Yes, I would like some horseradish sauce."

The maid hurried out of the room as Lucy popped the bite in her mouth and chewed thoughtfully.

Hershel grabbed his bag of Chinese takeout as he got out of the van, unaware he was on Lucy Taft's radar. He was halfway up the stairs when Louise screamed in his ear. It startled him enough that he dropped the sack. It fell between the steps and down onto the concrete below.

"What the fuck? Look what you made me do!" he yelled, and then looked nervously toward the house as he went back down the steps and began gathering up his food.

Go home! Go home!

"I *am* home," he muttered as he picked up the little cartons one at a time.

None of them had come completely open, but he could only imagine what a sloppy mess they were now. Sauce was dripping between his fingers, and some rice spilled out onto his shoe as he put everything back in the bag. By the time he walked into his apartment, he was in a fit of pique. He could control everything in his life but Louise. How could you argue with someone you couldn't see coming?

That man is helpless. You just can't do that.

Hershel lined the cartons up on the counter and opened them, then got a plate and began spooning out food from the dripping boxes.

"Look what you made me do," he muttered. "About ruined my dinner is what you did."

You plan death and then eat as if nothing was wrong. There is a devil in your brain. I don't like you anymore.

"As if I didn't already know that," Hershel said as he set the plate in the microwave and hit Start.

The hum of the microwave matched the vibration in his body. Sometimes he felt as if he was coming apart, and that, when the vibration got strong enough, he would shatter. When the microwave dinged, he actually jumped, half expecting to implode. It took a moment for him to realize it only meant his food was hot.

He opened the door, his hands shaking, and then carried his plate to the living room and sat down to eat. He aimed the remote, upped the volume and ate blindly, unaware of the taste or the show while waiting for a scream that never came.

Ten

Laura tossed the duffel bag with her workout clothes in the backseat, and then got in and buckled up. She popped in a CD as she drove away from the house. The drive to work was anything but smooth, but the upbeat music of Maroon 5 dulled the frustration of morning traffic. By the time she pulled into the parking lot at Red Cross headquarters, she was ready for the day.

As usual, it took a while to get to her office. Inevitably, someone stopped her to ask a question or, lately, to congratulate her on her upcoming nuptials. By the time she was in her office, she had half a dozen requests to check on.

Her secretary had entered the day's agenda on the iPad on her desk, and there was fresh coffee in the pot on her credenza, along with a cinnamon-raisin bagel and cream cheese. Within minutes she was returning phone calls and routing emergency supplies across the country between bites.

There was a flood in Colorado, a forest fire in California and a massive train derailment in New England. Two of the locations already had Red Cross shelters in operation, and the last one was in the process of setting up.

She got a text from Cameron before lunch telling her he would be out of town for the rest of the day but back in time to meet her at the gym that evening, and he signed it with a kissy-face emoticon. She sent a smiley face back and kept working.

It was almost quitting time when she got another text from Cameron letting her know he was back in the city and at the gym. She texted him back that she was leaving the office, and then did so in haste, wanting to get ahead of the traffic.

The first vehicle she saw as she drove into the parking lot was Cameron's SUV. Anxious to see his sweet face, she grabbed her bag from the backseat and headed inside.

She spotted him at the weight bench and paused to watch the play of muscles in his arms and chest. Her eyes narrowed as she realized Tate was spotting him, and Wade was on a treadmill nearby. Either she'd walked in on a regular workout, or they were all here on her behalf.

She stopped at the desk, got a key to a locker in the women's dressing room and went to change. She came out a few minutes later wearing tennis shoes, stretchy bike shorts and a T-shirt. Her hair was tied back, her chin was up and she was ready to take whatever they dished out.

Tate saw her coming.

"Hey, buddy, here comes your girl," he said.

Cameron finished the lift and grabbed a towel as Laura approached.

"Looking good," he said, eyeing her trim body beneath the figure-hugging clothes.

She glanced at Tate. "Are you and Wade here because of me, or is this your usual time to work out?"

"Busted," Tate said.

Wade came up behind her and tugged the ponytail hanging down her back.

"Hey, short stuff. How's it going?"

She shrugged. "It's good. It's all good," she said.

Cameron gave her a quick hug and led the way into a room he'd already reserved. Normally it was used for yoga classes, but this evening it was theirs. There was a wall of mirrors running the length of a long wall with long bars mounted end to end for warm-ups, and a large mat in the middle of the floor.

They walked out onto the mat, and then all of a sudden Wade turned and grabbed Cameron from behind. Before she could register what was happening, Wade was on his back on the mat and Cameron was free.

Cameron turned to Laura. "If you get him down, that's when you run."

Laura's eyes widened. "You think I can do this?"

"You can absolutely do that," Tate said. "Even to someone as big as Cameron."

A calm feeling washed over her. If they said she could do it, then she could, and she wanted to know how.

"Show me," she said.

And they did.

For the past two days Mr. Charles Trent, Esq., had been arguing a case at the federal courthouse in D.C., and the ruling had finally come down with a judgment in his client's favor. After congratulations all around, he went back to his office, elated with the win and the fat fee he'd received for his efforts.

Joan, his secretary of twelve years, was finishing up some paperwork when he rolled in the door. His briefcase was in his lap, and there was a big smile on his face,

When she saw him, she smiled.

"Congratulations! I knew you would win this."

Charles was more than a little pleased himself.

"I have to admit, it was satisfying to see big business take a fall on this one, but I'm glad it's over. Look, I'm going to dictate some final notes before I leave, but you can type them up tomorrow. Call it a day and go home, beat the rush-hour traffic for a change."

"Thanks. I think I will, although you know if I go home early, it means I'll have to take Killer for more than a walk around the block."

He laughed. Killer was Joan's Yorkie, a tiny hairball with feet and the heart of a lion, the antithesis of mean.

A few minutes later Joan was gone and Charles was at his desk tying up loose ends for the night.

Hershel was on stakeout near Charles Trent's office. He'd followed him there from the courthouse, and from where he was parked he had a clear view of who came and went. He already knew that Trent had a security alarm on his van, so breaking in ahead of time wasn't going to happen. But the alarm was always turned off when Trent opened it to get inside, and Hershel had a ready ruse to stop the lawyer from pressing any kind of alarm before he could get to him. That would give him all the time he needed.

Sweat was dripping down Laura's face. She had a burgeoning bruise on her arm from stepping into a hand chop instead of away from it, but there was a glint in her eye that meant business. They kept the lesson down to just a few basic moves, and then, for practice purposes, kept repeating them over and over until she had them down pat. Each time they repeated the steps, Cameron would let her break free of his grasp. Sometimes Wade would step in for Cameron, and sometimes Tate, getting her accustomed to how it felt to be accosted by different-size men with different body types. They had been at it nearly two hours when Cameron tossed her a towel.

"Is that it?" she asked as she wiped the sweat from her face.

His eyes narrowed. "We're going to do this one

more time, only this time you have to get free on your own."

She wiped the palms of her hands on her sweat-pants and widened her stance.

Cameron eyed his partners and grinned.

"I don't know about you, but I think I'm scared."

Laura glared. "Don't make fun of me, damn it."

"Are you pissed?" Wade asked.

She narrowed her eyes warningly. "I might be."

"Good, because that's what's going to keep you alive," Wade said.

She straightened up and slowly put her hands on her hips.

"You were goading me on purpose, weren't you?"

"Forgive us?" Tate asked as he extended his arm in a gesture of peace.

Within seconds she had him on his knees, one hand cupping his crotch.

"Holy shit, woman, I did not see that coming," he muttered.

Wade rushed her.

Laura reacted instinctively as she let out a blood-curdling scream and stepped sideways, aiming a kick toward the side of his knee rather than at his kneecap.

He dodged just in time and spun, grabbing her from behind.

She stomped his instep as she jabbed an elbow in his ribs. When she heard him grunt, she knew she'd landed a solid blow.

Wade backed off and frowned. "I was going to take it easy on her. I just didn't expect the scream."

"Enough," Cameron said.

"Good job," Wade said as he got to his feet.

Tate gave her a thumbs-up.

Even though they'd planned to pull their punches, she was pleased to know she'd taken them by surprise.

"So Tate and I are out of here," Wade said, and both of them patted her on the back as they went to the dressing room to change and go home.

"That was really good," Cameron echoed.

She stopped. "For real?"

He held out his hand. "Yes, honey, for real—but this only works if he doesn't use the Taser. You're powerless if he does."

She shuddered. "Will we do this again sometime?"

"As often as you like until you feel safe."

She looked away quickly, but not before he saw the tears in her eyes.

He tilted her chin. "What is it, Laura?"

She touched the cross beneath her shirt and then laid her face against his chest.

"Honey?"

"I never feel safe anymore. Not really."

He groaned as he pulled her closer, holding her tight against his body.

"I would give a year of my life to make what happened to you go away. I will never understand what you went through in the crash, or the hell that came after. All I can do is love you forever and promise I won't let you down."

"I know. I'm sorry."

"Nothing to be sorry for." When he leaned down for a kiss, he tasted her tears. "Don't cry. It kills me to see you cry."

"I want to go home. Can we go home now?" she asked.

"Yes, baby, we can go home. You go change, and I'll meet you at the front desk."

She walked away, swiping tears as she left the room.

It was long past dinnertime when Charles Trent locked up his office and wheeled out of the building. His battery-powered wheelchair rolled smoothly through the lobby as he waved goodbye to the security guard on duty.

"See you tomorrow," Charles said.

The guard waved back.

A cold wind enveloped Charles as he exited the building and then wheeled around the corner to the employee parking lot. It was nearly empty, save for a few scattered cars and the vans that belonged to the cleaning crews.

He glanced up at the sky, frowning. Not a star in sight, and there were a couple of lights out in the parking lot, as well. He made a mental note to mention it to the building superintendent tomorrow.

He headed across the lot toward his van. The keys

were in his lap, and as he got closer he used the remote to turn off the security alarm and unlock his van. When the headlights came on he steered into the light, using it to guide his way. Once he'd rolled over a pothole in this lot and turned over, then had to make a call to the security guard to help him get upright. Damn embarrassing moment he didn't want to repeat.

Facing into the light, he didn't see the van parked behind his vehicle or the man standing just between them.

He hit another button on the remote. A side door slid open and a hydraulic lift emerged and began to lower. Charles's mind was on dinner and his eyes were still adjusting to the dark after the glare of the headlights as he wheeled himself onto the lift, just as he'd done a thousand times before. And then out of the dark he caught a glimpse of movement, then heard a man's voice.

"Mr. Trent?

Charles frowned, his thumb firmly on the alarm.

"Yes?"

"I'm from Speedy Courier Service, and I'm really sorry to do this so late, but it just came in. I have a special-delivery envelope you need to sign for."

All Charles saw was the big manila envelope the man extended and not the Taser he was holding beneath it. The moment he put the keys in his lap, Hershel shot him in the face, then dropped the envelope and glanced around the parking lot before he stepped out of the shadows.

For Charles, the pain was excruciating, and when his body began seizing he lost his balance and fell out of his chair. His worst fear had just come true. He was fully paralyzed.

He saw the stranger coming toward him and tried to cry out, but his muscles were locked in spiraling pain. Spit was running down his chin, and try as he might, he couldn't talk.

He watched in horror as his assailant took out a length of nylon rope and wrapped it around his hands. Charles cringed inwardly at the rough feel of the spiky fibers against his throat as his attacker wrapped the rope around his neck.

God, oh, God! He was going to die!

The rope grew tighter, then tighter still. Charles was praying for a miracle, but it wasn't happening. He could barely hear the man breathing behind him, and his assailant's silence was almost as frightening as the fact that his own life was about to end. Why was this happening? Why? Why? Why?

Hershel ended the man's misery quickly, not out of kindness, but for fear he might be seen. He knew the moment the man quit breathing, but he still held his grip for a few more counts before he let go of the rope. Then he put it in his pocket and yanked the electrodes out of the lawyer's face. He used the wheelchair to move him to the back of his van, then abandoned it afterward.

It took exactly three minutes from firing the Taser

to driving away. Hershel took care to stay in the shadows and back alleys all the way to the next intersection before he merged out onto the street.

He headed out of town with Trent's body hidden beneath the drop cloths, always driving with his eye on time and traffic. When he realized traffic was getting heavier and slowing down, he took the next exit and found a new way to get to the same place. Just when he thought he had it made, he drove up on a wreck and this time got caught in a traffic jam. There was nothing to do but sit through it.

About thirty minutes into the wait his anxiety rose as a cop started walking toward his van. All of a sudden there was a scream in his ear, and he jumped as if he'd been shot.

"Damn it, Louise, you are going to get me caught! Shut the fuck up," he hissed.

All he could hear was her crying. It was so loud that he imagined the cop would hear her, too. But the cop passed by without a glance, and Hershel breathed a quick sigh of relief.

A quick check of the rearview mirror showed him the cop directing traffic to allow the rescue vehicles to get through. The tow truck had finally arrived.

When traffic began to flow again, he was so nervous he was shaking. It took almost an hour to reach the drop site once they got moving, and then when he got there he was in such a hurry to be gone that he dropped the body. The man hit headfirst on a rock, his skull cracking like an egg on the side of a bowl before he flopped onto his back.

"Son of a bitch," Hershel muttered.

He grabbed the body by the legs and began dragging it toward the water. His own legs were trembling, and the pulled muscle in his back was reminding him it was there by the time he reached the water's edge. Relieved that it was over, he gave the body a shove.

"Bon voyage," he said, and stumbled back to the van.

After checking the interior to make sure nothing had fallen out of Trent's pockets, he drove away, relieved the job was over.

It was almost midnight when he got back. He drove past Lucy Taft's house to his apartment, breathing a quiet sigh of relief that he was home. As he got out, he grabbed the sack with his burger and fries. He was halfway up the steps when he began smelling smoke from somewhere in the distance. He looked over his shoulder toward the house and caught a glimpse of someone in an upstairs window. When he realized it was his landlady with a pair of binoculars, his heart skipped a beat.

He ran the rest of the way up and quickly locked himself inside. Instead of turning on the lights, he made his way through the rooms, using the glow of moonlight to see. He changed clothes in the dark and then settled down to eat by the light of the television.

He felt uneasy, knowing she'd been watching him, and wasn't sure what that meant, but he had no qualms about killing her, too, should the need arise. In fact, the more he thought about it, the better the idea sounded. It would be the perfect way to tie up loose ends before he left. Satisfied that he'd solved another problem, he stuffed a couple of French fries in his mouth and then reached for the salt.

Lucy Taft had been sound asleep when she was awakened by a loud explosion. She threw back her covers and rushed to the windows, immediately horrified by a huge orange glow over the housetops and pillars of smoke billowing into the distant night air. She ran to the library to get William Harold's binoculars and then hurried back to her bedroom. The orange glow was getting bigger, but even with the binoculars, she was still unable to see what was burning. She was still standing at the window when Paul Leibowitz drove in.

She registered him glancing her way but didn't care as she glanced at the time. The air was filling with sirens, and she knew whatever had happened, it was bad.

"God's blessings and healing upon you," she whispered, then put down the binoculars and crawled back in bed.

Charles Trent's abduction was discovered when two members of the cleaning crew came out to their van for supplies and saw the door of his van standing wide-open, the lift still down, and the wheelchair tipped over a short distance away.

The police were on the scene within minutes. They bagged the manila envelope and his keys and briefcase, and started looking for witnesses.

The guard on the night desk confirmed the time Charles had left the building. They looked at security footage, but the parking lot was too dark for them to tell what had happened. Trent showed up on the footage when the headlights came on in his car, but when he passed the bumper, he disappeared. A few minutes later they could see a van leaving the parking lot, but with no identifying marks and no way to see the color or the tag number, it didn't further the investigation.

They called his secretary and asked when she'd seen him last. When she learned about her boss's disappearance, first she cried, and then she went into duty mode and came back to the office to help Detective Jenkins, the cop who'd caught the case. She went through Trent's files with steel-eyed diligence, giving Jenkins a list of names and backgrounds on past clients who might be holding a grudge. The man *was* a lawyer, and lawyers pissed a lot of people off.

Cameron and Laura were eating late after their session at the gym. She was quiet all through dinner. All the joy of her upcoming wedding had been crushed by what was happening.

Cameron knew her well enough not to push. If she wanted to talk about something, she would let him know. When they began cleaning up the kitchen, he turned on the television to catch part of the late news. He was drying pans and putting them away when the local newscast was interrupted by a breaking story. They both stopped to watch.

"...just now on the scene of what appears to have been an abduction. Local lawyer Charles Trent, who was paralyzed from the waist down over twenty years ago, has disappeared. A cleaning crew in the building where his office is located noticed his vehicle door open and his wheelchair lying on its side in the parking lot."

Charles Trent's picture came up on the screen as the newscaster continued to talk.

"Police are looking into his past cases, searching for disgruntled clients."

"I know him," Cameron said as he walked up behind her. "I've seen him trying cases in court. Nice guy. Never let his condition get him down."

Laura leaned against him without comment.

He wrapped his arms around her and kissed the back of her ear.

"We're nearly through here, honey. Why don't you go take a nice hot bath...soak the soreness out of some of those muscles? I'll finish up."

She turned around and hugged him.

"You're the best, and I'm sorry about your friend. Maybe they'll find him alive."

Cameron frowned. "It's not likely. When cops and lawyers go missing, it's usually because they've pissed off the wrong bad guys. So go soak your sweet self. I'll be in to check on you later...just to make sure you haven't fallen asleep in the tub."

He watched her leave, eyeing the drag in her step and the slump in her shoulders, and wondered if the self-defense lesson was the cause of this sadness. Had it put her back in that victim mind-set she'd tried so hard to get past?

Laura stripped in the bathroom and clipped her hair high on her head so it wouldn't get wet. She eyed the silver cross hanging between her breasts as the tub filled, then turned away and added some of her favorite bath salts. She slowly eased down into the heat with the bath pillow behind her neck, then took a deep breath and closed her eyes, all but floating in the hot, steamy depths.

Five minutes turned into ten, and she was trying to decide whether to get out or add some more hot water when an explosion rocked the house. The lights flickered as she climbed out of the bathtub in a panic. She grabbed a large bath towel, wrapping it around her body as she bolted out of the bedroom screaming Cameron's name.

Cameron was in the living room watching television when the explosion sounded. He jumped up from the sofa and ran to the windows as flames began spiraling up above the housetops nearby, then heard Laura scream. He turned just as she came running down the hall, dripping water as she went.

He caught her in midflight and swept her up into his arms, then headed back into the bedroom.

"Hey, honey. You're going to freeze out here like this. Let's go back and get you dried off and dressed, okay?"

Laura was shaking as she clung to him.

"Did you hear that explosion? Are we in danger? What happened?"

"Yes, I heard it. I don't know what happened, but I'll find out in a bit. Right now, let's get you dried off."

He handed her a towel and went to get some sweats out of the dresser while she finished drying.

She was sitting on the closed lid of the commode when he came back into the bathroom. She was staring at the scar on her leg and the bruises on her body, wondering how much all of that would show when she went for the fitting for her wedding dress in a couple of days.

He frowned. "Did you get all those bruises this evening at the gym?"

"I guess," she said.

"Son of a bitch."

She blinked and then looked up at the devastation in his eyes.

"You didn't hurt me. I wanted to do it."

He shook his head and then handed her the sweats.

She put on the pants and was pulling the top over her head when they began hearing sirens.

Cameron rushed out of the bathroom with Laura right behind him.

The moment she looked out the window and saw the flames for the first time, her training kicked into gear. She grabbed the landline phone and quickly called the police.

"Reston P.D."

"Please connect me with the officer in charge of this shift."

"One moment, please."

Laura waited a few moments and then heard a click, followed by a gruff voice.

"This is Lieutenant Sharp."

"Lieutenant, this is Laura Doyle with the American Red Cross. I live in Reston and just heard an explosion. I can see the flames from my home. Can you tell me what happened? I need to know what, if any, emergency services might be needed."

"I don't know details, Ms. Doyle, only that a gas main exploded. We've had conflicting reports of two, maybe three, blocks being leveled, but I can't confirm that."

Laura closed her eyes, imagining the devastation.

"Thank you. This was very helpful."

She hung up.

"A gas main exploded in a residential neighborhood. Initial reports are that two or three blocks have been leveled. I have to get down there and see for myself what's needed."

She started back down the hall toward the bedroom, but Cameron was right behind her.

"I go where you go on this one," he said.

She didn't argue.

Within ten minutes they were in the car and on their way toward the blaze. Cameron moved quickly through the streets, taking alleys and small side streets to get closer to the fire, and then they ran into a roadblock.

Laura got out of the car, leaving Cameron behind the wheel, and flashed her credentials as she looked for someone in charge.

She was directed to an officer another block down the street and gave Cameron a quick wave before jogging toward him.

Cameron never took his eyes off her, and when she returned a few minutes later, he was waiting.

She leaped in the car, buckling her seat belt as she talked.

"Take me home. I have enough information on my home computer to initiate emergency services, and then I'll go from there. If I have to drive into D.C. to my office later, then so be it."

Cameron quickly turned around and headed home.

"What happened? Does anyone know?"

"I doubt it, but I saw live footage on the lieutenant's laptop. Four blocks on both sides of the street are leveled, the worst I've seen. They can't search for bodies because of the fire, and they're evacuating at least ten blocks in every direction until the gas has been shut off. It looks like a war zone."

Cameron shook his head, thinking of all the people

who had been eating dinner, watching TV or sleeping in their beds. They probably never knew what hit them.

The next morning dawned cool and brisk. It was Lucy Taft's favorite time of year. She dressed in a pair of old wool slacks and an even older fuzzy sweater. She added her favorite corduroy jacket, and took her pruning shears and a basket as she went outside to deadhead the last of the flowers in her garden.

The garden was too large for her now, but she refused to give it up. She hired people during the hot weather to help with the weeding and mowing. But when the days began growing shorter, the nights colder and Mother Nature began putting her babies to bed, it was all hers.

She set the basket aside and began clipping old blooms from her chrysanthemum bed with a steady snip, snip. She'd been at it for at least fifteen minutes when she heard footsteps behind her. Thinking it was probably Mildred coming to urge her back inside, she ignored them.

"Excuse me," Hershel said.

Lucy stood up and turned around. "Oh, Mr. Leibowitz! I thought you were Mildred coming to talk me into going inside, and I didn't want to go. It's so nice out this morning."

"Yes, ma'am, it is nice," Hershel said, eyeing her pruning shears. "Those are some wicked-looking scissors you have there."

She glanced down and then shrugged. "I guess. I've had them for ages, and they do the job. Do you garden? I love to garden. I like to do my own dead-heading, too, don't you?"

She didn't wait for him to answer as she moved on to the next patch in need of cleaning up.

He stuck his hands in his pockets and began following her along the path.

"Yes, ma'am, I'm a strong proponent of taking care of my own business. I don't butt into other people's business, either."

Lucy missed the double entendre as she reached across a bed of marigolds to snip off an old rose hip she'd missed before. It didn't do to let them go to seed like that. William Harold always believed it weakened the main stalk.

She put the clipping in her basket and thought about her grandson, William Herman. Someone had done too much pruning on him back when he was young. He didn't have a lick of William Harold's backbone, and it was a damn shame.

Her thoughts turned to the explosion she'd heard last night and something occurred to her. She stopped and turned around, eyeing Paul with such intensity that he thought she was about to out him.

"You were out late last night."

Breath caught in the back of his throat. He frowned.

"Yes, I was. And you were up late, as well. I saw you standing at the window looking through a pair of binoculars."

Lucy was so curious to learn what had been on fire that she missed the sarcasm.

"I know. The explosion was so loud it woke me, but I couldn't see anything but an orange glow over the rooftops, even with my binoculars. I mentioned your late arrival hoping maybe you'd seen it on your way home and knew what had happened."

Hershel was so relieved he wasn't going to have to kill her—yet—that he almost laughed.

"Oh, so that's what you were looking at. I thought you were looking at me."

Lucy's heart skipped a beat. All of a sudden she felt threatened and had a sense that this conversation could have turned out much differently.

"Well, yes, of course I saw you drive in, but I'd been at the window for at least fifteen minutes. So you didn't see the fire?"

"No, ma'am, although I did smell smoke when I got out of my car. Maybe it will be in the morning paper."

"It wasn't. I looked. Probably happened after they'd put the paper to bed. I should have stayed inside to watch the news this morning. I'm sure it's on TV, but I wanted to do this while the day was young." Then she shrugged. "No matter. I'll call one of the boys. They always know what's going on."

"Oh, your sons live in the area?" Hershel asked.

"Not *my* sons. The boys…you know…CIA. I still have connections. William Harold was one of them once."

Hershel's belly rolled. Good thing he'd found out

now. He did not want the spooks on his ass, too. He gave her what he hoped was a congenial smile.

"Yes, ma'am. Well, I'll say good morning and be on my way. I need to do a little grocery shopping."

"Good morning to you, too," she said, and went back to deadheading.

She heard the engine start, but she didn't turn around. He didn't seem to like being watched—at all.

Eleven

Laura had been on the phone most of the night calling some of her local volunteers as well as suppliers, making sure the basics would be on-site. Then she called her boss to let him know she wouldn't be coming in. This was her hometown. She wasn't going to abandon it to someone else when she'd spent the past ten years going all over the country helping other communities just like this.

She left her house just before dawn dressed in jeans, a long-sleeved T-shirt and a red hoodie that zipped up the front. She'd learned a long time ago that noticeable colors helped people find her more quickly. Although Cameron was still at home, he promised to stop by before he left town, just in case she needed his help. He was still dragging his heels about going, although this day trip to Virginia for a follow-up on a case had been in the works since last week.

Laura didn't argue. She hadn't been out on a disaster site since before the plane crash and was hoping this didn't trigger an anxiety attack.

Daylight was only moments away as she drove up to the blast site. She needed to see what they were dealing with before heading to the shelter. After flashing her credentials, she went past a barricade that an officer moved aside for her.

Having a local volunteer who had offered the use of a very upscale motor home for a temporary headquarters was a coup. She couldn't count the times she'd bunked in a tent or in the building with the evacuees, which often made it difficult to work. Having privacy and a place to sleep was invaluable to her job.

She saw the motor home parked less than a block down and drove up behind it to park. She got out with her iPad and a travel mug of coffee, and knocked on the door. Laura recognized the owner, Bea Thomas, a sixtysomething ball of energy.

"Laura! Come in, come in. There's coffee on the stove."

Laura smiled as she climbed the steps. "Hi, Mrs. Thomas. Thank you so much for offering the loan of your motor home."

"Call me Bea, and you're very welcome. It's just been sitting in the driveway since my husband died. I'm happy to put it to good use."

Laura was impressed that a woman so small could handle a vehicle this large.

"Thanks again, Bea. And getting right down to business, have you heard anything from the first-shift volunteers? Last night I told them all to meet here. That was before I had confirmed the Wesley Methodist Church as our first shelter."

Bea dug through some paperwork on the table and handed her the list.

"These are the ones who have already reported in. I did what you asked me to do this morning and sent them to the church. Also, there was a man here earlier, said his name was Kevin Holmes."

"Good. He works for the Red Cross, too. Where did he go?"

"He went to the blast site."

Laura nodded. "I'm going to go find him, but I'll be back soon. If anyone else shows up, send them on to the church, as well."

"Will do," Bea said.

Laura looked up Kevin's number and called it as she began walking. The smell was sickening, and the smoke from the smoldering debris hung motionless in the air.

He answered on the first ring.

"Hello?"

"Kevin, it's me, Laura. Where are you? I'm walking into the area right now."

"I'm all the way down at the other end. I'll head your way. There's nothing we can do here other than leave word with the searchers as to where we'll set up."

"Who's in charge?" she asked.

"Right now there's a fire marshal and an arson investigator here, so probably them."

"Are there any survivors?" she asked, and then heard his breath catch.

"No."

"What's the death estimate?"

"Not sure yet, but four blocks of personal residences on both sides of the street are gone. You do the math."

"Dear God," Laura muttered. The smoke was making her eyes burn, but it wasn't the only thing that brought on the tears. It was the sight of all this devastation and the thought of being a witness to the final resting place of so many dreams. "Are there any bodies?"

The catch in his breath was more pronounced this time.

"Not a whole one."

Laura stopped. She wiped the tears away and took a deep breath.

"We can do this, Kevin."

"I know. I'm sorry," he said.

"Never apologize for empathy. Why don't you go ahead to the church and start setting up? I see some men in fire gear. I'm going to talk to them, and we'll meet up at the church later."

"Will do. The truck should be there with the cots. Are we expecting to shelter the people who were evacuated from the surrounding areas?"

"Yes, or at least most of them. See you soon."

Laura pocketed her phone and increased her speed, anxious to finish here as quickly as possible. After introducing herself and meeting the fire marshal, who corroborated everything Kevin had just told her, she left her card and information on where the Red Cross would set up and asked them to direct anyone in need of food or lodging to the church.

Her steps were dragging as she sidestepped bricks and melted metal on her way back. She passed the hulks of burned-out cars, the top half of a child's swing set and a broken bathtub that had been thrown clear during the blast, things that meant families had lived here.

All she had to do was look at the debris and she felt like throwing up. She kept flashing on the sound the plane had made when it hit the trees on the mountain, and the memory of waking up to the smell of smoke and burning electrical wiring. These people never had a chance of coming out of this alive.

Then she shook off the sadness. There was too much that needed to be done for her to dwell on the past. She decided to send Bea on to the church as well, and made a quick call.

"Hello."

"Bea, it's me, Laura. You can drive over to the church now. I think there's a hookup for you in their overflow parking lot. A lot of traveling evangelists use motor homes these days, so they had one installed for their use. I'm on my way back to my car."

"Will do," Bea said. "Oh, a half-dozen more volunteers came by. I sent them to the church, the way you told me to."

"Thank you. I'll talk to them when I get there." She disconnected, then made yet another call, this time to the local television station. She gave them her name and contact number, in case they needed more information from her later, and asked them to broadcast the location of the shelter for those in need, then called the radio station and requested the same thing.

She was almost back at her car by the time she finished the last call and had just pocketed her phone when she looked up to see Cameron standing by her car. She waved and walked faster.

Cameron had seen her coming from over two blocks away and started to meet her halfway when he realized she was on the phone. That meant she was in business mode, so he stayed put, feeling good about the purpose in her expression, the jut of her chin and the length of her stride. She meant business. When she looked up and finally saw him, he hurried toward her.

"Hey, honey, I see you're already busy," he said, and greeted her with a quick kiss.

But Laura didn't want quick and leaned into the feel of his mouth on her lips, regretting the necessary briefness of the moment.

"This is such a tragedy," she said.

"It is," he said, gazing down the street at the chaos the explosion had left behind. "Were there any survivors?"

"No."

He slid his hand under her hair and cupped the back of her neck.

"That's rough, but you have several hundred displaced people who need you, right?"

"Yes, and I have to go. Call me anytime. I'll be at the Wesley Methodist Church and then possibly spending the night on-site."

He frowned.

She started to explain. "You know this is part of the job, and I've done it for years. This time someone donated the use of a really nice motor home for an on-site office, and if need be, there are beds in there."

He didn't want to remind her that it wasn't about her ability to handle her business but that Hershel Inman could be alive and in town. However, she had a job that needed doing, and that was something he understood.

"I'll call you later. If you need something, call me. Love you most."

"Love you back," she said, then stayed to wave him off as he got in his SUV and drove away.

A chill wind lifted the hair from her neck as she stared up the street, marveling at the houses so close to the blast site that were still intact. But the longer she stood, the more it felt as if she was being watched.

She slowly turned, checking out her surroundings, and even though the feeling didn't go away, she saw nothing suspicious.

She shivered, hoping it wasn't an omen of things to come, and then decided it was the energy from this place of sadness that she was feeling. Suddenly anxious to be away from this horror, she got in her car and headed for the church.

Hershel found out what had led to the fire when he stopped to buy gas. He was intrigued by a disaster of that magnitude that had not been caused by weather and drove around the area until he found the site. The streets were blocked off all around it. He parked a distance away from the barricades but close enough to still be able to see the devastation and smoke hanging in the air.

It looked like footage from a war zone, which made him wonder what had happened to the people who'd been inside those houses, then whether they had found anything left to bury. It looked nasty, and he did not envy anyone the job of making sense of this hell. At the same time, a piece of him wanted to make it worse. But this wasn't his niche.

He started up his van and shifted into gear, intending to drive away, when a car drove past him, then was allowed past the barricade. It looked like the car Laura Doyle had been driving the other day. Out of curiosity, he waited. When he saw it park behind a motor home a few yards down, he looked closer. It *was* Laura Doyle getting out of the car. At that point he put his van back in Park.

Here she was again! What the hell was going on? Fate kept shoving her in his face, daring him to take advantage of the opportunities. But like before, there was no way he could kill her now and make it work.

He shut off the engine, pulled the hood of his sweat-shirt up over his bald head and slumped down in the seat, curious as to what would happen next.

A few minutes later he saw her come out of the motor home and walk down toward the blast site. She was just like he remembered, and yet different. He couldn't put his finger on what it was, but it was there. He watched her walk farther and farther until she was almost out of sight.

A few moments later an SUV drove up to the barricade, and like before, the guard let the car pass. He watched as the driver parked behind her car, and when the driver got out, his heart skipped a beat.

Cameron Winger!

Now he wished he *had* driven away, because he was too damn close to the man for his peace of mind. He reached down to start the engine, and then realized Winger would hear it and might turn around to look. Even if the man didn't recognize him, he didn't want to put the image of this van into his mind. So if he stayed, he needed to be doing something besides gawking. On impulse, he took out his cell phone and then looked down as if he was texting, watching from under lowered lids, and he didn't look up.

Not once.

Not when the motor home turned around and drove right past him.

Not when Cameron Winger did the same thing as he drove away.

He waited for Laura to leave as well, but when her

car didn't move he looked up and saw her staring up the street in his direction, looking at the empty houses as if she'd never seen them before.

That was when he got a really good look at her face and finally figured out what was different. He didn't know what had happened to her since they'd last met, but she'd aged, both mentally and physically. The little blond ingenue look was gone. Her chin was up, her shoulders back, and she had a "don't mess with me" attitude that was impossible to miss.

His eyes narrowed. This could change everything about how he took her down, and he was glad that he'd played the voyeur. He waited until she got in her car and drove past, and then he followed, just because he could.

When he realized where she was going and that she would most likely be there for a while, he decided to push his luck. The universe had been throwing them together, and he wanted to see how close he could get without giving himself away.

Even though it had been months since Laura had been on a disaster site, she fell back into the rhythm of the job like a pro. Kevin was supervising setting up cots and folding tables while she began checking invoices against the supplies being delivered. She had one volunteer out front taking donations of food, clothing, blankets and other necessities while another volunteer was taking personal information from the first wave of arrivals, most of whom were evacuees.

She'd thought it would bother her, being around so much tragedy again, but instead her anxiety settled. This was something she was confident in doing, and it needed to be done.

Hershel drove up to the church in a stream of vehicles and flashed back on Queens Crossing, Louisiana, and helping Laura Doyle set up for the flood refugees in the high school gym. He finally found a place to park, but instead of getting out, he stayed in the van, watching the chaos until he began to see a pattern in the rhythm of all the coming and going. And in the midst of the turmoil, there she was, steadfast and calm, with a phone at her ear, busy puzzling out the latest emergency.

It made him antsy. He needed to rattle her cage, so he left and drove until he found a grocery store, then made a quick purchase and drove back to the church site.

He grabbed the two commercial-size packs of diapers he'd purchased and got out of the van, counting on his appearance to help him blend in. He was at least fifty pounds lighter than when she'd seen him last, and the dark slacks, long-sleeved white T-shirt and dark hoodie made him look even smaller. He had the hood pulled up over his bald head, and his face had a slightly different shape after all the surgeries to remove the scarring. The last bit of his disguise was the sunglasses. He was literally betting his life she wouldn't know him, and the risk gave him a high.

He started walking toward the donation site with a packet of diapers in each hand, daring her to look up. She was standing near the doorway talking to a uniformed police officer as he walked up and got in line.

He liked hearing her voice. It sounded calm and full of confidence, but he would change that. She would be begging him for mercy—if he decided to let her talk. He kept thinking about the movie he'd seen, and pictured what it would be like to watch her hang. When she disappeared, they would be looking for her body to wash up in the Potomac like all the others, but she wouldn't be there. She would be swinging from the rafters in some long-forgotten building. By the time someone stumbled onto her body, her flesh would have rotted away and her skeleton would be in pieces. The possibility even existed that they would never find enough to bury, which would suit him just fine. He liked the thought of them never finding the body, and of Cameron Winger spending the rest of his years wondering what had happened to his girl.

Laura glanced up as the policeman walked away. The line of donors kept growing, which was amazing this early into the setup. The announcements had just gone out through the media, and yet here they were. It was times like this that reminded her of the good in people. She walked over to the line to make sure her volunteer wasn't overwhelmed.

"Hey, Sue…do you need anything?" she asked.

Sue turned around and whispered in her ear, "I could use a potty break."

Laura smiled. "Go. I'll handle things until you get back."

Sue rolled her eyes in mute appreciation, handed Laura her iPad and bolted.

Laura stepped up, smiling at the next person in line.

"Hello, what have we here? Oh, this is great! Mini bottles of shampoo."

The man shrugged as he handed her the plastic bag he was holding. "I travel a lot."

Laura laughed. "I definitely can relate. This is wonderful, and we'll put them to good use."

"I'd like to donate a hundred dollars, too."

"That's very generous. Just a moment and I'll give you a receipt for your tax records."

"No, no need for that," he said, and moved on as the next person in line moved up. In the process, two more volunteers showed up to help with the donations, which made the line move faster.

When Laura Doyle stepped up to take donations, Hershel flinched. This wasn't what he bargained for. He didn't want to see her face-to-face, not yet. She'd already seen him at the stoplight. What would she think if she saw him here, as well? Suddenly he was nervous again, which made him reconsider the recklessness of what he was doing. While he'd been basking in retirement, it appeared that he had also lost his edge. He was making bad decisions and pushing himself in a public way that he hadn't done before. Either he left the diapers at the curb and walked away, which might cause more attention than he wanted, or he stood his ground and faced her. If he did and wound up talking to her, he would have to disguise his voice, too.

But then the arrival of the extra volunteers made the line move faster, which was good. Now there was just a one in three chance he would draw her.

One by one, the people ahead of him made their donations and left, all while his heart beat faster. He was making bets with himself as to who he would end up talking to when all of a sudden it was all bets off, and he was up next. The diaper packs he was holding suddenly became heavier, and his legs felt weak. To his chagrin, it appeared Laura would be it. And then the woman she'd been talking to stopped and backed up to talk to her again, and that was what saved him.

One of the other volunteers waved him up. He donated the diapers and then glanced sideways as he turned to walk away. Laura was looking straight at him.

He nodded politely and shoved his hands in the front pockets of his hoodie as he headed back to his van. He didn't have to turn around to know she was still looking at him, because he could feel it. Once inside the van he looked back, but she wasn't there. Did that mean that she'd ID'ed him and was calling the police? She would know what he was driving. Why had he done this?

His thoughts were spinning as he sped away. His first instinct was to switch license plates with another vehicle, but then he stopped. No. He'd done that time and again before, and was sure they were on to that now. He needed to get rid of this van altogether and get something else to drive. Then he realized Lucy Taft would still know what he'd driven before. Whatever new car he chose, she would notice the change, so he would have to develop a lie for that. He'd lied a lot as a child, and every time he got caught in one, his mother had wagged her finger and made him repeat, "Oh, what a tangled web we weave when first we practice to deceive." She'd made him say it ten times, after which she washed his mouth out with soap. Obviously the punishment never took. His whole life was one very big lie.

The moment Laura saw the man in the dark hoodie, she felt uneasy. Maybe it was the black clothes and dark glasses, and the fact that she couldn't really see his face, but he seemed familiar. As soon as Sue returned, Laura went back into the church. But every time there was a lull in the work, she thought of him again. By the end of the day she decided he just looked like someone she knew and forgot about it. Then, to make her evening even better, Kevin volunteered to stay on-site, and she headed home, glad for the reprieve. It wasn't until she braked for a red light that it dawned on her why the man in the dark hoodie had looked familiar. He'd been sitting beside her in his

van at a stoplight the day before. That was it. Just a
stranger she'd seen in passing who'd come to donate
to the shelter. She laughed at herself and the fuss that
she'd made and headed for a supermarket to pick up
some things for dinner.

Washington, D.C., police department

Detectives Ron Wells and Sam Burch were desperate to find a solid connection between the deaths of
Patty Goss and Megan Oliver. The women's careers
didn't connect. They didn't know each other. They
didn't have memberships at the same gym or go to the
same church. All they knew was that they were both
in their late twenties, had dark hair, lived in Reston
and worked in D.C.; they had nothing in common.

Plenty of people died in D.C. on a weekly basis, so
had it not been for the Taser marks, the fact that they
had both died from strangulation and their bodies had
been pulled out of the river, there would have been no
real reason to assume the murders were connected.

For a while, the media had been all over their
deaths, but when Charles Trent went missing, that
changed. Now it was all about the handicapped lawyer, well-known in the area for taking cases against
people and corporations who abused their power. The
fact that he'd just won a big case against a drug cor-
poration in the morning and gone missing the same
night put the drug company in the headlights.

A Detective Jenkins from D.C. Homicide caught

the case. Trent had plenty of enemies to choose from, and Jenkins was working the list of suspects, with help from fellow detectives in the department.

Lucy Taft hadn't been able to get the creepy feeling she had about Paul Leibowitz out of her head. If she had a way to do it without causing a scene and ticking him off, she would give back his money and tell him to get lost. But after the brief conversation they'd had this morning, she was a little afraid to challenge him.

So, taking a leaf from her dearly departed William Harold's book, she opted to get him on the authorities' watch list and made a call to the D.C. police, asking to speak to whoever was in charge of the murder cases of Patty Goss and Megan Oliver. Her call was transferred, and she waited through two rings before it was answered.

"Homicide, Detective Burch."

"Detective, my name is Lucy Taft. I am a longtime resident of Reston, and I might have information about those women who were murdered."

Burch sat up in his chair and reached for a pen.

"Yes, ma'am. What's your address and a phone number where you could be reached?"

She gave him what he asked for as Burch made note.

"So what information do you have?" he asked.

Lucy settled in her favorite chair and put the phone in her other hand. If she held things too long with the left one, her hand would inevitably begin to shake.

"Since my husband passed, I have a garage apartment I rent out, and I recently rented it to a middle-aged man from out of town. He paid cash up front for two months, even though he said he wouldn't be here that long, and my husband always said not to trust a man who pays for everything with cash."

Burch rubbed the bridge of his nose against the disappointment. He could already tell this wasn't going anywhere.

"Is there anything else?" he asked.

"Yes," she said in a conspiratorial whisper. "He stays out late at night. I make notes. And every time a woman goes missing, he comes home late the very same time. He was even out late last night, and I heard a lawyer went missing."

Burch frowned. "Ma'am, one thing has no bearing on the other. Have you see him do anything illegal, or overheard him talking to someone about the murders?"

"No, but I'm telling you something is fishy about him. Why, just this very morning he came up to me in my garden, and I felt threatened, very threatened, by the way he behaved."

"Did he try to harm you?"

"No, but I was holding my gardening shears. I think he was afraid."

Burch sighed. "If he *is* afraid of you, then why do you think he's the one committing these murders?"

She spluttered, then frowned. "You don't believe a word I'm saying, do you?"

"It's not that, ma'am," Burch said. "It's just that we

need more than the fact that he comes home late to accuse a man of murder. So unless you witness something, there's nothing we can do."

"You could follow him," she said. "If you did, you would find out what he's doing. I'm sure it's illegal, whatever it is."

"There's nothing illegal or even suspicious about what you've told me, ma'am, and I'd have to have a better reason to stake out a citizen than just the fact that he keeps late hours."

Lucy sniffed. "Fine, then. You'll see. Mark my words, I know he's bad." She hung up, disenchanted with the police department, thanks to their lack of interest. "I should have known better. If this happens again I'll just call one of the boys. They'll know what to do."

She glanced at the clock and then rang the bell for Mildred.

"Yes, ma'am?" Mildred said.

"Mildred, I'm a little stressed right now. Would you please bring me a glass of my favorite merlot?"

"Yes, ma'am. Right away."

Lucy leaned back in her chair and closed her eyes. All this drama had worn her out.

Back at the P.D., Burch hung up the phone and shoved his hand through his thinning hair.

"That was a monumental waste of time," he said as he got up to refill his coffee cup.

Wells had just received a copy of Megan Oliver's

autopsy and was pinning some new information to the murder board. He heard frustration in his partner's voice.

"What do you mean?" he asked.

Burch shrugged.

"Oh, some old lady in Reston claims her renter is acting suspicious and thinks we should follow him to see where he goes at night."

Wells frowned. "Is she saying he's connected to the murder victims?"

"She says that he comes and goes at all hours, and has come in late both times one of our murder victims went missing, and since he was out late last night, too, she also blamed him for Charles Trent's abduction. I told her staying out late wasn't against the law. She got pissed and hung up on me."

"Does he live in her house?" Wells asked.

"No, a garage apartment," Burch said.

Wells shrugged. "Then obviously she's up late, too, or she wouldn't know what time he comes in. Sounds like a busybody with too much time on her hands. Still, treat the call like we do every other tip. You never know what might happen."

Twelve

Hershel left the Methodist church intent on looking for used-car dealers in D.C. He pulled over to check the Yellow Pages app on his iPhone, found several addresses and then started driving.

He was disgusted that he'd put himself in this position and tried to think of another way to solve this problem without trading cars. The only thing he could come up with was just to kill Laura Doyle now and leave, but then he wouldn't be playing the game with the Storm-chaser team. He wanted to win the game and make the FBI look bad, or he wouldn't have his revenge.

Once he got into the city he quickly found the first car lot, but he didn't like what he saw there and never pulled in. He needed a van, but all the ones they had there were junkers. He couldn't be driving something prone to breaking down with a body in the back. It wasn't until he drove past the fourth dealer that he saw what he was looking for.

The salesman came out of the office with a spring in his step and a smile on his face as Hershel pulled up and got out.

Hershel knew the drill. He would let the guy talk. No need to draw attention to himself by being rude. There were three—a white one, a beige one and a black one. He was thinking black. It would easily get lost in the shadows on dark nights.

"Welcome to Roberts Used Cars. I'm Roy. What are you looking for today? Car? Truck?"

Hershel shook the man's hand. "Paul Leibowitz. I want another van, but I'm looking to trade up."

Roy beamed. "We have three nice vans on the lot. Now, my personal recommendation would be the beige one. It's the newest and—"

Hershel was focused on the dark one. "Since the one I'm driving is white, I wanted a change. I think I'd rather look at the black one," Hershel said.

Roy rubbed his hands together. "Sure thing, but let me go get the keys to all three, just in case."

Hershel walked toward the black van as the salesman ran inside. He liked that this van sat a little higher off the highway. It would make a difference driving over rough roads to get to his dump site. It was a shame that he had to change vehicles now when he only had one more to grab before Laura Doyle, but necessity demanded the switch. He would sell this one before he left the States, and that would be that.

The tires had plenty of tread left, and he didn't see any dents or dings. There was a scrape on the back bumper, but nothing bad. He was guessing it was five or six years old. The one he was driving was eight years old. Not a big difference in money.

He was looking through the rear window, checking to see how much room was in back, when the salesman returned.

"Here you go," Roy said, handing the keys to Hershel. "Let's take her for a ride."

Hershel climbed in behind the wheel, adjusted the seat to his shorter leg length and checked all the controls before he started the engine. The engine turned over like a charm and ran smoothly.

"Nice and quiet, right?" Roy said.

"Not bad," Hershel said, and buckled up.

They drove out of the parking lot and down the street, with Roy talking faster than the speed limit. He was getting on Hershel's nerves, but he let him talk. It saved him from having to answer.

Hershel drove around for about five minutes and then headed back to the lot. As he did, Roy finally stopped talking and began watching him like a mongoose staring at a cobra, waiting to make his strike.

Finally Hershel spoke up. "What was the price of this one again?" he asked, and watched Roy's eyes narrow as he named the price.

"Well, obviously that's without trade-in," Hershel said.

Roy blinked. "I'll have to check the Blue Book to get the going price on your van."

Hershel pulled back into the lot and parked beside his van.

"Let's go inside and talk," he said.

The salesman smiled. This was going to be the easiest sale he'd made all week. Sometimes it happened like that.

It took nearly an hour to finish the paperwork, but when it was over and all Hershel's belongings had been put into the new van, he drove off the lot, pleased with the outcome.

He went straight to the DMV, put the new tag on the van and then drove to a Lowe's home improvement store. As he walked inside, he paused to take a deep breath. He could smell new wood, and the faint odor of paint and glue. Stores like this made him want to build stuff, but that way of life was behind him. He grabbed a shopping cart, paused a moment to get his bearings, then headed down the aisles. He was looking for step stools and spools of rope. What he wanted was a flimsy stool and thin nylon rope, something strong enough not to break, but thin enough to cut right into the flesh if a body hung there too long.

It was after dark by the time Laura finished shopping and started home. Since Cameron wasn't home yet, she didn't hurry. She was exhausted, but happier than she'd been in months. It made her realize how much she'd missed working on-site, although she knew if this wasn't happening in her hometown, her opinion would be different. She didn't want those long stretches away from home and Cameron anymore; plus the extra money that had come with her promotion was nice, too.

She thought about Tate and Nola, and how coincidence and a killer had turned their sad past into an amazing future. Jo and Wade's news was exciting. They had a baby on the way. She could envision their lives through the ensuing years, raising their children together and sharing both the good and the hard times. The dream was something to build on if they could just put Hershel Inman behind them.

The motion-detector light on the porch came on as she pulled into the drive. The sky was overcast again. Fearing rain, she drove toward the back of the house and parked beneath the portico. She sorted out her house key, grabbed the groceries and got out. The air was cold and damp as she unlocked the door and went inside. With a click of the lock and a flip of a light switch, she was home.

She set the sacks on the counter and turned up the thermostat as she went, depositing her work things in the office and her coat in the hall closet. After a quick change into something more comfortable, she went back into the kitchen, turned on the television and got to work making dinner.

Within the hour the wind started to blow. Laura turned the burners down, covered up the food in the pans and then went to the living room to look out the windows. A metal bucket was rolling down the street, an artificial flower arrangement still in it. She recog-

nized it as part of her neighbor's autumn porch decorations. She thought about going outside to chase it
down and then decided against it, since it was already
on the next block and still rolling.

She stepped out onto the porch for a bit of fresh
air, then immediately wrapped her arms around herself against the wind's blast. Lord, it was cold, but
surely too early in the year for snow. If she closed her
eyes, she could almost pretend she was back in school
again, waiting with Sarah on the covered porch for
their daddy to come home from work and take them
to the football game.

She could hear a dog barking, probably at the rolling bucket, and there was a television playing too loud,
most likely belonging to her neighbor across the street
who was almost deaf.

Even though the night was dark and miserable, she
didn't feel threatened. She'd grown up on this street.
She knew its sounds and the people who made them.

The first sprinkles began to fall just as she saw car
lights turn down her street. Cameron! When he turned
up the driveway, she went inside and ran through the
house to the back door, knowing he would have pulled
up under the portico, as well.

He was all smiles as he came in with the cold. "I'm
so glad to see you," he said, dropping his stuff on a
nearby chair as he swung her off her feet.

Laura wrapped her arms around his neck. Cold
lips, warm heart, her granny used to say. She sighed
as Cameron kissed her, but when he turned her around

and pinned her back against the wall, passion went from zero to flight within seconds.

She slid her arms beneath his coat.

He groaned. "Can dinner wait?"

She nodded, her pulse pounding, her knees growing weaker by the moment. She wanted to be naked beneath him in the very worst way, and she could tell he felt the same. His heartbeat pulsed beneath her palm, and the throb of his erection was hot against her belly.

All of a sudden she was in his arms and on the way down the hall to her bedroom. The room was dark; only the night-light in the en suite bathroom gave off a dim glow, but they didn't need to see to know what to do.

Shoes came off. Clothes went flying.

Cameron put his hand in the middle of her chest and pushed.

She fell backward onto the bed, and seconds later he was between her legs. Hard muscle wrapped in silken skin pulsed within her. She sighed and closed her eyes as he began to thrust. There was no hesitation about what he wanted or in case it was too soon. When she wrapped her legs around his waist he fell deeper into the heat and kept pumping until the room began to spin.

Overwhelmed by the heat of their lust, Laura came first. Flooded by the sudden burst of her climax, she swallowed a soft moan.

Cameron continued to pound the swollen nub between her legs until he felt the tremor of her muscles contracting around him and let go, spilling seed into the heat without thought of what might grow. At that point, nothing mattered but the ride.

Time ceased.

Laura was motionless beneath the weight of his body, her arms wrapped around his shoulders, her legs still locked around his waist.

Cameron couldn't move. The passion they shared was tinder dry and caught fire with little more than a touch.

He brushed his lips across her mouth and then whispered against her ear, "Are you okay?"

She sighed. "I am now."

He tucked his cheek against the curve of her neck and smiled.

It was long past sundown when Hershel finally drove home. He made a point of waiting until dark to go back because he didn't want to deal with any of his landlady's questions about his new ride.

He'd picked up fresh bread and lunch meat to make sandwiches, as well as a couple of honey buns and a six-pack of beer. He wasn't in the mood for takeout, and this was his idea of cooking.

The upstairs lights were off at the Taft house. He took the turn up the drive with his headlights off and drove the rest of the way in the dark.

He grabbed the groceries as he got out, locked the door to his new van and headed up the steps. At the landing, he turned and looked up at her window. He thought he saw the curtain move. but couldn't be sure.

"Yes, I'm home, you nosy bitch."

Lucy had turned off the television and the lights, and had been in bed less than five minutes when she heard a car drive past her window. She glanced out, thinking it would be Leibowitz. But when she saw the unfamiliar vehicle driving toward the apartment without headlights, she frowned.

"What's going on here?"

If someone was planning a robbery, she was going to have to call the police.

The driver parked where Leibowitz always parked. When the driver got out carrying a bag, she recognized her renter and relaxed. So he'd traded vehicles. That was interesting. She couldn't see the plate number in the dark, but she would deal with that tomorrow. She stepped away from the window before he turned to look up, made a note about the new car in her journal and then went back to bed. She didn't know what was going on, but she'd spent enough years with a man who'd lived his life as an international spy to know when something wasn't right.

The rain continued to fall long after Cameron and Laura had gone to bed for the night. The clock ticked loudly, the only sound to break the silence, while the lemon-scented dishwasher soap wafted faintly throughout the house. Laura slept curled up on her side with Cameron spooned against her back, his arm lying loosely around her waist. Even in sleep, he continued to protect her.

The next morning a police helicopter was flying over the Potomac, tracking a D.C. car chase in progress, when the pilot spotted what looked like a body. After all the rain from the night before, it was moving swiftly downstream.

Within a couple of hours the case of the missing lawyer had come to an end. Charles Trent was no longer missing, and his case had been handed off to Homicide, but it wasn't until the medical examiner saw the Taser wounds on the body and the strangulation marks around his neck that he realized they'd just gotten a third body with the same cause of death. Now everyone could say what they'd all been thinking. They were dealing with a serial killer. He made a quick call to Detectives Wells and Burch, which shot every theory they had on the women's murders straight to hell.

Wade was the first to find out the lawyer's body had been recovered from the river, and after following a hunch, he called the M.E.'s office to ask if there were Taser or strangulation marks. The affirmative response sent a cold chill up his spine. There was only one way this was heading. He called Tate.

The phone rang three times before Tate answered. "Benton."

Wade could tell his partner was distracted, and this wasn't going to make things better.

"They found another body with the same cause of death," he said.

"Who? I didn't know another woman had even been abducted."

"It wasn't a woman. It was a man, that lawyer who went missing."

"Charles Trent?"

"Yes."

"Taser *and* strangulation?"

"Yes," Wade said.

Tate sighed. "Does Cameron know?"

"I called you first."

"Okay, we've let this go long enough. I need to notify the director. I'll call you both back as soon as we've settled a few things. The D.C. police need to know what we know."

"They won't like us messing with their cases," Wade said.

"It won't be the first time feathers got ruffled," Tate said. "You call Cameron. Tell him to wait for my call."

"Will do," Wade said, and disconnected, then called Cameron.

Cameron was in his office doing research for a fellow agent when his phone rang. He glanced at the caller ID before picking up.

"Hey, Wade."

Wade didn't mince words. "We have a third body and it's the same killer. That missing lawyer was fished out of the Potomac this morning, and he'd been Tasered and strangled, just like the two women."

Cameron felt sick. "Son of a bitch."

"Tate is talking to the director, but it looks like the Stormchaser team is about to reactivate."

"The D.C. police aren't going to like this."

"I said the same thing to Tate, but like he said, they have to know what we know. He told us to sit tight and he'd call us back soon."

"Will do. Does Jo know?" he asked.

Wade frowned. "If she doesn't already, she will, and Tate will have to tell Nola, too. With all three of our women in the same area, it's too damn handy for Inman and my peace of mind."

"I'm calling Laura. She needs to be extravigilant now, too," Cameron said.

Laura was overseeing the unloading of a food truck when her cell phone rang. She was about to let it go to voice mail when she saw it was Cameron, and instead excused herself and stepped away.

"Hello, honey! Everything okay?" When he hesitated, she got a funny feeling in the pit of her stomach. "Cameron?"

"There's a third body with the same Taser and strangulation marks. There's definitely a serial killer out there, and we're about to resurrect the Stormchaser team."

All of a sudden her knees went weak.

"Well, hell," she said, backing up against a wall to

keep from dropping where she stood. "What should I do?"

"Just be more aware. Never trust anyone you don't already know, and don't go anywhere alone."

"I can do that," she said.

"You're fine, honey. I won't lose you."

She felt for the chain and the cross beneath her shirt. "Yes, I know. I'll pay attention. Call me when you get an update."

"I will. Love you most," he said softly.

Laura bit her lip to keep from crying.

"Love you, too."

The first thing Lucy Taft did when she woke up was get William Harold's binoculars and make note of the make, model and plate number of Leibowitz's new van. Then she went to the bathroom to take her shower, so it was late afternoon before she heard the news that a third body had been discovered.

Thirteen

Detectives Ron Wells and Sam Burch were in the process of adding Charles Trent to their murder board when Burch's cell phone rang. When he realized the call was from the chief of police, he frowned. This couldn't be good.

"Detective Burch, Homicide."

"Detective, this is Chief Warden. I'm giving you a heads-up. Three special agents from the FBI are on their way in. They have pertinent information regarding the man they believe is our serial killer, and yes, we have now officially designated these murders as serial killings. There will be a press conference within the hour notifying the public of that fact."

Burch's heart sank. "You're giving our case to the feds?"

"No, and they don't want it known that they're even working with you. They will explain. You will give them everything you know, and they will, in turn, tell you who you're most likely dealing with and his motivation."

"You mean they know who the killer is?"

"They think they do, and I will say, they made a convincing case. Regardless, you *will* cooperate. Is that understood?"

Burch sighed. "Yes, sir." The line went dead. He looked up.

Wells had overheard enough to know something was up.

"Well?" he asked.

Burch shrugged. "The feds are getting involved in our case. Supposedly they know our killer's identity, but they intend to stay in the background. They're on their way here with information, and we're supposed to share what we have in return."

"Son of a bitch," Wells muttered.

Burch shrugged. "Look, we don't know shit. If they have a lead, I'm willing to listen."

He heard footsteps behind him and turned around just as the lieutenant entered with the agents. The first thing Burch noticed was that they weren't dressed in the traditional dark suits, and they weren't smiling. He wondered if they were as pissed to be here as he was to see them coming.

Cameron saw the disgusted expressions on the detectives' faces and didn't really blame them, but they would soon understand.

Lieutenant Scott gave Burch and Wells a warning glance, and then began introductions.

"Detectives, these are Special Agents Benton, Luckett and Winger. Gentlemen, two of my best homicide detectives, Ron Wells and Sam Burch. I expect cooperation from all parties."

Wells and Burch nodded.

"Yes, sir. No problem," Wells added.

"Then, I'll leave you gentlemen to get to work," the lieutenant said, and walked out.

Tate quickly held out his hand. "Tate Benton. Wade Luckett is the one built like a linebacker. Cameron Winger is the rangy one."

Detective Wells shook his hand. "I'm Ron. He's Sam. So you're seriously sure who this killer is?"

Tate sighed. "About as sure as we can be without a visual identification. His name is Hershel Inman."

"Should that ring a bell?" Wells asked.

"Are you familiar with the Stormchaser, the killer who tore across the country picking his victims from the survivors of natural disasters?"

Burch eyes widened. "Are you serious? Why would you link him to these deaths? There were no natural disasters involved."

Tate proceeded to fill him in, and when he was finished, he handed him a USB drive.

"Everything we know about Inman is on that—the cases we worked, the different locations…everything. And here are the photos we have of him, though they're on the drive, too. The first is an older DMV photo from Louisiana. The second was taken by a hotel security camera. The last one is an artist's rendering of how we think he looks now."

"Wow. What the hell happened to him?" Burch asked, eyeing the scars.

"Those are scars from surviving a boat explosion and living through a tornado. He's a master of disguise, damn hard to find and even harder to kill," Tate said.

Cameron added, "We were hoping he'd gone somewhere and died. There haven't been any killings fitting his M.O. since his disappearance last year in Missouri."

Wells glanced at his partner and winced. They were over their head on this.

"What makes you think the murders here in D.C. are connected to him?" he asked.

Tate explained about the flowers left at Louise Inman's grave, the first hint that Inman was alive.

"There's also a link between your murders and our guy," Wade added. "He likes to use a Taser to subdue his victims, and then he strangles them. At least, that was his M.O. the second time around."

Ron shook his head. "But why would he come here? Why isn't he choosing victims at the site of a natural disaster?"

Tate hesitated. "That's what we don't know, and why we didn't say anything until the lawyer's body turned up in the river. He isn't picky about the sex of his victims. It's always about making a statement, and we think he's making a statement this time, as well. We just don't know what it is yet. He developed an attachment to our team as we pursued him. Over time it became an issue, and he wanted us to pay. He's targeted both my wife and Wade's wife, Jo, who's also an agent. Within a month, Agent Winger here is getting married, and the woman he's engaged to is someone Inman knows. She's with the Red Cross and was in charge of one of the disaster sites early on. Before we had identified him, he'd volunteered there to be closer to his victims, so at one time she was his boss. We don't know if any of that will play into what he's doing, but we can't take a chance that it won't."

"So why did he start killing to begin with?" Wells asked.

Tate shoved a hand through his hair. "That's the tragedy of it all. He and his wife were victims of Hurricane Katrina. They were stranded on the roof of their house, waiting to be rescued, but it didn't happen in time. His wife was a diabetic. She needed her insulin and couldn't get to it. She died during the second night and slipped off the roof into the water. They didn't find her body for several days, and Inman went crazy. He blamed the authorities for her death. He blamed the government for not acting quickly, and he's turned himself into God's nemesis. If God wouldn't save his wife, he's not going to let the ones God did save live."

"Holy shit," Wells said, and sat down with a thump. "But that scenario about storms and letting people live doesn't fit here," he added.

Tate nodded. "And that's why we hesitated to interfere. However, this isn't the first time he's changed his M.O., so we can't rule him out. The facts we do have on these killings are too close to his handiwork to ignore. You read the files we gave you, and if we're right and it *is* Inman, you can understand why we'd rather he not find out we're back on the case," Tate said. "We'll do everything we can to help. We'll work with you night and day, but we don't want to be at the forefront of anything. Understood?"

Burch nodded. "Understood."

"So what do you want to know?" Wells asked.

"Why don't you two check out the info on that drive, and we'll familiarize ourselves with your murder board. If we could have access to your case files, as well, it would be helpful. If anyone has questions, just ask," Tate suggested.

"Deal," Ron said. He sat down at his computer and pulled up the files for them to read, handed them the hard copies as well and gave up his desk and chair to Tate as he and Sam headed for another computer with the USB.

Hershel had a dilemma. Choosing the last victim, the one to the east, had posed a problem. Since he'd chosen his victims by location, he'd had no idea when he'd marked the last location that it was actually a three-story condo with a different resident on each floor.

The resident on the top floor ran a boutique in downtown Reston.

The resident on the second floor worked in D.C. as a barista at a coffee shop.

The resident on the ground floor was a thirtysomething professional dancer who taught classes at his studio in D.C. It was ultimately the location of the dance studio that marked Lionel Ricks as the fourth one to die.

Hershel knew the days and times of Lionel's classes, and that he also gave private lessons every evening from four to six.

Hershel's window of time would come right after the last lesson was over, when Lionel stayed behind to get ready for the next day.

Hershel had been in the parking lot of the strip mall where the studio was located all afternoon, listening to the radio and watching students coming and going. He was swallowing the last bite of the burger he'd been eating when his radio station segued to local news. He didn't pay much attention until he caught a sound bite from the D.C. police chief.

"The Washington, D.C., police department has determined that the murders of Patty Goss, Megan Oliver and Charles Trent were committed by the same individual. At this time we do not have a description of the person we have identified as a serial killer, but rest assured, we will not stop until he or she is apprehended."

Hershel smiled. Finally. So where were the feds? Why weren't they working this case?

He waited for the chief to say that the FBI had been called in, but he didn't. It pissed Hershel off and at the same time made him antsy. He needed the Storm-chaser team. They had to know it was him. The bodies had his signature all over them.

He thought about giving Tate Benson a call like before, but it would be risky, and he wasn't sure if that would make it too easy for them. They had to be aware of the way the victims had died, and they weren't stupid. He had a suspicion they were already looking for him, playing the same game he was. So there were two foxes in the henhouse. Which one was going to come away with the hen?

The music resumed, but the announcement had spurred his intent to get this finished, so he went back to his stakeout. From the number of students arriving with flowers, bakery boxes and happy birthday balloons, it appeared Ricks might be having a birthday. At that point Hershel revamped his plan and drove away.

The throb of the bass matched the young dancer's moves as he worked through his routine in front of the mirrored wall at Studio Ricks. For the boy, hip-hop was where it was at, and for Lionel, making money at something he loved was where *he* was at. He had over eighty students in six different group classes per week, plus the private lessons at the end of each day. He was grossing over four thousand dollars a week. Not a bad place for a man to be on his thirty-fourth birthday.

His students had been more than generous today. The studio was full of flowers, cupcakes and cookies, and a lot of balloons. It was going to take a moving van to get everything home tonight, except the balloons. They were definitely staying behind.

He glanced up at the clock, then back at his student, and stopped the music.

"No, no, J.J., not like that," he snapped. "You were sloppy. You have to make your moves almost robotic. They need to be short, jerky, in rapid time. And don't grab your damn crotch. That's tired and old school. Remember how I showed you?"

"Yeah, but—"

Lionel pointed. "No buts."

J.J. sighed. "Sorry."

"Now do it again, and do it right this time."

Lionel hit the switch and was once again assaulted by the music. It was all he could do to stay still. It would feel good to cut loose and show the kid up. Instead, he stifled the need to move bubbling within him and watched as J.J. went all the way through the routine, this time doing it perfectly. Lionel stopped the music again, but this time he was grinning.

"All right, that's what I'm talking about," he said, and gave the kid a high five. "Time's up. Hit the road, Jack."

J.J. grinned. "So I'll see you next week."

"Yeah…next week, and practice those moves. You need to be even sharper."

"You got it," J.J. said.

He wiped the sweat off his face, tossed the towel on the bench and grabbed his jacket as he danced out the door.

Lionel laughed as he watched him go. The kid was good, but he wasn't going to tell him so, at least not yet. And thank God it was finally time to set up for tomorrow and go home. He picked up the dirty towel and headed for the back room.

Hershel had a dozen birthday balloons in the back of the van. He had purchased them one at a time in twelve different locations. If the cops started looking for a man who'd bought a dozen balloons, they would never be able to find him. The balloon bouquet would get him in the door and put Ricks off guard, and that was all he needed.

He waited impatiently until the last student left and then waited again until the boy's motorbike cleared the parking lot before driving up to the studio and backing into the parking spot right in front of the door.

The door was all glass, which meant Ricks could look out and see him coming. The boutique next door had closed at six, and the space on the other side was empty. He glanced around to make sure no one was watching, then jumped out of the van, opened up the back doors and grabbed the helium-filled balloons.

The Taser was fully charged and in his pocket, but

as he started to enter he noticed a camera mounted at one end of the room and stopped. Either it was a security camera or one they used to film dance routines. He couldn't take a chance that it wasn't on, so he paused to pull the hoodie over his head, then held the balloons closer to help hide his face as he entered. The moment he was in and realized he was alone, he took the Taser out of his pocket.

Lionel was still in the office when he heard the bell on the door and thought J.J. must have come back. He walked out grinning.

"Hey, kid, what did you forget?" Then he stopped, saw the huge bouquet of balloons and the man who was holding them, and smiled. "Sorry, I thought you were one of my students."

"Delivery for Lionel Ricks?" Hershel said.

"Yeah, that's me," Lionel said as he jogged across the dance floor.

He was four feet away when Hershel raised the Taser and fired. The electrodes went into Lionel's chest, dropping him like a rock. The moment he hit the floor, Hershel spun and turned out the lights. A dozen happy birthday balloons drifted up toward the ceiling in the dark as Hershel went about the task of murder.

Lionel Ricks was grunting and twitching, although he was no heavier than the two women had been, but when Hershel bent down to pick up the body, a sharp pain cut across the lower part of his back.

"Son of a bitch."

He dropped Ricks and grabbed hold of his knees as the muscle spasm rolled through him. Ricks was vibrating like a high wire in a windstorm, still grunting and moaning from the electrical current shooting through him, but Hershel couldn't be bothered. He had his own hurt going on. When he tried to lift the man again a few moments later, the pain was worse.

"Damn it, not now," he muttered.

He couldn't get Lionel off the floor, let alone sling him over his shoulder, but he had to move him. Headlights swept through the door and across the wall of mirrors, momentarily highlighting the ongoing drama. When Hershel saw the face of the man hunched over the body on the floor, he staggered backward in horror. Not only had he not recognized himself, but it was the first time he'd gotten a glimpse of what his victims had seen. It was a sobering sight.

"It doesn't matter, it doesn't matter," he mumbled, and stumbled back toward Ricks.

The man's eyes had rolled back in his head. For all Hershel knew, he was already dead, but it didn't matter. He had to get him up and into the van.

He gritted his teeth as he slid his hands under Lionel's arms and began dragging him backward out of the studio, then toward the open doors at the rear of his van.

As Hershel shifted to lift Lionel upright, another muscle spasm nearly sent him to his knees. Groaning and cursing, he kept lifting until he had Ricks upright against the opening and then pushed. The body fell backward into the van. When Lionel's head hit the floor, the impact yanked the electrodes out of his chest.

Hershel grabbed his Taser as he climbed in, and then pulled Lionel the rest of the way inside, shutting the doors behind them. Hershel was in misery and sweating from the pain in his back, and Lionel was in the process of wetting himself when Hershel put the rope around his neck.

Hershel wrapped it tight, pushed his knee against the man's neck and pulled until he heard a pop. He felt for a pulse and then grunted with satisfaction when there was none.

The pain in his back shifted to his hip as he settled into the driver's seat, but he wasted no time leaving the parking lot, anxious to be gone.

He drove through D.C. with caution, intent on literally staying under the radar while the pain pulsed with every heartbeat. This was a setback he hadn't expected. Even though he'd been injured before, this was the first time his own body had betrayed him. It felt like more than bad luck. He'd made one foolish mistake after another since his arrival in D.C., and now this. He couldn't finish what he'd come here to do if he couldn't move.

The sudden sound of hysterical sobbing was so startling that at first he thought his victim had come back from the dead. When he realized it was Louise, he read her the riot act.

"Dang it, Louise. You nearly caused me to run off the road."

Your pain is my pain. My pain is your pain. You are a crazy man, Hershel, or don't you remember?

"I remember plenty, damn it. All this time I've been doing this for you, and you have been nothing but ungrateful."

You have done nothing for me. This is for you. You're always telling me I'm dead, so why blame me for these warnings? Have you ever seen me?

He braked for a stop sign, then eased through the intersection and kept driving on the dirt road.

"No, I haven't seen you, but I've heard you plenty."

Are you sure it was me you heard and not your own guilty conscience? Your pain is my pain. My pain is your pain. It's one and the same.

He frowned. Why would she say that? It was stupid. She'd been bawling and praying and carrying on from the start, and he'd been trying to explain why he was doing what he was doing. He'd heard her, by God. He wasn't imagining it. He couldn't have been imagining it. He tuned out the sound of her voice and concentrated on just getting to his drop site. He needed for this to be over with.

When he reached the little landing, he backed up to the slope and killed the engine, hobbling with every step as he went around to the back.

By the time he dragged Ricks' body out of the van and into the water, he was bawling. The pain in his back was so severe he wasn't sure he could get back to the van, and so he stood for a few moments to catch his breath, watching as the body sank out of sight.

It was quiet out here, with just the sound of the water lapping against the shore. He could hear an owl somewhere in a tree nearby, and the faint sound of a dog barking in the distance. He shoved the hoodie off his head and closed his eyes, letting the cool night air dry the sweat from his face.

He allowed himself a few moments of satisfaction that he was so close to being done. Lionel Ricks was the last clue they were going to get. As soon as the man's body showed up, Laura Doyle was next.

He glanced at his watch. He needed to get home, but there was that business about walking up the slope with his back in this kink. He turned around and was about to give it a try when he began to hear the sound of an airplane high overhead. He looked up, saw the flashing lights on the wingtips and guessed it was a plane just taking off from Washington National.

Sliding back into a brief moment of madness, he pictured passengers looking out the windows down into the darkness, and even though he knew it was nonsensical to think that they could see him, the urge to hide was impossible to ignore. He headed for the van with a stiff, hobbling gait.

He drove back to D.C. with his gut in a knot, went to an all-night pharmacy for a bottle of muscle-relaxing pain pills and headed for home. By the time he pulled into the drive, Lucy Taft was the last thing on his mind.

It wasn't until he started up the steps that he realized he couldn't lift his leg high enough to reach the next step without making the pain in his back worse. Left with no options, he dropped down to his hands and knees and crawled up, moaning and cursing as he went.

When he got to the top, he used the doorknob to pull himself upright, then unlocked the door and stumbled in. Just as he reached for the light switch, he realized the painkillers were still in the van. If that wasn't enough, Louise had to add insult to injury.

No more than you deserve. No more than you deserve.

He moaned. "If you're not real, then shut the fuck up, Louise."

You're the one who's crazy. You're talking to yourself.

Hershel cried all the way back down the steps to get the pills, and then crawled all the way up again. By the time he locked the door, he was hyperventilating and on the verge of passing out.

He staggered to his bedroom, shook a good half-dozen pills out into his hand, chewed and swallowed them without a drop of water, and fell into bed.

What if you overdosed?

He gritted his teeth and closed his eyes.

"Then I die, Louise, and it won't matter anymore."

Lucy Taft liked sleeping with fresh air, and now that the nights were getting colder, she left the window open about an inch, just enough to satisfy her fancy.

She woke as the van came up the drive and opened her eyes as the lights flashed across her bedroom wall. When she heard the tires popping the acorns that had dropped from the oak trees onto the drive, she knew her renter was home.

She slipped out of bed to look and knew immediately something was wrong. Leibowitz was walking as if he was drunk. Yes! He must be drunk. He was actually crawling up the stairs.

Disgusted with such low-class behavior, she was about to go back to bed when she saw him come back out of the apartment, sobbing and cursing all the way down the steps. He got something out of his van and then crawled back up again.

She made a note of the time of his arrival and the condition he was in, then got back into bed and said a prayer that he would pack up and leave.

Lionel Ricks' disappearance became evident once his ten-o'clock class showed up the next morning and found the door unlocked and the studio in the dark. But even more worrisome to the students was the fact that the cake and flowers were still there from yesterday, the ceiling was covered with balloons and their teacher was nowhere in sight.

Then they found his car keys in the office.

That was when they called the police.

Laura had gone to work early and was already set up in Bea's motor home and fielding calls. Within an hour of her arrival she received a call from the City of Reston, along with a follow-up fax, informing her that they had expanded the evacuation area, and until the gas company finished rerouting the gas lines, no one would be allowed to go home. They were looking at three more days, minimum.

When Kevin came out of the bedroom where he'd spent the night, she pushed the fax across the table.

"Take a look at this," she said.

He scanned it quickly, then looked up.

"What do you want me to do?" he asked.

She was already working on the new problem.

"The shelter here is too full, and we're going to be hit with an influx of new evacuees. We're going to have the fire marshal to deal with if we don't move some of these people today. I've got a phone call in to a community center on the west side of the city. If we get the okay, I want you in charge at the new location. It has a large office on-site, so you can set up a bed and your computer and lock up when you're out and about."

"Perfect," he said. "I'll go ahead and pack up my stuff just in case."

Laura went back to reading email. The next one was a confirmation letter from a supplier, so she gladly checked that off her list. So far, things were moving smoothly on-site, which was a blessing, because the rest of her life was on hold.

When Cameron had called her yesterday to confirm the Stormchaser team had been reactivated, she had been dealing with a plumbing problem at the church. Even though they'd talked about the possibility that the team would go active, it had startled her when it actually happened. It was shocking to think that Hershel Inman was once again in their midst, and it had been the last straw in her day. Something had to give, and the least important thing on her current agenda was the final fitting for her wedding gown.

She'd called the bridal shop right then and rescheduled the fitting, then gone back to trying to find a plumber. Eventually the situation was resolved, but that was yesterday, and here she was with a whole new set of problems to solve and not a lot of time to make it happen.

When her phone rang again, it was with good news. The community center would be available to them for as long as they needed it, and there was a manager on-site waiting with keys.

She got up and walked toward the back of the motor home.

"Hey, Kevin!"

He opened the door to the back bedroom.

"Yeah?"

"We have the okay on the community center, and the manager is waiting with the keys. If you'll head that way and get started, I'll send some of the volunteers to help you set up. Don't worry about supplies. Just call me. I'll get whatever you need."

"Thanks, Laura. You're the best," he said, and disconnected.

She sighed. It was good to be appreciated, but it would be even better if she wasn't so distracted by her personal life.

Fourteen

The FBI team showed up at police headquarters with two boxes of doughnuts and a new can of coffee. Considering Wade's bottomless appetite, they felt it only fair to bring their own food. Even with Ron temporarily out of the office, by the time they'd finished going over the murder board trying to glean new information, one box was already empty.

Wade was on his third bear claw as he studied the locations where the victims had disappeared, while Tate was talking to Burch.

Cameron was going through crime scene photos when he stopped and turned around.

"Hey, Sam."

Burch turned around. "Yeah?"

Cameron tapped a photo from the first abduction site.

"If I remember correctly, you guys interviewed the deliveryman from the Chinese restaurant, right?"

Burch nodded. "Yes. Patty Goss was a regular customer. When she worked late, she often ordered food to take home."

Cameron nodded. "So that explains the food cartons at the back door of the boutique, but at the second abduction you have flowers." He pointed to the crime scene photos of bedraggled flowers scattered around and beneath Megan Oliver's car. "Then here at Trent's abduction you have a manila envelope between the van and wheelchair, but I think I read that there was only blank paper inside. Is that correct?"

Burch nodded. "Yes, we figured it was something Trent had in his lap while he was getting on the lift, and then it fell off when he was attacked."

Cameron's eyes narrowed. "So what about the flowers at Megan Oliver's abduction site?"

Burch frowned. "There were hundreds of cars in that parking lot. There's no telling where they came from, because we got a rainstorm during the night she disappeared. They could have blown in from anywhere."

"But they're not all over the parking lot. They're right near her car," Cameron argued.

Burch's frown deepened. "What are you getting at?"

"Let me ask you this," Cameron said. "If you were a perp and you needed to take someone out with a Taser, how would you get close enough to them without alerting them they were in danger?"

Now Tate and Wade were listening, too.

Burch's eyes widened slightly as he walked closer, focusing on the photos as a group.

"Fake someone out with a delivery…maybe something they have to sign for. But wait. We know the delivery guy from the Chinese restaurant isn't Inman, and he did make that delivery."

"Yes, but clearly the killer took advantage of the fact that Patty's arms were full and it was pouring down rain."

Tate walked up and pointed at the flowers. "Megan Oliver was single but had a boyfriend, right?"

Burch nodded. "Yes, but he was out of town when she disappeared."

"So we need to find out if he sent her flowers that night," Cameron said.

"I'll get his info off the report," Wade said, licking sugar off his fingers as he went.

"That leaves Trent," Cameron said. "Yes, he's a lawyer, but why would he take home a manila envelope full of blank paper? Unless it wasn't his—unless someone approached him under the guise of being a courier."

Burch turned around and stared at the pictures again, and then put his hands on his hips.

"Well, shit. How did you see this and we didn't?"

Cameron knew he had to backpedal a little or risk the fragile cooperation between the two departments.

"Hey, it's just new eyes and us knowing as much as we do about this particular perp. He's wicked smart and full of deceit. Everything he does has a message.

It's always about the game with him. We were on the lookout for him in Louisiana nearly two years ago, and I let myself get suckered. Wound up in the hospital with a concussion and nearly got Tate's wife killed. However, I will say on my behalf, we still didn't know who he was or what he looked like at the time."

Burch's attitude shift was noticeable. "I see what you mean."

Wade walked back into the room. "The boyfriend never sent any flowers."

Cameron shrugged. "Someone did."

Burch's phone rang. He glanced down at the caller ID. "It's Ron. Hang on a minute," he said.

"We have another missing man," he said without preamble.

Burch frowned. "And what makes that our business?"

"Missing Persons seems to think something about it falls into the same category as the other three. We need to check it out. Meet me in the parking lot."

"On the way."

"What's going on?" Tate asked as Burch hung up.

"Another missing person. My partner's waiting. We're heading out to see the crime scene."

Tate hesitated. "We'll follow…but at a distance. If there's a back entrance, make sure we can get in."

"You got it," Burch said.

The detectives headed directly to the designated address while the FBI team took another route. When Tate and his team drove past the strip mall where the dance studio was located, there were two news crews and at least eight or nine cop cars at the site.

They circled the lot and drove up the alley, coming to a stop behind the studio. The door opened as they were getting out. It was Burch.

"Inside—and hurry. The news crews smell blood. Now that they know there's a serial killer abducting his victims, we weren't the only ones to assume this might be connected."

The team hurried inside, entering a narrow hallway that led to a small office, and from there into the studio, where Wells was waiting with the information they'd gathered so far. They glanced toward the front door, anxious to remain unobserved, and noticed a policeman standing guard outside the door, which blocked the view well enough to keep their presence unobserved.

"Missing man is Lionel Ricks, a resident of Reston. He's had the dance studio for ten years. Yesterday was his thirty-fourth birthday." Wells pointed at the flowers and cake boxes on a table at the far end of the room. "The kid sitting in a chair beside the flowers is J.J. Danson. He had a private lesson last night that was over at 8:00 p.m. He said when he left, everything was fine."

Tate tapped Cameron on the shoulder. "Go talk to him. See if there's anything different about the room that wasn't here when he left last night."

Cameron walked over. The kid looked scared, as if he'd been crying. He felt sorry for him, but he had to talk to him now, while everything was fresh in his mind.

He pulled up a chair, flashed his badge and sat down.

"I'm Special Agent Winger, FBI. Is it okay if we talk a minute?"

The boy nodded.

"So your name is J.J. Danson."

"Uh-huh."

"How do you know Mr. Ricks?"

"He's my dance instructor."

"When did you see him last?"

The boy wiped a shaky hand across his face, swallowing nervously.

"Last night. I left right after 8:00 p.m. when my lesson was over."

Cameron glanced at the table of gifts next to where they were sitting.

"I understand yesterday was Mr. Ricks' birthday."

J.J. nodded.

"Looks like quite a party."

"Not a party, not really. We just decided that whoever wanted to bring him something would do it when they came for class."

Cameron eyed the table again, and then glanced up at the ceiling.

"Looks like a lot of his students brought presents. Did you bring something, too?"

J.J. ducked his head. "No. I ride a bike. Didn't have a way to carry anything."

"No matter. The reason I asked is because I need you to do something for me. It's really important, and since you were the last student here, then you're probably the only one who can help us."

J.J. sat up a little straighter.

"I'll do anything to help find Lionel. He's a good guy and a sick dancer, for sure."

Cameron smiled. "Sick? That means good, right?"

"Right. So how can I help?"

"I need you to walk the room with me and tell me if you see anything unusual, something that's here now that wasn't here last night."

"I already know one thing," J.J. said, and pointed to the ceiling. "There weren't that many balloons when I left."

Cameron's heart skipped a beat as he looked up. "Are you sure?"

"I'm positive. You can ask around. There are at least ten or twelve more than when I left."

Cameron kept looking. "How can you be that certain?"

"The ceiling is low. I'm short. I danced in front of that dang mirror for two straight hours trying to get my routine down, and every time I looked up I could see them bouncing against the ceiling. There weren't more than eight or nine. Now look."

"Good eye, J.J.," Cameron said.

"Did that help?"

"Yes. It helped a lot."

"Can I go home?"

Cameron put a hand on the boy's shoulder. The kid was shaking.

"The detectives will let you know. Thanks again for your help."

"Do you think Lionel is okay?"

"I don't know, son. I sure hope so," Cameron said. "Sit tight, and I'll send a detective over."

The boy sat down again as Cameron headed back across the room. He stopped to talk to Wells, who was directing the crime scene photographer to get the shots he wanted.

"Tell him to take pictures of the balloons," Cameron said.

Wells paused. "Why?"

"I talked to the kid. He said there are at least ten or twelve more here now than when he left last night."

Wells looked up, then back at Cameron. "Maybe another delivery? I'll get some guys on that. We could get lucky and find a place that sold someone a dozen balloons last night."

"Good idea," Cameron said. "Oh, the kid wants to know when he can go home."

"I'll go talk to him," Wells said, then told the photographer, "Hey, Pete, get me some shots of the balloons, too."

Cameron went back to the office.

Tate was going through a day planner on the desk, and Wade was watching the last recordings made on the security camera.

"Hey, Tate, I think we've got something," he said.

Tate looked up.

Wade pointed. "I think we're looking at a balloon delivery here. Oh, wait. Damn it."

"What happened?" Tate asked.

"Just a second," Wade said as he ran the footage back a couple of seconds and then hit Play.

They got their first glimpse of Ricks as he waved goodbye to J.J. and turned toward the office.

"Nice-looking guy," Cameron said.

"And fit," Tate added.

Wade pointed. "Now he disappears, which means he came in here. Now watch the front entrance. It's dark out, but you can see movement through the glass door."

Their gazes were focused on the door as it began to open. But instead of a person, all they saw was a deluge of balloons being herded inside. There was a brief glimpse of the top of a dark hoodie, and then a man's chest and legs. From the angle of the camera, the balloons completely obliterated his face.

"The bastard knew about the camera," Tate said.

"This guy is skinny. He's not built like Inman," Wade said.

"Wait! Look at his legs," Cameron said.

"I'll be damned! They're bowed! Good eye," Tate added.

"There's Ricks again," Wade said as Ricks appeared on camera again, walking toward the front door. Then the deliveryman fired a Taser. "And down he goes," Wade added.

The deliveryman suddenly pivoted. They had a brief glance of his back as the balloons floated upward. All of a sudden the room went dark.

Wade grunted. "He turned out the lights."

"Is that all?" Tate asked.

Wade nodded.

"So what's your call?" Tate asked.

"It's Inman," Cameron said. "He may have changed his build, but he couldn't hide those bow legs."

"I agree," Wade said.

"Let's get back to the P.D.," Tate said. "If he follows the pattern, once Ricks' body shows up, he'll take his next victim. We have to figure out how he targets these people beforehand, or someone else will die."

"Why do you think he hasn't contacted us?" Cameron asked.

Tate shrugged. "Because he's pissed. I think something made him angry. I'm not sure what, but these killings are quick and brutal. They mean nothing to him. They're just a means to an end. The message is that he can do what he wants, when he wants, and we can't do anything about it. He doesn't want to talk to us anymore. He's telling us he's through with the game."

"But we're not in charge of the investigations like before, so it's really not directed at us," Wade said.

Tate took a deep breath and then looked at his partners.

"Not yet it's not. But if this *is* Inman—and I fully believe it is—he'll find a way to draw us in."

Cameron suddenly shivered. "By taking someone we love."

Tate pointed to the security camera. "Bag the disc and let's get out of here."

Hershel woke up feeling as if he'd been on a two-day drunk and needing to pee. His head was spinning, his back was killing him and his mouth tasted as if he'd been eating shit. It was just after ten in the morning, and he'd been asleep almost nine straight hours. He rolled over to the side of the bed, and then slowly swung his legs off the mattress and got up. It hurt like hell to walk, but he hadn't wet the bed since he was four and wasn't going to start now.

After he was finished, he thought about getting in the shower and letting the hot water loosen up the muscles in his back, but he needed coffee worse.

He had just started the coffee when there was a knock at the door. The unexpected sound made him jump, which sent the muscles in his back into a spasm. He felt like hell, and considering the fact that he'd slept in his clothes, he probably looked like hell, too. Whatever. *If someone comes unannounced, they get what they get.*

A second knock sounded as he shuffled slowly to the door.

"I'm coming!" he yelled, cursing beneath his breath.

He opened the door to find Lucy Taft on the stoop. Her cheeks were pink from the exertion of climbing the steps, and she had her gardening shears in her hand again.

"I'm so sorry to bother you. Hope I didn't wake you up," she said in a rush.

"It's okay," he said. "I was up, but I'm moving slow. I hurt my back a couple days ago, and it keeps getting worse."

Now Lucy understood his behavior from last night and felt somewhat guilty that she'd tarred him so quickly with the drunk brush.

"I'm sorry to hear that. Is there anything I can do for you? Do you need to go to a doctor? I can recommend one."

Hershel was surprised by the offer. "No, thanks. I'll be fine."

"Well, the reason I came up is only going to add fuel to the flame of your discomfort. I was in the garden when I noticed your back right tire has gone flat. I thought you would want to know."

Hershel groaned, thinking of the pain of lifting and changing a tire.

Despite her distrust of him, Lucy felt bad for his discomfort. "I can make a call, if you like. There's a garage that I use for oil changes and tune-ups. They fix flats. If I called them, they would come out and remove the tire, then fix it and bring it back, if you were willing to pay a little extra."

Hershel sighed. "That would be great, and paying extra is no problem."

She nodded primly. "Then I'll get right on that.

Have a nice day, and I do hope your back gets better soon."

"Yes, ma'am, thank you," he said.

He watched until she was safely down the stairs before he shut the door. The scent of freshly brewed coffee pulled him back to the kitchen, and within an hour he heard a truck pull into the drive and park at his apartment. He heard footsteps coming up the stairs again, but this time he was wearing clean sweats and had given himself a half-assed shave for a face that grew a half-assed beard. Filled with more pain pills, coffee and cereal, he answered the door, then shivered from the chill of the wind.

The mechanic quickly introduced himself.

"Hey. I'm Frank from Georgio's Garage. Mrs. Taft called us about fixing a flat on your van."

"Paul Leibowitz," Hershel said. "I really appreciate this. I hurt my back a couple days ago, and I'm barely mobile."

"We'll get you fixed up," Frank said. "Do you have a spare?"

Hershel's heart skipped a beat. It was inside the van, but he wasn't sure if there was anything obvious in there that might incriminate him.

"I'll get my keys and meet you downstairs," he said.

The mechanic nodded and headed back down as Hershel went to get a jacket and his keys.

He descended the steps slowly, taking care not to hurry, and made it down with a minimal amount of pain. When he unlocked the van, he opened the back door and looked in. Nothing seemed out of place. He pointed at the tire lying against the side.

"There it is, but I'm not sure it's good. I haven't owned the van very long."

The mechanic pulled the tire out and then let it go. It bounced. He nodded.

"It's holding air. Do you want me to switch it out and bring back the one I fix as your spare?"

"That would be great," Hershel said. "I think there's a jack somewhere."

"I brought a jack. This won't take long," Frank said.

Hershel shut the van and locked it.

"I'll have your money ready when you come back," he said.

"Boss said a hundred bucks, seeing as how we're making two trips, plus fixing the flat."

"That's fine," Hershel said. "I'll pay cash."

He watched for a couple of minutes and then went back upstairs, grateful he didn't have to do this himself.

Laura was on her way into the church when her cell phone rang. When she saw it was Cameron, she smiled and stopped under a tree to take the call in privacy.

"Hello, my darling. How's your morning?" she asked.

"Hectic. Another call came in the morning about a missing person. Someone else has been abducted, and we're on our way back to the P.D. now."

The smile slid off her face. "Oh, no. Who was it?"

"A dance instructor from Reston named Lionel Ricks. He had a studio in D.C. where he gave lessons. He disappeared sometime after eight last night."

"Wow. Yet another resident of Reston," she said.

Cameron frowned. That fact had already been noted, but maybe they were missing the obvious.

Laura lived in Reston.

"Yes, another one," he said. "I don't have to tell you to pay attention to your surroundings."

"I'll be fine. There are more than a hundred people here."

"Still—"

"I'll pay attention," she said.

"That's all I needed to hear. Love you most."

She smiled. "Love you, too," she said. But as soon as their call ended, she called Nola.

Nola was in her art studio, working on a commission, when the phone rang. When she saw who it was, she laid down her brush and quickly wiped the oil paint from her hands.

"Hey, Laura. How's it going?"

"Another person has gone missing. That makes four."

Nola groaned beneath her breath. The anxiety was getting to all of them.

"This is maddening. I can't believe this is happening again, and right here in our area."

"I know. Before, the Stormchaser team went to the killer's chaos. This time he brought it to us," Laura said.

"Are they sure it's Inman?"

"I don't know. But they have to operate under that assumption, don't they?"

"Yes, I suppose they do. Are you on your own? Are you scared?"

"No, I'm still at the Red Cross shelter here in Reston with the people who were evacuated after the gas explosion."

"That was just awful," Nola said. "Did you know any of the victims?"

"I don't know," Laura said. "I don't think they've even released a complete list of the deceased yet, because it's been so difficult to confirm who was lost."

Nola gasped. "Good Lord. You mean...?"

"Nothing intact," Laura said softly.

"How awful."

"Yes, it is. Anyway, I need to get back to work, but I can't talk about this mess to just anyone, and I needed to hear a sane voice."

"I hope to God they catch the beast who's doing this, whether it's Inman or not. Call me anytime."

"I will, and thanks," Laura said.

This time when she hung up, she felt better. She made herself focus on the task at hand and hurried back into the church, for the time being pushing Hershel Inman to the bottom of her to-do list.

It was nearing four o'clock, and with so many children who'd been forced to evacuate with little more than the clothes on their backs, Laura had to improvise old-fashioned entertainment. Without their usual Xbox games and televisions, they'd gotten bored.

She was sitting cross-legged on the floor with four girls ranging in age from eight to twelve, showing the girls how to play jacks, when she saw a teenage girl walk in wearing a miniskirt and stockings, a turtleneck T-shirt and a bejeweled jean jacket. Her short brown hair was purple on the tips, and her eyes were red rimmed and welling with tears.

Laura handed her ball and jacks to one of the children.

"Here you go. You give it a try. Sorry, girls, I'm going to have to get back to work. Do you think you've got this now?"

"We've got it," one of them said.

Laura smiled as she got up, brushing off the seat of her jeans as she went. The closer she got to the purple-haired teen, the more certain she became that the girl was on the verge of hysteria. She had a duffel bag in one hand and a cell phone in the other, and she was trembling from head to toe.

"Hi, I'm Laura Doyle. What's your name, honey?"

"Lisa Welch."

"How old are you?" Laura asked.

"I'm fifteen."

Laura frowned, hoping she wouldn't have to call the police about a runaway.

"Are you looking for someone, or do you need a place to stay for a bit?"

The girl took a deep breath. "I had a fight with

Mommy and Daddy, so I ran away from home. I just wanted them to hear my side, but they wouldn't listen. I thought if I ran away, they would be so scared that when I came back they would listen to what I was trying to say. I bought a bus ticket to South Carolina. We used to live there when I was younger. But I didn't stay. I just wanted to go home."

"Do you want me to call them for you?"

Lisa began to shake harder. Tears were rolling down her face now, and her words were coming out in thick choking sobs. She held up her phone.

"They didn't call me. Even after two days, when I got scared and was running out of money, they didn't call. I sent them a text, but they never texted back. I called and called, and no one ever answered. I thought they were so mad they didn't want me anymore."

Laura was beginning to get an awful feeling. She knew, even before Lisa said it, what had happened. "Come, sit with me," she said softly.

Lisa took a deep shuddering breath and followed Laura into her office. The moment she sat down, she closed her eyes. When she opened them again, the horror of her reality was reflected through the tears.

"I begged money from strangers to get enough to come home, but home isn't there anymore."

Laura pulled a handful of clean tissues from her shirt pocket. "I'm sorry, honey. I am so sorry. How did you know to come here?"

The girl swayed where she sat, too shocked to pay attention to gravity.

"There was a guard where the street was blocked off. He told me to come here. I asked him if this is where the survivors were. He said there weren't any. Is that true?"

Laura cupped Lisa's cheek, and then pulled her into her arms.

"Yes, it's true."

It was Lisa Welch's last straw. She moaned, and then threw back her head and screamed.

Laura caught her as she collapsed, cradling Lisa's head in her lap. The girl's eyes were closed. Heartsick and in shock, she'd gone as far as she could go.

Fifteen

Laura called Child Protective Services. And then the media caught wind of the story and descended on the Wesley Methodist Church like locusts eager for the next big meal.

Everyone wanted the girl's story.

The girl who'd run away from home only to find upon returning that home wasn't there. It was something straight out of a Lifetime movie, and everyone wanted their own sound bite.

Laura fielded the reporters like the pro she was. It wasn't the first time she'd been inundated with media, and it wouldn't be the last. The media were always about fresh blood.

She was so involved in her job that she never thought about what Hershel Inman might do if she wound up on the local news. Her only thought was to protect the girl. And because of her diligence, *she* became their sound bite, along with a few moments of film footage on the teenager as the authorities finally arrived and whisked her away.

Cameron was in Homicide adding a new map to the murder board when Tate stuck his head in the door.

"Your girl is on TV," he said, and then ducked back out.

Cameron bolted for the break room.

"What happened?" he asked.

Wade pointed. "Hell of a deal. Some kid who lived in the area of the explosion ran away from home that night. She got scared and came back after not hearing from anyone, and turned up at the Red Cross shelter at the church. Laura is holding her own with the news crews, but I wish the police had gotten there before the media."

Cameron's heart sank. He knew exactly what Tate was getting at. Every time anyone connected with the team got more news coverage than Inman did, it increased his rage.

"Is that live?" he asked.

"No, taped from about an hour ago," Tate said.

Cameron kept telling himself not to panic, but he was already calling Laura as he walked out of the room.

After the girl was gone, Laura retreated to the motor home with Bea, leaving the police to move the news crews along. She couldn't shake the emotion filling her at the girl's plight, and kept remembering how the teen had fallen into her arms, devastated by despair. She'd heard Lisa tell a social service worker that she had an aunt and uncle in Colorado, and two sets of grandparents, one in New York State and one in Massachusetts. It was the only saving grace to her situation.

One day the girl would realize that she wasn't meant to die that night and hopefully find reason for her life. But she knew that right now Lisa Welch's only thought was for what she'd lost.

As Laura finished up some reports, she was vaguely aware of Bea puttering quietly about the kitchen. But when she suddenly appeared at the little table where Laura was working and set a frothy mug of hot chocolate at her elbow, the ache in her chest began to subside, a reminder that the world does go on.

"I thought you might like something warm," Bea said.

Laura looked up and smiled. "And sweet makes it even better. Thank you so much. Did you make yourself some?"

Bea nodded.

"Then, get it and come sit with me. I need some company right now."

Bea settled in on the other side of the table and took a quick sip from her mug.

"Mmm, that hits the spot. I've felt chilly all day. I think the weather must be going to change."

Laura looked out the window. The sky did look a little gray.

"This is certainly the time of year for it. So tell me,

Bea. Where did you grow up?" She noticed absently that when Bea smiled, her eyes almost disappeared.

"I grew up in Vermont, the baby of eight. I had five brothers and two sisters. I was a twin, but my sister died in an accident years ago."

Laura frowned. "Oh, my goodness. I'm so sorry. That's how my sister, Sarah, and I lost our parents. One day they were there, and then they weren't."

Bea nodded. "Yes, I've thought a lot about death lately." Then she laughed. "I don't mean in the sense of offing myself. What I meant was that the older one gets, the more solid the knowledge that it comes to all of us."

"Is it true what they say about twins having a special connection?" Laura asked.

Bea nodded. "Leah and I sure did. I knew she was gone before the phone call ever came. Before, I'd always felt her inside me, so when I felt her absence, I knew. Even though I was married, it was scary, wondering if I would know how to live without her."

Laura put her elbows on the table and leaned closer.

"That's amazing. You really felt it?"

Bea shrugged. "It was normal to us, the knowing. We always knew when the other one was sick or had been injured. We could feel each other's emotions. We just didn't know what caused them."

"What a gift, to be that connected to someone," Laura said.

Bea's smile softened. "I was that connected to my Robert, as well. In many ways, losing him was worse than losing Leah. She was my blood, but he was my heart."

Laura leaned back, struck by her honesty.

"I think I know what you mean about that. After meeting and falling in love with my fiancé, I can't imagine life without him."

Bea patted her hand. "That's the way love is supposed to feel. Now drink your chocolate before it gets cold."

Laura smiled and did as she was told.

Bea finished hers and had left in a borrowed car on a grocery run when Laura's cell phone rang. She smiled when she saw Cameron's name pop up on the screen. "Hi, honey."

"Hello, baby. I'm just checking in on you. We caught some of the footage about the runaway. That's a really tough place for her to be in. Does she have other family?"

"Yes. Both grandparents, and an aunt and uncle."

"Thank goodness for that," he said.

Laura could hear the tension in his voice.

"Why did you really call?" she asked.

Cameron sighed. "Busted."

"Did you find Lionel Ricks' body?"

"Not yet. What time do you think you'll be home tonight?"

"We had to set up a second site today, and Kevin is over there now, so I was thinking I should stay here tonight."

"Then send your roommate home and I'll come stay with you."

She smiled. "You don't have to."

"I know, but maybe I want to."

"Would you bring me a change of clothes?" she asked.

"Absolutely. Text me later and tell me what you want me to bring."

Laura waited. "You still haven't said why you really called."

"You were on TV today. Inman isn't going to like playing second fiddle to a story connected to you."

A wave of fear washed over Laura so fast it took her breath.

Cameron frowned. "Laura?"

Her hand was shaking as she wiped it across her face.

"I'm here. I just never thought—"

"You didn't do anything wrong. I just want you to pay very close attention from now on."

She felt the first stirring of true panic. It was the same kind of fear she'd felt when the wolves were outside the plane, trying to get in. This was the same thing. She was alive, but until someone found Inman, there would always be a wolf waiting to take her down.

It was late afternoon before Hershel ventured out of the apartment. He had an appointment with a chiropractor Lucy had recommended and was hoping an adjustment would help whatever was wrong with his back.

He found the address without any problem but was a little surprised by the neighborhood. It was very residential. Obviously the doctor had an office in his home.

There was a small sign near the doorbell that read Enter. The line below read Ring After Hours. He opened the door and walked in. As he did, a buzzer sounded. Moments later a heavyset man walked in wearing a white lab coat.

"Good evening. I'm Dr. Payne. You must be Mr. Leibowitz."

"Call me Paul," Hershel said.

The doctor smiled, and handed him a clipboard with a paper and pen.

"If you'll fill this out on both sides, I'll be with you shortly."

"I intend to pay in cash," Hershel said.

Payne was still smiling, but it had yet to reach his eyes.

"That's fine, but I'll still need your medical history. Wouldn't want to make a bad situation worse. I'm sure you understand."

"Yes, of course," Hershel said.

"I'll be back in a few minutes to answer any questions you might have," Payne said, and left the room.

Hershel began reading the form. He had no intention of responding to anything truthfully and began randomly checking off boxes, making sure that whatever he marked wouldn't cause a denial of services, no preexisting conditions that would preclude manipulation. He needed this pain to go away.

A short while later he was on the table, grunting with every manipulation Payne made.

"I just realized the irony of your last name," Hershel muttered as the doctor pushed against a knotted muscle.

"Eventually, everyone gets it," the doctor said, and then moved to the end of the table and put effort into pulling first one foot and then the other, until Hershel actually felt the pain release.

"Oh, wow. Whatever you just did felt good."

"Pinched nerve, I think. You'll need to alternate heat and ice packs when you get home."

"I can do that," Hershel said.

"And no lifting. Definitely no lifting anything over five pounds until this stabilizes."

"I hear you," Hershel muttered, which was the truth. He just didn't have any intention of obeying.

He left twenty minutes later with seventy-five dollars less in his pocket and a considerable reduction in pain. It was enough. He stopped at a pharmacy to buy some ice and heat packs, then at a bank ATM to get some more cash before moving on to a fast-food restaurant for a meal to take home. He planned to take it easy for the next two nights. Hopefully Ricks' body would wash up somewhere within that time frame, and then he could finish what he'd come to do.

* * *

The urgency to find out what triggered Inman's choice of victims was growing. The more time that passed, the more people who wound up dead, and still they had no more notion of why the first one had been picked than they did why he'd picked the last. There were no witnesses. They had no leads. They didn't truly know what Inman looked like anymore. They didn't know what he drove.

The official police report that a serial killer was at work in the D.C. area had sparked a flood of phone calls. The P.D. was following up on them as fast as possible, but so far every one had wound up a dead end.

The two detectives that Burch and Wells sent out on a balloon hunt had turned up nothing. Almost every place that sold helium-filled balloons sold the same brands and styles. It was not lost on the team that Inman had done the same thing when he'd purchased the flowers for his wife's grave. He'd made sure there was nothing unique about the flowers or the card, and now he'd done it again. The balloons were as generic as they came.

After receiving a list of the places nearest the dance studio that sold the balloons, Wade left to follow up on an idea. When he came back hours later, he was grinning from ear to ear.

"Got the little bastard," he said.

Every man in the room stopped what they were doing and turned around.

"Pull up a chair," Wade said as he popped a disc into the computer. "This is a supermarket. The floral department is small, and the balloons are already blown up. All you do is walk in and buy one, which is what he did. I didn't catch this at first until I saw the same man in a dark hoodie and jeans show up on the security footage from four other places. After that, I quit looking and went back to get copies. There's no need looking for all twelve purchases. Not now. Watch this."

The scene was typical of a grocery store, shoppers pushing carts, kids tagging along behind or crying for something they couldn't have. And then the camera caught the back of a man in a dark hoodie and blue jeans walking toward the floral desk. Within minutes, he exited carrying a happy birthday balloon.

"Can't see his face," Tate said.

Wade popped in the next DVD. "Bear with me," he said.

The next scene was inside a flower shop. A man wearing the same dark hoodie and jeans bought a happy birthday balloon and walked out with his head down and the balloon clutched firmly in his fist.

"He's making sure we can't get a good look of his face," Cameron said.

Wade grinned and popped another disc into the computer. "Another supermarket buy."

This time they got a better look beneath the hoodie. It wasn't definitive, but they could see the man was the right age.

"Okay, we can all agree this is the same man who delivered the balloons to Ricks' studio. But we really need a facial shot. Do you have one?" Cameron asked.

Wade handed the last disc to Cameron with a smile. "You do the honors."

Cameron slipped it in and hit Play.

"This one is from another grocery store," Wade said. "There he goes, straight toward the floral department. He makes the buy, he turns around to leave, now watch...watch...*boom!* How do you like them apples?"

"What happened there?" Tate asked.

"Some kid knocked down an entire end cap of soda. Glass bottles exploded all over the place. It was still sticky walking on that floor, even though it happened last night. Obviously the noise distracted him from his need for secrecy. Like everyone else, he looked up."

Cameron froze the shot on Inman's face. They couldn't quit staring.

"He's lost at least fifty pounds, wouldn't you say?" Tate said.

"He's also had reconstructive surgery on his face. Those burn scars are nearly gone," Wade added.

"And we've got a bald head and a little black mustache," Cameron muttered.

"Wade, make copies of that shot. I want them distributed to every beat cop," Tate said.

"What about alerting the media?" Cameron asked.

Tate was the profiler, the one with the inside knowledge of how killers behaved. He shook his head.

"If he knows he's been made, I think he'll run,

and then he'll start all over somewhere else and more people will die."

"So no to the media," Cameron said.

"For now," Tate added.

Wade hit Print and the first of two hundred copies started to emerge.

"Great job," Tate added.

Wade grinned. "Got anything to eat around here?"

Everyone laughed.

Having their first real lead was a high they would be happy to repeat.

It was after eight before Cameron arrived at the shelter. He had just parked beside the motor home and gotten out carrying a take-out bag from one of Laura's favorite Chinese restaurants when he heard her calling his name. He turned around just as she came out of the church at a lope.

"I was watching for you," she said as she threw her arms around his neck for a quick kiss. When she saw the bag, she grinned. "Ooh, spring rolls?"

He chuckled. "Yes, and a few of your other favorites, too."

"Thank you! I'm starved."

"Are you okay to leave right now? We can go inside if you need to be there. Lord knows I've spent plenty of time in shelters with you."

"No, it's okay. I called in another worker to take the night shift. And it looks like this is going to come to an end sooner than we thought. If nothing happens to change the situation, we got word they'll be allowed to go home sometime tomorrow afternoon or evening. So let's go to the trailer. It's chilly and feels like rain."

"Good news. Lead the way."

She unlocked the door to the motor home and walked in, leaving him to lock up behind them.

"I'm going to wash up," she said, and made a beeline for the bathroom as Cameron set the bag onto the little table. He took off his jacket and began looking around, impressed by the luxuries that had been downsized to fit such a small space.

A few moments later she was back.

"I'll get the plates and forks if you'll set out the food. Do you want me to make coffee or—"

"Maybe later. I'm good with a soft drink or water."

"I have bottles of lemon iced tea."

"Perfect," he said, and began pulling the little boxes out of the bag.

A few minutes later they were sharing a meal and the events of their day. They were almost finished when he laid his fork down and looked up.

"Have you heard anything more about your runaway?"

Laura nodded. "They contacted her grandparents in New York State, who of course thought she was dead. They're ecstatic."

"Oh, wow. Talk about a miracle for them." He reached for her hand. "That's how scared I was when your plane went down. I thought I'd lost you. And then we found the wreckage, and the first person we saw was the pilot. Then the two bodies that had fallen against the door, and even as I was looking for you, I was afraid of what I would find."

Laura had stopped eating, and her hands were in her lap.

Cameron frowned. "What's wrong? I'm sorry. I shouldn't have brought up such a—"

"I dragged the bodies there," she said, and without realizing it, she began rocking where she sat. "The wolves were trying to get to Ken…to the pilot. The windshield was broken. I was afraid they would get in and get me."

Cameron felt sick. All this time, and he hadn't known.

"The door wouldn't stay closed. I guess it was sprung or something after the crash. I pulled their bodies against the door to keep it shut. I thanked them for helping save me. I told them I was sorry."

Cameron jumped out of his seat and pulled her into his arms.

"I'm sorry. I'm so sorry. I didn't mean to resurrect your nightmare. And don't feel guilty, baby. Not ever. You did what you had to do to stay alive. That's how the strong survive."

Laura was crying again, but she didn't want to.

"I'm sorry. I ruined our dinner, and I didn't mean to—"

"Come, sit," he said, and tugged her hand as he led her to the sofa. "I don't know about you, but I need a hug, and I have some news to share, too."

Laura leaned against his shoulder, taking comfort in the hug and the deep rumble of his voice near her ear.

"Tell me something good," she said.

"I can go you one better. I'm going to *show* you something good. Hang on."

He jumped up from the sofa, got a paper from the inside pocket of his jacket and then dropped it in her lap as he sat back down.

"Take a look at that," he said.

She unfolded the paper, stared at the face for a moment and then looked up.

"I think I've seen him. Once sitting in a van in traffic, and again making a donation after the gas explosion."

Cameron's gut knotted. If Inman was lurking around Laura, that most likely meant she was the target. He would have to tell the team.

"You said he was driving a van. Do you remember what color?"

Laura frowned. "Light color, maybe. I didn't pay attention, because I didn't recognize him. He looks so different now."

"Yeah, that's Inman, fifty pounds lighter, bald and mustached. He's had some reconstructive surgery on the facial scarring." Then he handed her another photo. This time all she could see was a man's body from the chest down, holding a bunch of balloons. "Check out the bow legs. It's hard to disguise a body feature like that."

Laura felt sick, knowing Inman had been scoping her out.

"So now you know for sure he's here. But why? How is he choosing victims? They aren't storm survivors. Why has he targeted them?"

"We're still working on that," Cameron said. "But I wanted you to know this face. When you know your enemy, then you know who to fight...and you've turned into a pretty good opponent."

She nodded, thinking of what he'd taught her about self-defense.

"Hang on a sec," he said. "I'm going to call Tate and let him know about this. I'll be right back."

He left the room and made the call, filling them in on everything she'd said, but without anything solid to go on, Inman was still in control.

Going back to face her was hard. He hated the tension on her face, but it was better to be safe than sorry. Even so, he changed the subject.

"Hey, we still have fortune cookies," he said. He got up again and dug them out of the sack. "Pick one," he said, holding them out in his palm.

Laura chose one, opened the little cellophane wrapper, then cracked the cookie and read her fortune.

"'Your life is about to undergo great change.'" She frowned. "I hope that means I'm still here when the change is over."

"You're getting married. That's a great change, so quit looking for the bad stuff," he said, and kissed the side of her cheek to take away the sting of the words.

"What does yours say?" she asked.

He opened the cookie, read it, then laughed as he repeated it aloud.

"'You are one tough cookie.'"

"It does not say that," she said, then snatched it out of his hand and read it aloud.

"'You are wise in the ways of man.' What's wrong with that?"

"Nothing. I just like being one tough cookie better."

Then he pulled her up on his lap and proceeded to kiss her senseless.

Sixteen

The threatening storm finally moved in while they were asleep.

Cameron woke in the night to the sound of rain on the roof of the motor home, with Laura curled up behind him, as always with her nose so close to his back he could feel the warmth of her breath against his skin. He knew he was her touchstone to safety, but with Hershel Inman back in their lives, the pressure to keep her out of that madman's hands was overwhelming.

He turned over carefully until she was facing him, then slipped his arm beneath her neck and cradled her close against his chest. She shifted unconsciously in her sleep and then sighed. When he felt her body relax, he closed his eyes.

The next time he woke it was morning, Laura was gone and the alarm was going off. Then he heard the shower running and got out of bed.

* * *

Laura was standing completely under the shower-head with her eyes closed, rinsing the soap out of her hair. When she heard the shower door slide open, she fumbled for her washcloth.

"It's just me," Cameron said as he stepped up behind her and cupped her breasts with both hands. "I didn't think we should let all this water go to waste on one little blonde."

She was laughing and trying to wipe the soap out of her eyes when his hands slid from her breasts to the juncture of her thighs.

"I don't know if this shower is big enough for two of us," she said, and then groaned at the feel of his erection pushing against her backside. Just the thought of it inside her made her ache.

"Don't move," he whispered. "Let me."

Bracing both hands against the wall, she leaned forward. The water was pummeling her back, and Cameron's hands were on her hips.

He was hard and hot.

She was soapy and wet.

It was a match made in heaven.

A short while later, Cameron left the motor home for the D.C. police department while Laura walked across the parking lot into the church and went to work.

Hershel woke up as close to pain-free as he'd been in days. He was almost afraid to move and aggravate his back, but he needed to pee and once again had no other option. He got out of bed without a muscle spasm ripping through him and smiled as he walked to the bathroom. He was better.

"Halle-freakin'-lujah," he muttered, and peed off his erection.

It never occurred to him anymore to want a woman beneath him in any other way but dead. He had long since channeled his sex drive into hate and revenge. His high came in knowing when he'd made fools of the people who'd let him down.

He opted for a long hot shower, letting the jets of hot water pummel the sore muscles in his back, and then dressed to go out. Sometime today he needed to go shopping. Laura Doyle was getting married, and even though they hadn't invited him to the ceremony, he wasn't going to hold a grudge. He was still going to get them a present. It was the honorable thing to do.

Every patrol cop in D.C. was carrying a picture of Hershel Inman, and even though they weren't flashing it around, they gave an extra glance at anyone fitting the profile.

The Stormchaser team was still staying in the background and concentrating on the info coming in, and now Jo Luckett was back on the team. She was working from the field office, searching online through the banking and credit-card systems for connections to Inman's old aliases. Wade had filled her in on the victims' info, as well.

Charles Trent's autopsy report was on Tate's desk, but it was the same as the first two. All three victims had been Tasered, then strangled. And after seeing the video at Lionel Ricks' dance studio, his death, which would be the fourth, was already an assumption, even though his body had yet to be found.

Cameron was at the murder board, mentally moving info and pictures from one place to another, convinced the answer was right in front of them. Colored push pins on a D.C. map marked each abduction site, and he had added a smaller map of Reston, with pins corresponding to the victims' home addresses.

They had worked up the routes the victims took to work, the hours they worked, their quitting times. Nothing had been left to chance. They had two victims who'd been divorced and two who had never been married, one of which was Charles Trent, who happened to be gay. To their knowledge, the victims weren't people Inman would have known or held a grudge against.

All they knew for sure was that Inman had posed as a deliveryman to get close to his last three victims, perhaps inspired by catching his first just after receiving a delivery, and that the victims were dead before they hit the water. Somewhere there had to be a message or a pattern to his selection—they just hadn't found it yet.

Laura's day at the shelter had turned into a good one. They'd finally gotten the all clear to send the evacuees home, and it was none too soon. Between the grieving relatives who'd continued to show up searching for loved ones and the people who had been displaced, this had been a particularly difficult experience. She was so glad it was over and anxious just to get home. Tomorrow was Friday, and on Saturday morning she was going for her final fitting for her wedding gown. She kept thinking of the laundry that had to be done, groceries to be purchased and a house in need of cleaning.

She had so much to do that she was considering making a call to a cleaning service she had used before, and then decided against it. She'd had enough of strangers for a while. She just wanted to get on with the business of getting married, and enjoy the peace and quiet of home.

Now all she had to do was finish packing up and documenting what was being returned to the warehouse, and she could go home.

It was almost ten in the morning before Hershel got up the energy to go out. Buying a wedding gift would most likely require going to a mall, which made him nervous.

During his trip from New Orleans to Virginia he'd stopped along the way to replenish his stash of disguises, just in case, and he considered it time to pull one out. He was so close to ending this quest that it would be foolish to get careless now.

He went back to his bedroom and pulled a small duffel bag out of the closet. There were three wigs, two mustaches and a beard, all in different colors. He thought about it for a few moments, then tried on one curly gray wig but discarded it for a bushy gray mustache, matching eyebrows and a gray sock cap. Everything would all blend together and make him fade into a crowd.

Then he switched the jacket he'd been wearing for a denim one, changed his jeans to sweats, his hiking shoes to tennis shoes, and packed the mustache and eyebrows along with the spirit gum in a fanny pack. He'd started toward the door when he happened to look out. His heart skipped a beat.

Lucy Taft seemed to be inspecting his van.

"What the hell are you up to now, you nosy little bitch?"

The shriek in his ear was so startling Hershel jumped.

"Louise! What the hell?"

It's not about what she's up to. It's what you're about to do. You leave that woman alone. Do you hear me? Leave her alone!

Hershel spun away from the window, waving his arms in the air.

"Or what? Or what? You'll divorce me? Oh, wait! You can't do that, can you? Because you're fucking dead."

Louise didn't respond, and Hershel was done talking.

* * *

Lucy Taft had a case of what William Harold had always called cabin fever. After a breakfast of Mildred's buckwheat pancakes, she decided she needed to walk off the calories and opted for a leisurely stroll around her block. She'd done that often in her younger days, but not so much now. Still, it seemed the perfect opportunity while the weather was still nice.

She walked all the way down to the end of her block before meeting the mailman making deliveries and paused for a brief visit. After his departure, she turned right at the corner and moved down the next block, stopping often to admire the fall flowers.

As she turned the corner to begin the return journey, an old friend saw her coming and ran out to flag her down. After a brief chat and the unexpected gift of a loaf of still-warm banana bread, she moved on, wondering why she didn't do this more often.

She finished the last side of the block unimpeded and was on her way into her house via the back door when she saw something shiny lying in the dirt near the back of Paul's van.

She stopped, took another look and moved closer.

"Well, now, would you look at that," she said, and picked up a lug nut, obviously left over from changing the flat.

She glanced down at the tire to see if a lug nut was missing, but the hubcap hid the wheel. She was waffling what to do when the apartment door opened and Paul Leibowitz came out.

"Talk about timing!" she called, and shifted her banana bread closer to her body to keep from dropping it.

"For what?" Hershel snapped, hanging on to his temper by a thread.

"The weather is beautiful, isn't it? I just couldn't stand being indoors any longer and took myself a nice little walk. One of my friends even gave me a loaf of banana bread."

She held it up for him to see and kept talking.

"Anyway, I was on my way back in the house when I saw something shiny near your van. Here you go," she said, and dropped it into Hershel's palm.

"A lug nut," he said, then felt like a fool for stating the obvious.

"Yes. I looked to see if it was from your wheel, but I can't tell because of the hubcap. You best check it before you leave. It wouldn't be safe to drive for long if you're missing one."

Hershel was relieved the incident he'd witnessed had been innocent.

"Yes, you're right, and thank you."

"Glad I saw it. Nice talking to you."

She tottered off toward the back door of her house with her banana bread, leaving Hershel in the proverbial dust.

He could almost hear Louise saying, *I told you so,* as he unlocked the van to get a crowbar. He popped the hubcap, put the missing lug nut back on and then tightened it. He replaced the hubcap, tossed the tools into the van and then dusted off his hands.

He hated to admit it, but Louise was right. He needed to leave the woman alone. She didn't fit into his purpose, and above all, he needed to stick to the plan.

But watching her nose around the back of his van reminded him of how complacent he'd become. Besides switching vehicles and getting back into disguise, it was time to switch his tag.

Once inside the van, he took advantage of the tinted windows to put on the eyebrows and add a larger bushy mustache over the one he had, then drove away, as confident as he could be that he was still safe and sound.

He knew that malls were rife with security cameras, so he needed a less obvious place to lift a tag. He was trying to think of a place with easy access and was thinking of a junkyard when he drove right past a driving range. There were at least thirty cars in the parking lot and golf balls flying through the air behind the one small building that was the office. It had only a single window overlooking the parking lot, since all the activity took place behind the building, out on the driving range.

He drove a short distance down the road, then circled back and pulled into the parking lot, choosing an empty space between two vehicles near the back.

He sat for a few seconds, scoping out the building for signs of a security camera, but saw nothing obvious. Satisfied, he grabbed some tools from the glove box and then ducked behind the large SUV to his right as he got out. He had the license tag off in less than a minute and made short work of switching both plates. Then he walked calmly back to his van and drove off.

The next thing on his agenda was a place to dump Laura Doyle. He was still taken with the notion of hanging her and leaving her there rather than tossing her in the river. But he needed a location that was off the beaten path, like an empty farmhouse or an abandoned barn. He didn't want to leave her body in plain sight. He wanted her hanging until the body rotted and fell apart. That was what it would take before he felt free to return to Lake Chapala.

Instead of driving back toward the city, he drove farther into the countryside, but it was all so beautiful. He got all the pretty colors he could want down in Mexico. What he needed was something that was as abandoned as he felt.

There you go, feeling sorry for yourself again.

Hershel frowned. "I'm not talking to you, Louise. All you do is remind me of how awful I am. Please, go away."

Remind you? Remind you? *How could you ever forget the horrors for which you are responsible?*

Hershel's ears were burning, which meant his blood pressure was rising. She was going to be the death of him yet, but he told her he wasn't talking, and to his relief, she went away.

He was so pissed that he forgot to pay attention to where he was going and found himself heading northwest on Highway 267. He didn't see anything resembling abandoned farm buildings. He was getting ready to turn around when he caught a glimpse of a weather vane on top of an old roof off to his right. At first he didn't see a way to get to it to check it out, but then he saw an exit coming up and took it.

He found an old access road less than a mile from the highway, and the farther he drove, the closer he got to the barn.

He slowed down even more, searching for a way to get onto the property, and finally spotted a gate across an overgrown road. When he stopped to check it out, he saw it was only fastened with a chain looped over the post.

He pushed it aside and drove in, tentatively following the barely discernible road until it ended at what had once been a home. There was nothing left of the house but steps and a brick chimney, but now he could see the old barn. It was a two-story building with a rounded roof and large gaps where parts of it had caved in.

It was the barn that interested him. He waded through the grass to get to it, checking to make sure the path to it was free of anything that might ruin a tire. When he got to the barn, he paused at the entryway and peered in.

The floor was dirt, and there wasn't a blade of grass growing anywhere within. He stepped inside, then immediately sneezed.

The cocoa-colored dirt was face-powder fine and poofed up in the air with each step he took, turning his white tennis shoes into a dirty brown. But he wasn't looking down at his shoes. He was looking up to the rafters. They were high. It would take some time to get a rope over one and then tie it off, which meant he couldn't make this happen without some prior preparation.

He went back outside and looked around, looking for signs of a walking path through the grass or a road coming in from another direction, but as far as he could tell, it didn't look as if anyone had been here in years.

He thought for a bit, knowing he was taking a chance on setting things up ahead of time, then showing up with Laura Doyle and facing the possibility of not being able to get in. Then he decided to risk it. Nothing ventured, nothing gained.

He went back to get the van and drove out to the barn.

He began by making a hanging noose with the rope he'd purchased days ago, and then spent the next twenty minutes trying to throw it over the rafters before he gave up. He stood for a moment considering the situation, then drove the van inside the barn, used the stepladder to climb on top of the vehicle and easily threw the rope over the rafters.

He got down carefully to avoid reinjuring his back, put the step stool beneath the noose, then adjusted the length of the rope before tying off the other end to the rungs of a ladder running up the side of a granary that led to the loft. As he turned around, a rat ran out from beneath the rotting floor of one of the granaries and disappeared into the grass outside.

His eyes narrowed as he watched it run and wondered how many others were in here. Rats could climb. If there was something hanging from the end of that rope that they wanted bad enough, he wondered if they would think to chew through the rope, or just climb down to it and eat their fill. Either way suited him just fine.

He stood back, eyeing the setup, picturing how it would go when he kicked the stool out from under her feet, and decided it would suit just fine.

He got back in the van and drove out as carefully as he'd driven in, then stopped at the gate and fastened it shut. The tracks he'd made in the grass were already springing back up in the breeze, and this time when he drove away he took note of the distance in miles and all the landmarks, making sure he could easily find his way back.

He still had to buy a wedding gift, and find out how much longer Laura Doyle would be at that shelter. He'd tried to take Nola Landry down in one of those places and nearly gotten himself caught. His plan this time was to abduct Laura from home.

Once he got back to Reston, he drove until he found a mall, then went into a department store and went straight to bedding. It didn't take long to pick out a white, king-size comforter, and after he paid for it, he took it back to be gift-wrapped.

Less than thirty minutes later he left with the pres-

ent in the back of his van. The next stop on his agenda
was to see if his theory about the FBI team was correct. He was convinced they would be working the
murder cases, and since they weren't actively inves-
tigating things themselves, he was betting they were
working with the D.C. police department. He wouldn't
let himself believe that they'd ignored his signature
methods. They had to know he was back on the job,
and he was convinced they were actively trying to
find him.

He knew what kind of vehicles they drove. He
also knew that the feds and local governments were
rarely happy to work together. He was curious to see
if there were any government-issue vehicles parked at
the P.D., and if there were, it might be interesting to
stick around and see who was driving them.

His belly was grumbling from lack of food, his
mustache was itchy and the eyebrows he was wearing
felt weird. He stopped at a drive-through restaurant
long enough to pick up a chicken sandwich and some
fries, then headed for the police department. By the
time he arrived, his sandwich was cold. He slowed
down as he made the first pass, intent on scanning
the parking lot, but traffic forced him to speed up,
so he came back around for a second look. This time
the traffic was slower, allowing him more time. That
was when he saw three dark SUVs with even darker
tinted windows parked almost side by side near the
back of the lot.

"Just what I thought," he muttered, then started circling the block, looking to find a parking spot nearby that would give him a clear view of those vehicles. Eventually someone would have to claim them. He wanted to see who they were.

He finally found a place to park that suited his needs and settled down to eat. By then it was almost three o'clock, so he pushed the seat back for more legroom. Might as well get comfortable while he waited.

One hour passed into another, and he needed to pee. But if he did, he was afraid they would leave while he was gone. He dug around in the back for an empty drink cup from a quick stop and peed in that, then opened the door just enough to pour it out.

He could just imagine Louise's disgust if she'd been sitting there with him, then wondered why it mattered. While he was all about revenge on her behalf, he was somewhat disenchanted with her recent behavior.

Time slowed down to what felt like a snail's pace, and the longer he sat, the closer it came to sundown. If they came out after dark, even though the lot would be well lit he wouldn't be close enough to clearly see their faces. He was trying to figure out his next step when three men in street clothes suddenly walked across his line of sight, heading straight for the vehicles he'd been watching.

He smiled. There was no need for binoculars. He knew their build and their walk as well as he knew his own. It was the team, just as he'd suspected. They were working in conjunction with the D.C. police but keeping a low profile, undoubtedly thinking they would have him at a disadvantage if he didn't know they were around. One by one, they drove away, two going in one direction and one in the other.

He smiled.

"Thought you were playing me, didn't you? Giving the cops all your info without stepping into the media spotlight. You don't want the public to know it's me because I've made you look bad. Not once has the media mentioned the Stormchaser. I happen to think the public has a right to the truth."

He started the van and drove away with the full intent of buying a disposable phone to make his calls. Then he saw the gas gauge in his van and amended the plan. Gas first. Phone later.

The traffic was getting heavier. It was the end of the workday, and people were on their way home. He pulled into the first gas station he came to, but as he drove toward the pump, he realized there was a D.C. patrol car parked on the other side, having what appeared to be the beginnings of an altercation with a customer.

He started to drive away and then decided the cop was too preoccupied with that guy to pay any attention to him. He glanced over at the cop's car as he killed the engine, and because he was sitting up so much higher, he had a clear view of the clipboard lying on the console. There was a photo on it, and when he first saw it, he thought the guy looked familiar. Then he looked again, and at that point his heart nearly stopped.

Son of a bitch! It's me.

They had made him but hadn't said a word about it in the press. That meant they were purposefully keeping it under wraps to keep from spooking him. This changed everything. To hell with phoning the media.

He started the engine and very carefully drove away.

His hands were shaking as he stopped at the next gas station. He refueled his van and then headed back to his apartment as fast as he dared.

It was dark by the time he arrived. The security light was on outside, but he knew it was the time of evening when his nosy landlady was at her dinner table. He threw his clothing into his suitcase, packed up everything that was his, including food, and began moving it out to his van, but there was so much crap in there now, there wouldn't be room to haul a body. So he took out the ladder and paint supplies that he'd kept to back up his profile and repacked what was there. His back was beginning to hurt after he'd made the second trip, but it couldn't be helped. Once his picture hit the media, Lucy would recognize him and they would know where he'd been living, so trying to wipe away fingerprints was wasting time. He just needed to be sure there was nothing left to tell them where he lived.

He left the key on the coffee table and the apartment in darkness. He drove slowly past the house and didn't turn on his headlights until he was out on the street.

It was time to hide.

* * *

The morning sky was overcast and the wind was stiff, making the jogger's early-morning run that much harder. He was on the last leg of his route and about to head back to his apartment when he spotted something in the river. After taking a closer look, he realized it was a body and called the police.

Lionel Ricks had finally made it home, which was ironic timing, because Lionel's arrival coincided perfectly with Paul Leibowitz's departure.

Lucy Taft suspected Leibowitz was gone for good when she didn't hear him come home. When she woke the next morning and saw that the van was gone she guessed that he might have moved on, but she needed to know for sure.

She heard the breaking news about the discovery of the fourth body, and while Mildred was making breakfast, she took the extra key to the apartment and went out the back door, only to find the apartment unlocked. She walked in, found his key on the coffee table and pocketed it, then walked through the rooms. Everything he'd brought with him was gone. Even though he was finally off her property, she was still uneasy. She noticed a ladder and some empty paint cans near her garbage cans and frowned. He'd left something behind after all.

When she went back inside to have breakfast, she didn't say anything to Mildred about cleaning the apartment. She didn't want it touched until she'd called the boys. The fact that Paul Leibowitz had disappeared the same morning the last body was discovered was yet another fact to be added to her journal. She was convinced there was something shady about him, but this kind of stuff was better left to people in William Harold's field, not hers. As soon as she finished her breakfast, she took her coffee and went to the library. It made her feel good to sit in William Harold's chair, almost like sitting in his lap.

She took another sip of her coffee, then set it aside to get the old Rolodex from the bottom drawer of his desk. She took her time flipping through the cards, remembering each person fondly as she searched for one certain name. None of the names on the cards were real ones. They were all in code, and when she finally found the one she was looking for, she made the call.

Rambo Phillips was in the middle of the best morning sex he'd ever had when his cell phone began to ring. He would have ignored it had it not been for the ringtone. There was only one woman that went with the theme song to *The Golden Girls*. The minute he heard it, he gritted his teeth and rolled off the woman beneath him.

"What the fuck are you doing?" she asked.

"Sorry. Duty calls," he said, and headed for the bathroom to take the call in private, while the less-than-happy woman cursed his exit.

"Hello, pretty lady. How the hell have you been?"

Lucy grinned. She hadn't heard a man curse since

William Harold's death. It wasn't ladylike, but she had a fondness for the habit in others.

"I'm just fine, Bo. I hope you can say the same."

He glanced down at his erection and rolled his eyes.

"Yes, ma'am. I'm still wound tight and ready to blow."

Unaware of the significance of his statement, Lucy giggled, then cleared her throat and got down to business.

"I'm glad to hear that, but I called for a reason."

She proceeded to tell him everything she'd seen and how she'd kept the journal, mentioning the fact that Paul had switched vehicles only days after his arrival, then capped it off with the fact that he'd disappeared without a word last night and that a fourth body had surfaced this morning.

If it had been anyone else, Bo would have sweet-talked his way around the request, but he remembered hearing William Harold say many times that his wife had better instincts than he did.

"I'll tell you what, sugar. How about I get a buddy of mine and we come see you today? I'll take a look at your journal, and we'll fingerprint the apartment... see if any special names pop up, okay?"

Lucy sighed. Finally someone was taking her seriously.

"Yes, more than okay. I'll have Mildred make you one of those apple-crumb pies you're so fond of."

Bo's mouth watered just thinking about it.

"That would be amazing. See you soon," he said,

and hung up. When he got back to the bedroom, the woman was gone.

Whatever. He could jack off, which frankly was almost as good as the real thing, and still not break a sweat, which he proceeded to do.

A short while later he picked up fellow agent, Grant Whitelaw, who also liked pie and was up for the ride. It was close to noon when they reached the Taft residence, and when Bo pulled up in the drive, Grant leaned forward, looking toward the garage apartment in the back.

"So that's where the big bad man's been hiding out?" Grant drawled.

Bo frowned. "You do not make fun of Lucy Taft. She may be old now, but she knows her stuff. This isn't going to hurt us, and it will satisfy her mind."

Grant nodded. "Yeah, and there's that pie to satisfy *my* stomach."

Bo parked and got out, stretching his tall, lanky frame before heading for the front door.

Grant was shorter, but just as lean and mean, and followed suit.

Seconds after they rang the bell, a woman in a maid's uniform answered.

"Mr. Phillips and Mr. Whitelaw to see Mrs. Taft."

Mildred smiled primly. She knew Bo Phillips from prior visits, and even though he looked a bit like Elvis, he was also more than a little scary. The other one was a stranger.

"Come in, Mr. Phillips. She's expecting you."

She led the way into the library, where Lucy was waiting in a chair by the window. When she saw them come in she stood up, and just for a moment, with the sunlight coming through the window behind her, she looked like a tiny angel, which Rambo Phillips knew was a big misconception.

She smiled.

"Pretty as ever," Bo said, and carefully swung her up in his arms, planted a kiss on her cheek, then set her back on her feet. "Hey, sugar, this is my friend Grant Whitelaw. I thought it would be a good idea to have two sets of eyes on your info, instead of just mine. You know how difficult it is for me to keep my eyes off you, so I'll most likely be distracted anyway."

Lucy grinned. "You haven't changed a bit. You're still the disreputable rake you always were, and I love it. Nice to meet you, Mr. Whitelaw. I hope you know the company you're keeping."

Grant smiled. "All too well, ma'am. All too well."

"I insist you call me Lucy. All of William Harold's boys do."

Grant's smile widened. "Yes, ma'am…I mean, Lucy, and thanks."

"Now…where's that journal you've been keeping?" Bo asked.

Lucy took it from the top drawer of the desk and handed it to him. When he opened it and began to read, she still felt the need to narrate.

"I was put off almost immediately by the large amount of cash he was carrying and his claim not to like hotels. Who doesn't like a hotel? Room service, maids to make the beds…you know what I mean. Anyway, I began with his name and the date of his arrival. As you can see, I noted what he was driving and the tag number, although a few days in, he switched to another vehicle in a completely different color. Another van, though. Good for hauling bodies, you know."

Grant started to grin and then realized she was dead serious. He looked at his partner's face, and saw that he was serious, too. She continued to talk.

"He suffered some kind of injury a few days ago and could barely walk. I recommended a chiropractor, and I suppose he went, because he came back later a little better." She tapped the page. "But his injury occurred the same night the last victim went missing. Deadweight is heavy to move."

Bo was listening with one ear as he scanned the entries. He could see the case she was making, and it was damn intriguing. He glanced back up at the top of the page.

"Said his name was Leibowitz, did he?"

She nodded.

"Did you call this in to the D.C. police?"

She frowned. "Yes, and they blew me off like dust on a little black dress."

Grant stifled a chuckle. He liked Lucy Taft more and more by the minute.

Bo frowned. "Blew you off, did they? So give me the key to your apartment and we'll see if we can lift some prints."

She frowned. "Okay, but don't make a big mess for Mildred to clean up. Oh, he left a stepladder and some old, empty paint cans behind. They're beside my garbage cans."

"Yes, ma'am," Bo said.

Lucy rang for the maid, who led them out to the apartment the same way she'd taken Hershel. Grant went to their car to get a kit to dust for fingerprints, and after Mildred's assurance that nothing had been touched since his disappearance, she left them to their devices.

Grant was smiling as the maid left.

"That Lucy Taft is something, isn't she?"

Bo nodded. "So was her husband. At one time Taft was one of the best international operatives we had, and she was his cover. Cute little woman married to a rich industrialist. They were perfect. She was also smart enough to know not to clean this place until we could search it. So let's get started."

They lifted prints off the most obvious places. The bedside table, the bathroom mirror and the coffeepot in the kitchen, and then took pictures of the prints and emailed them in to NCIC to confirm what they already knew, so there would be no loophole for him to crawl through when they finally got him in court.

They were still poking around in the bedroom when Grant's phone signaled a call, but the caller ID was a blocked number.

"Look at this," he said as he held it up to Bo.

"That's weird," Bo said. "So answer and find out who it is."

"I'm putting it on speaker," he said, and then answered. "This is Whitelaw."

"Agent Whitelaw, this is Agent Jo Luckett, FBI. You sent a fingerprint into NCIC, and we'd like to know where you lifted it."

Grant's eyes widened. "Whoa," he muttered. "I do believe Miz Lucy hit the jackpot."

"I'm sorry, I didn't hear you. Could you repeat?" Jo said.

"I'll tell you where I got it if you'll tell me who it belongs to," Grant said.

Jo didn't hesitate. "Ever hear of a serial killer called the Stormchaser?"

Bo introduced himself and then joined the conversation.

"Agent Luckett, this is Agent Bo Phillips. I'm here with my partner, Agent Grant Whitelaw. Are you telling us that this print is a definite match for the killer?"

"Yes, and there is an active investigation involving the D.C. police and our Stormchaser team as we speak. I would ask that you take yourselves and your information down to the P.D. as soon as possible. I'll alert them that you're coming."

"Is it that urgent?" Bo asked.

"Yes. They can explain," she said.

"So who's heading up the team?" he asked.

"You'll be looking for Special Agent Tate Benton

and his team, along with Detectives Wells and Burch on the P.D. side."

"Okay. Tell them we're on the way and we're bringing along a witness."

"Stellar," Jo said. "I'm making the call now."

Grant logged off, then gave Bo a look.

"I wonder how close Miz Lucy came to being a victim?"

Bo frowned. "I don't like to think about it. However, let's get back to the house. We need to get our pie, and then take Lucy and her journal down to the P.D. ASAP."

Seventeen

Laura and Cameron were eating breakfast when her phone rang. "Hey, Laura, this is Tate. Is Cameron there with you? He's not answering his phone."

"Yes, he's here and it's on the charger. Hang on a minute." She handed Cameron the phone. "It's Tate, for you."

"What's up?" Cameron asked.

"Ricks' body turned up. A jogger spotted it in the river. The M.E. is on the scene."

"I'm almost through. I'll meet you at the P.D.," Cameron said.

"My best to Laura. Tell her to pay attention."

"Will do," he said, and disconnected.

Laura got up to refill her coffee, then carried the carafe to the table to top Cameron's off, as well.

"What's happening?" she asked as she slid back into her seat.

"The fourth body surfaced this morning."

She shuddered, the expression on her face suddenly haunted.

"We're going to stop him, Laura."

She didn't look up. It was her lack of faith that they could honor that pledge that hurt most, and he completely understood why. They'd been saying the same thing for far too long.

He reached across the table and took her hand.

"So what are you going to do today after you get everything shipped back?"

She made herself smile as she looked up to meet his gaze.

"Go home. The place has been sadly neglected. It needs a good cleaning. We're low on groceries, and laundry is piling up."

"Give me the grocery list. I'll shop before I come home today."

She shook her head. "Don't be silly. You have a whole new victim to process. It will be good to do mundane tasks. I want to get them over with before tomorrow."

"What's tomorrow…besides Saturday?"

She smiled again, and this time it was genuine.

"I'm going for the last fitting on my wedding dress."

The knot in Cameron's stomach tightened. He loved this woman so much, and, come hell or high water, he had to keep her safe.

"I don't suppose I'm allowed to go on this trip?"

"Of course you're not allowed. It's bad luck, remember?"

He frowned. "I don't believe in luck. I believe in blessings, and the day I met you was the biggest blessing of my life."

Tears suddenly blurred her vision of his face.

"I sure do love you, Cameron Winger."

"I love you most," he said softly as he got up to leave. "And if that slips your mind during the day, when I get home tonight, I'll be happy to remind you again."

Laura stood and put her arms around his neck.

"I could never forget my hero."

Cameron bent down to kiss her, but when he saw the tears she was trying not to shed, he groaned.

"Laura…honey…you break my heart."

Her voice was shaking, but she wouldn't let go of her smile.

"Just kiss me, Cameron. All I need is a kiss."

He could never tell her no.

Laura worked through the morning with her head down and didn't look up. It took her until early afternoon to finish the paperwork and get the unused supplies loaded back onto a truck before she could leave, but it was finally done.

Kevin had already signed off on the community center and was on his way back into D.C. to the main office.

She handed the church keys to the pastor, thanked

him for the generosity, then drove home in a daze, her mind still filled with images of lives lost and hearts broken. As always, it would take time for the shock and sadness of the disaster to dissipate. It was part of the job.

She was driving past a supermarket when she suddenly switched lanes and drove into the lot. Even though it was late and she was anxious to get home, it would be easier to do the grocery shopping now than have to deal with it tomorrow, and she'd wanted to get it done today anyway.

Once she found a place to park, she sat in the car making a grocery list, then glanced at the time. She couldn't remember the time difference between here and London, but she suddenly had the urge to hear her sister's voice. She made the call, then settled against the seat as she waited for it to go through.

The sun was warm against her face. The silence inside the car was hypnotic. If it wasn't for the constant movement of the cars and people around her, she could easily have fallen asleep. When the phone finally began to ring, she counted them. Just when she feared it was going to go to voice mail, Sarah answered.

"Hello?"

Laura frowned. "It's me. You sound terrible."

"That's because I was asleep. I've been sick with some bug for the past two days, so I went to bed early."

Immediately she knew she wasn't going to tell Sarah she'd already seen the killer—twice.

"Oh, no! Honey! I'm sorry. Have you been to the doctor?"

"Yes. I have meds. I'm taking them, but they make me sleepy, which is why I sound like a drunk." Sarah tried to laugh, but it came out in a cough instead.

"I'm so sorry. I feel bad that I woke you, but I was homesick to hear your voice."

Sarah shoved the covers back and sat up. She could hear more than loneliness in her younger sister's voice.

"Have they caught him yet?"

"No, but we know for sure it's Inman now, and he's killed four people so far."

"Why? How is he choosing them?"

"The team hasn't figured that out yet. It's worrying Cameron. He feels responsible for putting me in danger."

"I disagree! He didn't put you in danger. That creepy killer is the one putting people in danger, and you tell him I said that."

Laura smiled. This was exactly what she needed to hear.

"I'll tell him. Selfishly, I wish you were here. I have the final fitting for my wedding dress tomorrow."

Sarah groaned. "Oh, honey, I'm so sorry. I should be the one with you. Well, technically, it should have been Mom, but—"

"Oh, I'm not going alone. Nola is going with me. I'm not sure about Jo. They have her working on the case with the guys, so she might not be free. Please, don't feel bad for me. I was just talking."

Sarah sighed, then blew her nose.

"Sorry for the interruption. It was threatening to run away."

Laura laughed. When she was little and didn't think to blow her nose, Sarah used to tell her to blow it or it would run away.

"That's how you got me to blow my nose when I was little," Laura said. "I was afraid my nose was going to disappear if I let it run, so I blew it religiously."

Sarah giggled. "Looking back, that threat was kind of mean."

"Not really," Laura said. "At least I never had a snotty nose like Mike Gerlicky."

"Ick," Sarah said, remembering the kid who used to live next door.

When they both began to giggle, the knot in Laura's stomach began to ease. Sister talk was good for the soul.

"So what are you doing now?" Sarah asked.

"About to go into the supermarket. Ever since the explosion, I've let shopping slide."

"Explosion? What explosion?"

"Oh, that's right. I haven't talked to you since that happened. There was a gas leak here in Reston. Four blocks of houses on both sides of the street were leveled, with no survivors, and they evacuated blocks and blocks all around it until the gas company could cap off the breaks and make sure there wouldn't be another one."

"Oh, my God. Oh, Laura, how awful. Not one survivor?"

"Well, not anyone who lived through the blast. One poor teenage girl did show up at the shelter. She'd had a fight with her parents that same night and had run away from home before it happened. She didn't know about the explosion, and kept expecting them to call or text her. After several days she got scared, thought they didn't want her anymore and came back to find out her whole family was gone."

Sarah blew her nose again, but this time it was from tears. "Can you imagine what the rest of her life will be like? I mean, knowing the last thing you'd said to the people you love had been in anger and never getting a chance to say you're sorry?"

Laura was picking at a speck of dirt on the knee of her jeans, but she was thinking about what Sarah was saying.

"I kind of have a different take on that. When I thought I would never see you again, I was sorry for all the things I never said."

Sarah was quiet for a moment, digesting the poignancy of such a simple truth.

"Then say them to me now, little sister."

Laura swallowed past the lump in her throat. "For starters, I love you very much. You are the best sister ever, and I thank you for stepping in the gap when Mom and Dad were killed and never letting me feel like the orphan I actually was. We both were."

"Aw, honey, I love you, too. And yes, technically

I guess we *are* orphans, but at least we were nearly grown, and we weren't left homeless and destitute. Even though Mom and Dad are no longer here, they're still taking care of us. They left us a beautiful home that's debt-free. We have the stock portfolios Daddy started for us when we were born, and we have our educations."

Laura sighed. "I know, and I also know I need to hang up so you can go back to sleep. I'm sorry I woke you, and I'm very sorry you're sick."

"It's fine. I always want to hear from you. So be careful while that nut job is still on the loose, and I'll see you at the wedding."

Laura smiled. "I can't wait."

"Me, either, honey. Love you."

"Love you, too," Laura said, and disconnected.

She looked down at the grocery list in her lap, then grabbed her purse and car keys and got out, feeling lighter and better than she had in days.

Before the Stormchaser team even got to the P.D. that morning they were rerouted to the field office for a face-to-face meeting with their chief. He didn't read them the riot act, but it was evident by the time they left that he wanted this case brought to a successful end ASAP. It was nearly ten in the morning when they walked into Homicide.

Burch and Wells had gone out to the site where the body had been recovered and weren't back in the office yet, and after the discussion the team had just had with their superior, Tate didn't want to wait for Lionel Ricks' autopsy report to show up. He decided they needed to make a trip to the morgue to see the evidence for themselves.

Once they'd verified the ligature marks around Ricks' neck and the Taser wounds as identical to the ones on the other victims' bodies, they had the confirmation they needed. They were on their way back to the P.D. when Wade's cell rang.

"It's Jo," he said. "Excuse me while I breathe heavy into the phone."

They laughed. Wade wiggled his eyebrows and grinned as he answered.

"Hey, honey, tell me something good."

"I have more than good. Are you sitting down?" Jo asked.

"Is this business?" he countered.

"Yes, directly related to the case. Put me on speaker."

"Listen up, guys. Jo has news. Go ahead, honey. You have the floor."

"You know we had Inman's fingerprints flagged in case they ever came through NCIC, and we just got a hit not an hour ago. You won't believe who ran them."

"Who?"

"Two spooks named Phillips and Whitelaw. I don't know where they pulled the prints or why, but they're on their way to the P.D. now with a witness to tell you the particulars."

Tate sped up the car.

Wade was more than surprised. "The CIA? You're not serious."

"Yes, I am. Are you there?"

"We're almost there now. Thanks for the heads-up," Wade said.

"Maybe this is finally coming to a close," Jo said, and signed off.

Tate was driving as fast as the law allowed, and still it didn't feel fast enough. The men riding with him were silent. Almost everything they'd been through with this killer had been said and repeated far too many times already. They were coming up on the police station when Cameron finally broke the silence.

"I so need this bastard behind bars."

"We all do," Tate said.

Cameron shook his head. "Yes, I know, but we still haven't figured out the message in his kills. I know it's there, but I can't find it, and I have to figure it out before it's too late."

"What do you mean, 'too late'?" Tate asked.

"It's obvious he's coming after Laura. I can't prove it, but I know it."

"What makes you so sure?" Tate asked.

"Other than the fact that he's been stalking her? She was once his boss. Now she's hooked herself up to me, and he's mad at all of us. He took a shot at Jo and Nola, and they beat him. He won't try them again. Laura is the only one left. She's the obvious choice."

"Do you still have that tracking app connected to her necklace on your phone?" Tate asked.

"Yes, and on my iPad, too."

"We're here," Tate said as he slowed down and turned into the police parking lot.

They got out on the run, anxious to get inside. They met Detective Burch coming out and stopped him.

"Wherever you're going, cancel it," Tate said. "We have a break in the case, and they're bringing in a witness. Where's Wells?"

"In a meeting with the lieutenant. We're getting pressure, big-time."

"Get him back here. Everyone needs to be in on this."

Burch made the call as he followed them in.

They made it to the investigation room a couple of minutes ahead of Wells. He came in wild-eyed and breathing heavy from running part of the way.

"What's happening?" he said.

"CIA ran some prints through NCIC that came up as Inman's. They're on their way in with a story and a witness."

Wells rubbed his hands together in obvious delight.

"Oh, man, I hope this is what it takes to close this case. We need to get this sorry sucker off the streets."

Less than five minutes later the men from the CIA arrived with a little gray-haired lady in tow.

Tate knew Bo Phillips was CIA but didn't know the other agent or the woman.

Cameron recognized Whitelaw, who nodded in acknowledgment, as CIA, as well.

Tate glanced at the detectives and then stepped forward to take charge.

"Agent Phillips. It's been a while since I've seen you. I understand you have some information for us."

Bo grinned. "Hey, Tate. You're looking good. What have you been eating?"

"My wife's wonderful cooking," Tate drawled, and eyed the little woman with them. "Ma'am, I'm Special Agent Tate Benson. These are my partners, Special Agent Luckett and Special Agent Winger, and these are two of D.C.'s finest detectives, Detective Burch and Detective Wells."

"Lucy Taft. I'm pleased to meet you, and I do believe Detective Wells and I have already had a conversation recently. One in which I offered information on your serial killer that he didn't seem to think was relevant."

Wells stared in disbelief.

Bo shook his head. "Not a smart move," he said. "Lucy is wise in the ways of surveillance, having been married to one of our best before he passed. You screwed the pooch, boys."

Wells turned red from the neck up but didn't comment.

Tate pulled up his desk chair. "Ma'am?"

Lucy sat, smoothing her hands down the front of her dress and then patting her hair to make sure it was in place. It was like looking at a *Cosmopolitan* version of Granny Clampett from *The Beverly Hillbillies*.

"So talk to me," Tate said. "How did you come to run those prints?"

Bo winked at Lucy. "This pretty lady called me with a concern about a recent renter of hers, and Grant and I went to check it out. A man calling himself Paul Leibowitz did a Houdini act on her last night without letting her know. After reading the log she'd kept on him, we went to the apartment and lifted some prints. Not in a professional capacity, though. Strictly as a service to one of our own, you understand. One of your agents caught the flag and sent us here. She also told us to bring our witness, so we did. Lucy, honey, show them your journal."

She promptly handed it over.

The moment Tate opened it he could see it was circumstantial evidence that would actually stand up in court as corroboration. From dates and times to what might have seemed unrelated details to others, she'd been meticulous in documenting what had been going on.

"I'm impressed," he said as he scanned the entries.

Lucy sniffed and glared at Wells. "Thank you. I know my stuff."

Wells looked down and then walked off to keep his composure.

Cameron showed her the photo they had of Inman buying a balloon in the grocery store.

"Mrs. Taft, can you identify this man?"

She looked and then handed it back.

"That is the man who's been renting the apartment

over my detached garage. His name is Paul Leibowitz."

Wade moved as if he'd been ejected from his seat.
"Oh, man, we actually have an identification and an
active alias. Excuse me," he said, and left the room to
call Jo and let her know.

Cameron was anxious, too, but for Laura's sake.

"You said he left the apartment as of last night?"
he asked.

Lucy nodded. "I did not see or hear him come
home, which I always do. When I checked this morning, he was gone and so were his things. As I told the
boys, he's changed vehicles once since his arrival, and
both of them were vans—handy for hauling bodies.
He also complained of a back injury the same night
the last victim went missing. It was pretty serious.
I saw him crawling up the stairs to get to the apartment door."

"Did he ever threaten you?" Cameron asked.

Lucy glared at Wells again. "I believe I mentioned
in my phone call to Detective Wells that there was an
instance where he made me afraid, and that had I not
been holding my gardening shears, I'm not certain
what might have occurred."

"You are a very fortunate woman to have been in
such close contact with Inman and still be alive. You
need to be aware that he might take it in his head to
consider you an unwanted loose end," Cameron added.

Bo slid an arm across Lucy's shoulders.

"Don't worry about that. We've got her back," he said.

Burch touched the arm of her chair. "Mrs. Taft, I apologize for how casually we took your call."

She shrugged. "Two more people died because you ignored it. You might want to direct your apology to their families."

Burch felt as if he'd just had his butt paddled and his mouth washed out with soap.

"Yes, ma'am."

Burch was reading the journal entries when he paused and looked up.

"Here's something we need to get a BOLO on. You say he's driving a black Chevrolet van with this tag number," Burch said.

"Last time I saw him, yes," Lucy said.

Cameron shook his head. "If he's on the run, then he's either already changed vehicles again, or tags, or both."

Burch frowned. "What do you mean?"

"He swaps license tags like some people change shoes," Tate said.

"And you can bet he no longer looks like this," Cameron said, pointing to the picture in Lucy Taft's lap.

It was good news and bad news. They knew where he'd been, but they didn't know where he'd gone.

Hershel's motel room in D.C. was nothing like Lucy Taft's apartment, but he'd checked in late last night—

or early this morning, however one chose to look at the fact—without a care for décor.

He'd fallen asleep on top of the covers without removing his clothes, and when he woke up hours later, a maid was knocking on the door. He got up to let her in, asked for more soap, towels and washcloths, and then told her he was going back to bed and to come back tomorrow.

But once he was awake, he had a chance to see the room in a better light. It was not nearly as clean or quiet as he had hoped, and damn sure not nearly as comfortable as where he'd been. When he tried to turn on the television, it didn't work. Now he was faced with calling attention to himself by complaining, but if he couldn't stay abreast of the ongoing investigation, then he was going to have to move.

Finally he called the front desk.

The clerk who answered sounded sleepy, which irked him even more.

"The television doesn't work in room 124. I need one that does."

"Did you try unplugging it and plugging it back in again?" the desk clerk asked.

Hershel frowned. "No. Why would that have anything to do with the television?"

"The plug needs rewiring. The owner knows. It ain't been fixed yet is all."

"Is the place gonna catch on fire?" Hershel asked.

"I ain't got no way of knowing that," the clerk said. "Do you want I should move you to another room?"

"I'll let you know," Hershel snapped, and hung up in disgust.

He unplugged the television, then plugged it back in and turned it on. It worked like a charm.

"Worthless piece of shit," he muttered, and stretched out on the bed with the remote in his hand and began channel surfing.

Eighteen

Hershel drifted off to sleep in the middle of a game show and woke up in the middle of the latest news bulletin about the discovery of the serial killer's fourth body. He fumbled for the remote and turned the volume up.

The information officer for the D.C. police was typically noncommittal about where they were in the investigation, which was cop speak for they were fucked and they knew it.

Hershel grinned. He loved it when a plan came together.

"Okay, boys. That was your fourth and last clue. You are now on your own. I, however, am ready to bring down the curtain."

Then the news report segued to an update on the gas leak that had decimated a Reston neighborhood. Since this involved his next target, it was in his best interests to know about this, too.

There was a sound bite from the night of the explosion, some film of the explosion site the next day, and then a reporter doing a live shot of the area.

"...area has been cleared of any danger, and the residents of the surrounding houses are now free to return to their homes."

Hershel smiled. Damn but this day just kept falling into place. This meant Laura Doyle would most likely be going home. He glanced at the clock. It was almost noon, time to go get some lunch and then check out her whereabouts. If he was lucky, all this could be over today. He headed for the bathroom to wash up and get back in disguise.

The buzzer went off on the dryer, signaling a load was ready. Laura stopped to turn down the heat under the pan of soup she was making. She wiped her hands before heading for the utility room. She was tired, but in a good way. It felt wonderful to be home, doing ordinary things, surrounded by her own belongings, and she imagined all the evacuees who'd gone home today felt the very same way.

She took the load of towels out of the dryer, then stood and folded them on the worktable. This house was the place that stabilized her world, along with the man who slept beside her at night. That led to thoughts of her wedding. It had been almost two months since she'd last seen her dress, and she was anxious to see it on, fitted to perfection. She felt giddy with excitement and was still smiling as she carried the towels through the kitchen, then down the hall to the linen closet.

Cameron couldn't be still. Ever since the discovery of the last body he'd been battling a case of all-out panic. The only pattern they had was that a new abduction took place the day the body of the previous one was discovered. It was not lost on any of them that it could have happened already and they just didn't know it.

Burch and Wells were in a meeting with the chief of police, and the Stormchaser team sympathized. They'd already had their "come to Jesus" meeting that morning. For three years, law enforcement at all levels had been thwarted by one angry, crazy man, and they couldn't let him slip away again.

Tate felt certain this time was going to be different. Jo Luckett had notified him less than an hour ago that Paul Leibowitz, officially of Lake Chapala, Mexico, would not be allowed back into that country, and that the staggeringly substantial bank account under Leibowitz's name was frozen, along with his credit card.

They'd already found the van Leibowitz had driven into Virginia at the used-car dealer where he'd made his trade, and thanks to Lucy Taft's diligence, they had a BOLO out for the one he was currently—as far as they knew anyway—driving.

When Burch came running into the room with new information, their focus shifted again.

"Just got a report off the wire from a town north

of Reston. Some guy reported somebody took his license plate and put a different one on his truck. I just ran the number. It's the one that was on the black van Inman traded for."

Tate's pulse kicked up a notch. This just kept getting better.

"Do we have the number for the stolen tag?"

"Yes," Burch said. "Dispatch is sending out word as we speak. Now we know the color and plate number of the van he's driving. It won't be long. I can feel it."

"From your lips to God's ears," Cameron muttered, and turned back around to look at the murder board.

The victims' pictures ate at his conscience. Four more people dead because they kept letting the sorry bastard slip away. He was staring at the maps as he'd done a thousand times before when something about the Reston map clicked. His heart skipped a beat.

"I need a ruler," he said.

Wade turned around. "A what?"

"A ruler!"

Wells circled his desk and dug through the top drawer.

"Here's one," he said, and handed it to him.

Everyone turned around to watch as Cameron slapped the ruler onto the map and drew a line from the first victim's home to the second victim's. Then he drew a line from the third victim's home to the fourth.

Shit.

His breath caught in the back of his throat as he

stared at the point of intersection. He began tapping at the place where the lines crossed.

"What's this address? Who lives here?"

Even though the houses were represented by tiny squares, and side streets and house numbers were not visible, he knew the answer.

Tate pulled out his phone and synced the coordinates with a map of Reston.

"It's Laura's house! You were right! That son of a bitch *is* targeting her! He was showing us all along who the final target was going to be, and we didn't see it," he said. "Call her, Cameron. Tell her to batten down and stay put. We'll dispatch local police to her house until we can get there."

He needn't have bothered saying a word. Cameron was already making the call.

Laura had just put away the towels and was on her way back into the kitchen. Soup would be done by the time Cameron came home, but she still had cookies to bake.

She pulled out a mixing bowl and her mother's recipe box and began thumbing through the dessert section. She was just about to start assembling the ingredients when she heard a car pull into the drive. She wiped her hands and started toward the living room to see who it was when her cell phone began to ring. She backtracked to the kitchen to grab it. When Cameron's name came up on the caller ID she winced, hoping he wasn't going to tell her he'd be coming home even later.

She was in the living room and heading for the door when she answered. "Hello, honey."

"Where are you?" he asked.

She frowned. The urgency in his voice made her heart skip a beat. But she could see the tail end of what looked like a delivery van in the drive, and a delivery-man was carrying a beautifully wrapped gift up the steps toward her door, which made her move faster.

"I'm home. I've already done the grocery shopping and I'm almost through with laundry."

"Listen, Laura, there's something—"

The doorbell rang.

"Hold on a second, honey. Someone's at the door with another wedding present."

She was already turning the knob to open the door when she heard Cameron shouting, "Don't! Don't open the door! It's Inman!"

But it was too late.

The moment the door opened, Hershel dropped the box on the threshold and aimed the Taser.

Laura's scream was instinctive as she ducked behind the heavy door. The electrodes hit the wood instead of her flesh as she slammed the door on Hershel's foot.

He cursed as pain shot all the way to his knee.

Laura was screaming Cameron's name as she leaned all her weight against the door, trying to force Hershel out, but he wouldn't move his foot and pushed back. When it became apparent that she couldn't shut the door, she turned and ran.

Cameron's heart nearly stopped when he heard Laura scream.

"He's in the house!" he yelled as he grabbed his iPad.

Tate spun, shouting orders to Burch and Wells as he followed Cameron out.

"Call the Reston police. Tell the officers on their way to her address to run hot, and notify the state police that he might take her out of the city."

"I'm driving!" Tate yelled as they hit the parking lot.

They jumped in his SUV and flew out of the lot with their lights flashing and the siren running.

Cameron already had the tracking app up on his iPad. Once he located her position, it became apparent she was still in the house, but in motion, which meant she was running.

"She's still in the house."

Tate nodded and pressed harder on the gas pedal.

It was the longest drive of Cameron's life. All the way there he had a horrible feeling of déjà vu. It was just like the trip from D.C. to Denver, not knowing what he would find at journey's end.

The moment Laura turned and ran, Hershel pushed his way inside the house and chased after her. His foot was hurting, but his need to subdue her overrode the pain. He caught her in the hall, tackling her from behind. They went down in a tangle of arms and legs, with Laura screaming and Hershel cursing.

She threw an elbow backward as hard as she could, hitting him in the chest. She heard him grunt, then heard him cough and thought she might have knocked the wind out of him.

When his hold on her loosened, it was the break she needed. She bucked him off her back and then rolled to her feet. But when she tried to dart past him, he grabbed her by the ankle and yanked her back down. There was no breath left for screaming now. They were in a fight to the death.

When Hershel smashed his fist into Laura's face, the blow landed on her cheekbone just below her right eye and made her mad. She dug her fingernails into his cheeks and dragged them all the way through the scarred flesh to his neck, but he was so locked into what he was doing that the pain didn't even register.

Laura landed another blow to the side of his head, right on his ear, and when he moved sideways to dodge a follow-up blow, she kneed him between the legs. To her horror, he absorbed the pain without uttering a single sound.

All of a sudden his fingers were around her neck and she was choking. No matter how hard she still fought, no matter how many blows she landed, he bore them in mute defiance.

The last thing she saw before the world turned black was the reflection of her murder in his eyes.

* * *

Tate was less than five minutes from the Reston city limits when Cameron groaned.

"What?" Tate yelled.

"They're on the move!"

Wade was back on the phone, this time with both the local and state police.

"Feed me coordinates!" he said.

Cameron's mind had shut down to the possibilities of what it meant that Hershel had her and was taking her somewhere. They already knew that every other victim had been dead before he tossed the bodies— probably before he left the scene of the abduction. He couldn't bring himself to apply that thought to Laura. He kept staring at the blip on the iPad as Inman took her farther and farther away.

Tate gave his arm a push, jarring him out of his panic.

"You found her alive once before against all odds. Don't quit on her now."

It was all Cameron needed to hear. He started relaying information as they drove, keeping a running commentary of where Inman was going while Wade relayed the info to the cops as they went.

Hershel hadn't meant to kill her. He'd bound her hands and ankles with some of the leftover rope out of habit, even though he knew it wasn't needed.

He'd been so pissed when she'd screwed up the Taser that rage had overtaken everything else. He didn't want her dead. He wanted to see the fear on her face and hear her begging for mercy when he hung her up to rot.

His urge to speed was huge. He was so close to this being over that he couldn't think. He'd driven all the way out of the city before he realized he was low on fuel.

He couldn't believe it! He'd checked right before he headed to Laura's house, and now it showed less than a quarter of a tank. What the hell? The only thing he could think was that the gauge didn't register properly. He could assume it was fine and keep driving, or accept it might have been stuck and was now registering right.

He didn't know what to do. It was risky as hell stopping to refuel, but they had no way of knowing where he was going or what he was driving. He knew she'd been on the phone when she opened the door. He'd heard her scream Cameron's name. It made him feel powerful to know he had taken Cameron's woman. He hoped to hell Cameron was in a panic just like he'd been with Louise, praying someone would come rescue them before it was too late.

Less than a mile later, he saw a truck stop up ahead and decided to pull over and get fuel. It would pay off later on. Once he'd hidden her body, his next stop would be the nearest airport to catch a flight back home. He wondered if anyone had missed him, and if they would have a big get-together at the community center to welcome him back.

The truck stop was busy, so when he pulled up to a pump and stopped, he felt just as anonymous as all the others coming and going.

He glanced in the back, making sure the drop cloth was safely concealing Laura Doyle's body, and got out. He took a credit card from his wallet, swiped it through the pump, then waited for it to clear. When it showed up as having been denied, he frowned and did it again, only slower. It didn't change the result.

"What the hell?" he mumbled, and switched the credit card for his debit card, only to get the same result. It had to be the pump. There had to be something wrong with the pump.

He glanced inside the window to make sure she was still out, then jogged to the station to use the ATM. There was a man ahead of him, and the longer he waited, the more worried he became.

Finally the man moved away and Hershel calmly swiped the debit card through the ATM machine, punched in his PIN and waited.

When it came up declined again, his heart skipped a beat. He looked down at the card, then pulled out the credit card. It, too, was declined. He counted out the cash in his wallet while trying not to panic, then walked to the front desk and tossed two twenties onto the counter.

"Forty dollars on pump four," he said.

The attendant took the money and gave him a receipt, then set the pump as Hershel walked out the door.

His stomach was in a knot as he strode to the pump.

He wouldn't let himself believe this was anything but a glitch. Computers did stuff like this all the time. It didn't mean anything. It couldn't.

Laura came to in total darkness, immobilized, gasping for air, disoriented and in pain, but fully cognizant of what had happened. She was stunned that she was still alive and aware Inman had her. Since the vehicle was stopped, she imagined that he had taken her to the river to dump like he had all the others, then realized she could hear traffic and people talking, so that couldn't be true.

She did a quick recon of her situation, felt the thin nylon rope tied around her wrists and assumed that was what was binding her ankles, as well. She didn't know where Inman was, only that he wasn't inside the van, but he could open the door at any moment. When he did, her chances of surviving this would lessen even more.

She could feel the cross dangling between her breasts as she lifted her wrists to her mouth to try to get herself free. Cameron knew she was in trouble. They couldn't be far behind. All she needed was to delay Inman's plans, so she began biting at the rope, trying to loosen the knots with her teeth. She was making progress, but not nearly fast enough, when she heard a click. He'd unlocked the door with the remote. A wave of fear washed through her.

Oh, God, please, no.

And then it was too late.

Inman was back in the van.

She froze. Her only chance of staying alive was to play dead.

Hershel was sick to his stomach as he got inside the van. The moment he locked the doors he got out his credit card and made a call to customer service. It rang and rang, and when it was finally answered, it was nothing but an automated voice. He cursed as he went through the process, punching numbers and waiting to be connected, until he finally got to a living, breathing human.

"Customer service. This is Martha. May I have your name, please?"

"Paul Leibowitz."

"Thank you, Mr. Leibowitz, and how may I help you?"

"I just tried to use my credit card to get some gas and it was declined, so then I took it inside to an ATM and it was declined again. I want to know what's going on. I am not delinquent in paying. In fact, I don't owe any money on this card at all."

"One moment please, and I'll see what I can find out," Martha said.

He frowned when she put him on hold, and as the music began playing he started up the van and pulled back onto the highway, on his way back to the barn he'd found yesterday. Right now, he needed this money thing ironed out.

One minute passed, and then another, before Martha came back on the line.

"I'm sorry for your wait, Mr. Leibowitz."

"Did you get the glitch fixed?" he asked.

"I'm sorry, but your account has been frozen."

Hershel swerved, then dropped the phone as he overcorrected and almost rolled the car. When he finally had it back on the highway, he grabbed the phone from between his legs and started yelling.

"Hello? Hello? Are you still there?"

"Yes, sir. Is there anything else I can do for you?"

He was screaming. "You can fucking tell me why my account was frozen! That's what you can do!"

"I don't have that information, sir. I suggest you contact an attorney."

The line went dead.

Hershel began cursing and slamming his fist against the steering wheel. All he could think was that they must have finally aired his picture to the public and nosy-ass Lucy had called in. And then he groaned. He'd forgotten that identifying him would also give them access to the name he was living under. He'd been away from this for too long and made a terrible mistake that had just cost him every penny he had. He couldn't go back to Mexico. He could hide again, but it would be harder without money. Son of a bitch! This was not how he'd planned for things to turn out.

Don't pretend to be surprised. This is what happens to people who do bad things.

"Shut up, Louise! Just shut up! I need to think!"

You can't think yourself out of this mess. They're on to you. This is where your revenge has taken you, and this is where it will end.

"I don't care! I don't care!" he screamed. "I'll have the last laugh. She's dead, and after I get rid of her body, it won't matter what happens to me because I don't fucking care."

Laura's elation at finding out the FBI was in the process of shutting him down ended when the van nearly rolled. She'd come close to screaming before the van finally leveled out, and he began talking to his dead wife. Both Nola and Jo had warned her that this had happened. Now she was experiencing it for herself.

When she heard him screaming that he thought that she was dead, she took a chance he wouldn't notice any movement behind him and began trying to work the knots loose from around her hands again.

When the Stormchaser team realized Inman wasn't taking her to the river, it changed the whole dynamic. Once again, everything was an unknown as they followed the moving blip onto Highway 267 westbound out of Reston. Tate put the accelerator to the floor, turning the passing scenery into a blur. Cars on the highway ahead of them heard the screaming siren, saw the flashing lights and began pulling over on both the right and left shoulders to give them space.

Cameron's only focus was the blip. As long as it

stayed in motion he could let himself believe they still had a chance.

Wade was in the backseat relaying mile-marker information to the Virginia Highway Patrol, praying someone would get to Inman faster from the other direction.

Wade's staccato comments and the whine of the tires against the pavement were almost rhythmic, lulling them into a false sense of hope, and then Cameron suddenly groaned.

"He stopped! Inman stopped," Cameron said.

"Where?" Wade asked.

Cameron told him the coordinates.

Seconds later Wade relayed a message back from a Virginia Highway patrol dispatcher. "It's a gas station, Cameron. He just stopped to get gas."

Tears blurred Cameron's vision.

Nineteen

Laura could hear Hershel muttering and crying as she chewed at the knots in the rope around her wrists. She didn't know what was going on inside his head, but it was obvious that he was coming undone.

Over and over, she locked her teeth around the knot, pulling first one way and then the other, trying to get it to loosen. When it finally began to give, she almost cried out with relief. It was the impetus she needed to pull harder. The van was swerving all over the road again, and she was scared to death that they were going to crash before she could get free.

She didn't realize Hershel was driving with one hand and making a phone call with the other until she heard him talking again.

Hershel's theory was that if the credit-card account was frozen, then the bank account would be, too, but he had to know for sure. His fingers were trembling as he made the call.

"Fidelity National, how may I direct your call?"

"I need to speak to customer service, please," he said.

"One moment."

"Please, please, please. Please let it be okay," he mumbled.

"Customer service, how may I help you?"

Startled by the loud, brusque voice, he flinched, fumbling the debit card in his hand. It fell into the floorboard, and once again he had to pull off to the side of the road to find it.

"Just a moment, don't hang up!" he shouted. "I dropped my card." A few seconds later he was back on the phone. "Hello? Hello?"

"Yes, sir, I'm still here. How may I help you?"

He didn't realize he was sobbing.

"I tried to use my ATM card and it wouldn't work."

"What's your name and account number, sir?"

Hershel gave her the info, then waited agonizing minutes for an answer before she came back.

"I'm sorry, sir, but your account has been frozen."

Hershel hung up, and for a few seconds he stared blindly out the window without making a sound.

In the back of the van, Laura's heart was pounding so loudly that she was sure he could hear it, but she managed to keep herself from making a sound.

She was still motionless and praying to be found when she heard what sounded like a high-pitched howl. At first she thought of the wolves that had tried to get into her wrecked plane. When she realized it was Hershel, the hair stood up on the back of her neck as the howl morphed into a scream.

Seconds later the van began to move, and her panic rose. Whatever was happening, it was bad, which didn't help her chances of living through this. He sped up, the van going faster and faster, until the tires were whining on the pavement like the far-off whistle of a southbound train.

Cameron was on the edge of the seat, his gaze fixed on the highway before them. At any moment, he kept telling himself, they would top a hill and see Inman's black van in the distance. Every few seconds he would glance back down at his iPad just to make sure the blip was still moving, and then he would shift focus to the highway.

"How much farther?" Tate asked.

"We're about three, maybe four miles behind them," Cameron said, but when he looked down to check, his heart skipped a beat. "They've stopped again. What the hell? What's he doing?"

"Every time he stops or slows down, we get that much closer," Tate said.

Cameron was at the point of losing it. The guilt he felt for what was happening to her rode heavy on his heart. He knew for a fact that if she hadn't been engaged to him, this wouldn't be happening. For her sake, he had to pull it together.

"Yes, I know that, but it doesn't make this easier," he said, then looked down. "They're moving again."

"We're going to catch up," Tate said.

Cameron touched the moving blip with the tip of his finger.

Hang on, Laura, honey. We're coming to get you.

All of a sudden Cameron looked up and grabbed the dashboard, as if trying to push the car to go faster.

"He took a right! He's going straight north off 267, and this map doesn't even show a road there."

Wade relayed the message to the highway patrol dispatcher, who sent it down the line.

"They'll find us, and we'll find Inman," Wade said. "Have faith."

Less than three minutes later Cameron pointed.

"There! I see an exit up ahead. He had to go that way."

"I see it," Tate said, and barely slowed down as he steered off the highway.

Laura felt the pull of gravity against her body as Hershel took a sharp right, and then she felt the pavement give way to unpaved road. Dust was coming up inside the van, but Hershel wasn't slowing down. Twice the back end of the vehicle fishtailed in the loose dirt, but he kept on driving.

There was a coppery taste in her mouth. She was bleeding, most likely from the rough fibers of the rope, but she was still trying to get herself free. One moment she was still pulling on the knot, and the next thing she knew it was loose.

She swallowed a sob of thanksgiving and pulled more frantically at the second knot, which was looser. It came undone within moments, and then all of a sudden her hands were free. She bent down beneath the drop cloths, feeling the knots in the rope around her ankles. They were so loose they seemed to be after-thoughts.

Within moments she was completely untied. Her heart was pounding again, but this time with hope. She needed something to use as a weapon and won-dered if he still had the Taser, or if he'd left it behind at her house.

While she was trying to second-guess a madman, Hershel began slowing down. As he rolled to a stop at the gate, he put the van in Park and got out on the run.

The moment Laura heard him get out she crept out from under the drop cloth to look for a weapon. She saw a crowbar on the other side of the van at the same time she heard footsteps coming back.

It was now or never.

She grabbed the crowbar and slid back out of sight even as he was getting into the seat.

When the van began to move again, the crowbar was tight within her grasp.

Hershel was numb. He was about to achieve his ultimate goal, yet nothing was going right. It was unlikely that he would escape this time, and a part of him didn't really care. He was tired, so tired of cat-and-mouse games.

I told you that you would die.

When Hershel heard Louise's voice, it demolished the last of his restraint. He began to argue, and the more he said, the louder he became, until he was screaming.

"Yes, Louise, yes, you did, and you were right. Is that what you want to hear? That you were right? Then I'll say it again. You were right! You were right! You were right! So what? That just means I'll finally see you again."

You won't see me.

He didn't know what to make of that and no longer cared. He drove up to the old homestead and then all the way down to the barn and pulled the van inside like he had before. As he did, a pair of doves perched up on the rafters took flight.

He put the van in Park and killed the engine, thinking what had to be done. The body still had to be unloaded, and his back was already so damn sore he could hardly breathe. He couldn't decide if he wanted to give up and just leave her body on the ground and let the rats go at it, or go ahead with his plan and hang her high.

Truth was, the whole hanging thing had been interesting only if he could have watched her die. As it was now, he would just be hauling deadweight up into the air to watch it swing. He wished again that he hadn't killed her so fast back at the house.

Laura's thoughts were in free fall. She'd already considered trying to take him from behind, but if she messed up, she would still be trapped inside the van. If she had a chance of living through this, she had to take him by surprise, and she needed room to run.

Hershel's focus was on the noose he'd left hanging. Even though the day was windless, it was swinging slightly to and fro. He looked up and saw rats running across the rafters. They were what had set it in motion, and they would be the denouement to his final kill.

He pocketed the keys as he got out and, with purpose in every step, circled the van. The elation he'd expected to feel had been severely dimmed by his financial setback, but he was ending this his way, and that would have to be enough.

As he approached the back doors, a rat darted out from beneath the van. He kicked at it and missed, stirring up a cloud of dust instead.

"Nasty sons of bitches," he muttered, and opened the back doors.

He was still looking down when Laura swung the crowbar. Pain exploded in his head as he dropped where he stood.

She leaped out of the van and swung the crowbar one more time while he was down. His body jerked from the impact. When she heard him grunt, she bolted, running out of the barn and into the pasture with the crowbar still in her hand, following the set of tracks that he'd left in the grass.

Tate was flying down the dirt road as fast as the SUV would go when Cameron began pointing at the fencerow.

"Turn right! Turn right where the fence is down, and hurry. They stopped again. This is it!"

Wade was still relaying directions to the police as Tate shot through the opening. It was obvious some-one had driven through recently; the knee-high grass had been flattened into two distinct tracks.

In the distance they could see the rooftop of a barn, and in that moment Cameron realized Inman had never wanted her to be found. He was so damned scared he couldn't catch his breath.

The sun was warm on Laura's face. If she hadn't been running for her life, it would have been a beautiful place to be. But running in the overgrown field was like running through quicksand. The grass and weeds kept wrapping around her legs and tugging at her clothing like a little kid who didn't want to be left behind.

The first time she fell, she lost her breath. She was belly down and staring straight at a rabbit who was obviously as startled as she was. With no time to waste, she pushed herself to her knees, frantically gasping for air. By the time she got up she was in a panic. She looked back toward the barn, certain she would see the van coming for her, but it looked as abandoned as she felt. She started running again, but off the path into deeper grass, getting farther and farther away and closer to a band of trees.

One moment she was running, and the next thing she knew she was rolling and tumbling head over heels down a slope. She landed with a thump in a dry creek bed and didn't get up.

Hershel opened his eyes, convinced his brains were in the dirt beneath his head. He'd been so sure he'd killed her, and instead she had killed him.

He was flat on his back and looking up at the rafters just as he and Louise had looked up at the sky while trapped on the roof of their house. But then she'd died and rolled off when he wasn't looking. It would have been so simple if he'd died with her. He should have. Why didn't he?

It's over.

For once the sound of her voice was a comfort.

"Yes, Louise. It's over."

You will not kill again in my name.

Tears ran from the corners of his eyes, or maybe it was blood. It was difficult to tell.

You know they're going to find you now.

Pain rolled through his body, and then he felt another kind of pain. He turned to look and saw a rat chewing on his hand. He doubled up his fist, and the rat skittered away.

"That fucking hurt!" he yelled, then closed his eyes as he rode out a new wave of pain.

When he opened his eyes again he saw the noose swaying right above his head, back and forth, back and forth, and before he knew it he was caught in the hypnotic motion. All he kept thinking was that it was supposed to have ended a life. It was a shame to let it go to waste.

He rolled onto his side, then made it up on his hands and knees before dropping his head, too sick and dizzy to move farther. But he kept telling himself he couldn't quit now. He was tougher than this. It was the height of irony that he'd lived through a flood, an explosion and a tornado only to come to his end in such an ignoble fashion.

Gritting his teeth against the throbbing bone-deep pain in his head, he crawled to his van while the barn turned circles around him, and then managed to stand upright. He could hear sirens now. No time to waste. All he needed was the step stool.

He took a few staggering steps toward it, then stopped and threw up. By the time he was through, the sirens were louder, closer. He made another try at the step stool, and by the time he reached it, he was about to faint. He was seeing everything in triplicate, and finding it harder and harder to catch his breath. The sirens were screaming now, but it was okay. There was no breath left in him to scream for himself.

He pulled the step stool squarely beneath the noose and crawled on it, then stood up and made a last-moment grab at the rope to keep from falling. The barn was spinning faster as he pulled the noose over his head, settling it firmly around his neck.

The sirens tore holes in the air, shattering his concept of up and down. He closed his eyes and jumped just as the stool fell out from beneath his feet.

Tate drove past the broken foundation and the standing chimney toward what was left of an old barn.

Cameron had his gun out and his hand on the door when Wade pointed.

"There's a vehicle inside the barn!"

Tate hit the brakes, bringing the SUV to a stop a few yards back.

The state police were only seconds behind them, but they'd lost Inman twice already. Tate wasn't waiting.

"Fan out!" he ordered as they hunkered down in the grass to take cover and headed toward the barn in a crouch.

Cameron was less than twenty yards out when he caught a glimpse of something dangling from the rafters and stopped. The image was both startling and unexpected. If Inman was dead, then where was Laura? What the hell had he done to her first?

He started running, calling her name.

Wade saw him and yelled out, "Cameron! What the hell?"

"Inman's dead," Cameron said.

The state police cars came over the hill with lights

flashing. The high-pitched sirens sent birds into flight and animals into hiding as the trio entered the barn in a state of shock. After all of the grief and chaos Hershel Inman had caused, they would never have imagined the chase would end this way.

"He took himself out. Never saw that coming," Wade said.

Cameron was running through the barn, searching the granaries and behind every pile of junk, shouting Laura's name, but she didn't answer.

Tate spun on his heels and ran back to their SUV to get the iPad.

A half-dozen police officers swarmed inside with their weapons drawn. It didn't take long to figure out that they were still missing a victim, and when it appeared Inman had taken her location to his grave, they started searching through his van for clues.

Cameron's emotions were buried. The only thing on his radar was finding Laura. One way or another, he was taking her home.

He was about to climb up into the loft when Tate came running back into the barn.

"Cameron. Stop! Stop! She's not up there. Look at this!"

Cameron jumped down with a thud and grabbed the map. The blip was still there and motionless, but the location was off. Somehow she had moved since he'd looked at it last.

He ran outside with the map as the others followed. The pastureland in front of them was knee-high with brush, grass and weeds. According to the map, she was in there somewhere.

He thrust the iPad into Tate's hands and pointed. "She's out there somewhere! Fan out!"

Tate tossed the iPad in their car as he went past and then headed into the brush with the others. They were moving in tandem and only a few yards apart when Cameron began calling Laura's name.

Laura came to with the side of her face in the dirt and both arms flung over her head, obviously an unconscious attempt to break her fall. She rolled over onto her back, and the first thing she thought of was Inman. Was he looking for her now? Where was Cameron? Why hadn't he found her?

She felt for the necklace and when she realized it was gone, she sat up in a panic. If she lost that, he lost her.

She remembered feeling it between her breasts when she'd swung the crowbar at Inman's head but had no memory of it since. She saw the crowbar a few feet away. She must have dropped it when she fell. She crawled over to pick it up, and as she did, she saw something shiny in the dirt and rocks beneath.

It was the necklace!

This meant she hadn't lost Cameron after all.

The clasp was broken, but the cross was still there. Her hands were shaking as she put the necklace in the pocket of her jeans, then began to climb up the slope.

She was clinging to tree roots on the steep edge

of the drop, trying to get a better footing, when she began to hear a voice.

Someone was shouting!

She slid backward down the slope and hunkered down at the bottom, her heart pounding. It must be Inman, furious that she'd gotten away and in a rage to find her.

When the shouting got louder, she knew he was coming closer. She jumped to her feet, looking down the creek bed, then up the other way. Should she run, and if she did, which way should she go?

She was poised to bolt when the words became more distinct, and this time she recognized the voice. It was Cameron.

"Here! I'm here!" she screamed, and then started to climb.

Cameron froze in midstride and raised his arm, his hand open, the universal signal for stop.

"Stop! Everyone stop! I think I heard something!" He yelled again, "Laura! Where are you?"

"I'm here. I'm here!"

"Keep yelling!" he shouted, and started running. "Don't fall. I'm down here, but I'm coming up."

The men began moving forward at a lope, relieved that this was a rescue in progress and not a retrieval.

She was halfway up the slope when she heard noise above her and looked up. Cameron was on the ridge. Before she could call out, he was on his way down, running and sliding until he caught up with her. He rolled over on his back and took her with him, holding her tightly in his arms.

He couldn't talk without crying, and she couldn't quit crying long enough to talk. All that mattered was that she was safe. Twice she'd been lost, and twice he had found her. She didn't ever want to be lost from him again.

Twenty

The wedding day—September 28

Sarah had been home for two days, helping Laura with the final preparations, but time had gone all too fast. If there were details left undone, they would have to stay that way. The day was cold but clear. The church was packed, and Laura's phone was vibrating all over the table behind them. Who knew Cameron Winger would have turned into such an anxious groom? Did he honestly think, after all they'd been through, that she wouldn't show?

Laura glanced at the phone and smiled.

"Poor Cameron. Sarah, honey, hand me the phone—again—will you?"

Sarah stopped buttoning buttons long enough to pass the phone over, muttering as she went, "Dear

Lord, Laura! How many little satin-covered buttons are there down the back of this dress?"

"I believe there are fifty," Laura said.

Sarah looked up, her mouth slightly agape, as Laura winked at her and smiled.

"It's all about taking it off, not putting it on," Laura said, and then held up her finger as she answered the call. "Hello, my darling. I'm still here."

Cameron frowned. "I knew that. I was just checking to make sure you have everything you need."

"As soon as I have your ring on my finger I'll be perfect," she said softly. "I love you. Be calm. Everything will be fine."

"I love you most," Cameron said. "The pastor is here. He wants to know if—"

"It's all these buttons," Laura said.

There was a long moment of silence, and then she heard him clearing his throat.

"Buttons? There are buttons?"

"Yes."

"A lot?"

"Yes."

"Lord."

"Ten minutes, tops," Laura said.

"Got it," he said, and hung up.

"Just a few more to go and we're done," Sarah said.

Laura couldn't quit looking at the dress. She'd fallen in love with it the moment she'd tried it on. The slender line and lack of lace and ruffles was so her. A sweetheart neckline revealed just enough of her curvy breasts to be enticing and still demure. There was a slight flare at the hemline for easier walking. Sarah said it looked as if she had been dipped in white satin, then set out to dry.

There was a slight knock at the door, and then her bridesmaids, Nola and Jo, slipped inside.

"Oh, my stars, you look beautiful," Nola said softly. "Here, I have your 'something old.' Sarah said it's a handkerchief that belonged to your mother."

"There," Sarah announced, and stepped back. "The buttons are done, and the 'something new' is the garter she's wearing."

Jo kept watching Laura's face. After all she'd been through the past few weeks, Laura's expression of calm and stately peace was surprising. Laura Doyle was small, but inside she was an Amazon of a woman, and no one could deny it.

"I have your 'something borrowed,'" Jo said, and handed her a white leather version of the New Testament to carry with her bouquet.

"And I have your 'something blue,'" Sarah said as she put tiny blue topaz earrings in Laura's ears. The color perfectly matched her eyes.

"Are you going to leave the necklace on?" Jo asked, eyeing the little cross dangling between Laura's breasts.

"I'm here because of that necklace. It stays," Laura said.

"Then all you need is a penny in your shoe," Jo said.

Laura lifted the hem of her dress, revealing the heels she was wearing.

Jo gasped. "Are those Jimmy Choos?"

"Yep. Got a penny?"

Jo slipped the brand-new coin into the side of the shoe. Laura dropped the hem.

"You are so good to go," Laura said.

"We need the flowers," Sarah said, and dashed over to the table and began distributing bouquets. "What about the boutonnieres for the men?" she asked.

Nola smiled. "Tate's all over that."

Sarah handed Laura her bouquet, then leaned in and kissed the side of her cheek.

"I wish you and Cameron the best long and happy life ever, little sister."

Laura caught her sister's gaze. There were tears in Sarah's eyes, and Laura swallowed past the knot in her throat. They were both thinking about their parents, and wishing they were still there to share this day.

"Thank you, Sarah."

Her phone started vibrating again just as she turned around.

She rolled her eyes and laughed.

"Someone open the door and get me to the altar before Cameron has a stroke."

"Give me that phone," Wade said, then took it from Cameron's hand and laid it aside. "Just got a text from Jo. It's time, man. It's time."

Cameron bolted toward the door.

Tate put a hand on his shoulder and smiled.

"Walk, don't run."

Cameron stopped, then took a deep breath and started over.

He opened the door and stepped aside for them to go first.

"Let's do this," he said.

The pastor was waiting for them in the hall. He lined them up in the order they would enter the sanctuary, and then smiled.

"Gentlemen, if you would please follow me."

They walked into a church filled with their friends and coworkers, and went to stand before the altar.

Cameron's heart was pounding. His eyes kept tearing up, but he loved Laura too much to care who saw him cry. When the music began playing, they turned to look up the aisle toward the doorway.

Nola was the first to come down the aisle, holding a single white rose tied with a thin silver ribbon. The bridesmaids' gold silk dresses had been draped to fit their bodies in a soft, clinging style.

Jo came next, and the tiny bulge of her belly beneath the dress made the moment all the more poignant.

As maid of honor, Sarah was next, and the gold fabric of the dress was a perfect foil for her sleek blond hair. She walked with a bounce in her step and a smile on her face, happy for her sister's joy.

And then the music changed and everyone turned to look up the aisle.

The ache in Cameron's chest swelled as Laura appeared, resplendent in white satin with a bouquet of white roses clutched against her waist. Her long hair was piled high atop her head, with tiny tendrils falling down around her face and neck.

She looked so beautiful and so alone, standing at the end of the aisle without her father on her arm. Instead of waiting in place with the groomsmen, he took two steps forward until he was standing in front of the pulpit, and then held out his hand.

Laura had sailed through this day without a qualm until she saw Cameron standing at the end of the aisle. Tears came as the music swelled, and when he held out his hand, she started down the aisle, moving closer and closer to the rest of her life.

* * * * *

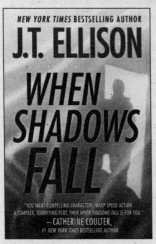

Book three in the heart-pounding
Brown & DeLuca series
from *New York Times* bestselling author

MAGGIE SHAYNE

To save innocent lives, they'll have to risk their own...

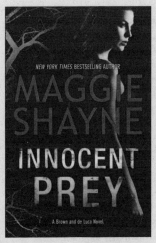

Rachel de Luca and detective Mason Brown have finally given in to their overwhelming mutual attraction, but neither one of them is ready for a full-blown romance. Then a judge's daughter disappears, and Rachel is certain it's connected to their most recent case: the abduction of her assistant.

The discovery of a string of missing women seems like a promising lead. But with no clear connection between these girls and the high-profile young woman, Mason will have to rely on his own well-honed instincts and Rachel's uncanny capacity to see through people's lies in order to catch the predator.

Available now, wherever books are sold!

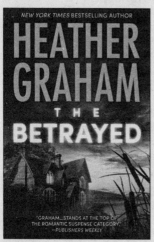

REQUEST YOUR FREE BOOKS!

2 FREE NOVELS
FROM THE SUSPENSE COLLECTION
PLUS 2 FREE GIFTS!

YES! Please send me 2 FREE novels from the Suspense Collection and my 2 FREE gifts (gifts are worth about $10). After receiving them, if I don't wish to receive any more books, I can return the shipping statement marked "cancel." If I don't cancel, I will receive 4 brand-new novels every month and be billed just $6.24 per book in the U.S. or $6.74 per book in Canada. That's a savings of at least 22% off the cover price. It's quite a bargain! Shipping and handling is just 50¢ per book in the U.S. and 75¢ per book in Canada.* I understand that accepting the 2 free books and gifts places me under no obligation to buy anything. I can always return a shipment and cancel at any time. Even if I never buy another book, the two free books and gifts are mine to keep forever.

191/391 MDN F4XN

Name _____ (PLEASE PRINT)

Address _____ Apt. #

City _____ State/Prov. _____ Zip/Postal Code

Signature (if under 18, a parent or guardian must sign)

Mail to the Harlequin® Reader Service:
IN U.S.A.: P.O. Box 1867, Buffalo, NY 14240-1867
IN CANADA: P.O. Box 609, Fort Erie, Ontario L2A 5X3

Want to try two free books from another line?
Call 1-800-873-8635 or visit www.ReaderService.com.

* Terms and prices subject to change without notice. Prices do not include applicable taxes. Sales tax applicable in N.Y. Canadian residents will be charged applicable taxes. Offer not valid in Quebec. This offer is limited to one order per household. Not valid for current subscribers to the Suspense Collection or the Romance/Suspense Collection. All orders subject to credit approval. Credit or debit balances in a customer's account(s) may be offset by any other outstanding balance owed by or to the customer. Please allow 4 to 6 weeks for delivery. Offer available while quantities last.

Your Privacy—The Harlequin® Reader Service is committed to protecting your privacy. Our Privacy Policy is available online at www.ReaderService.com or upon request from the Harlequin Reader Service.

We make a portion of our mailing list available to reputable third parties that offer products we believe may interest you. If you prefer that we not exchange your name with third parties, or if you wish to clarify or modify your communication preferences, please visit us at www.ReaderService.com/consumerchoice or write to us at Harlequin Reader Service Preference Service, P.O. Box 9062, Buffalo, NY 14269. Include your complete name and address.

SHARON SALA

32792	TORN APART	___ $7.99 U.S.	___ $9.99 CAN.
32785	BLOWN AWAY	___ $7.99 U.S.	___ $9.99 CAN.
32677	THE RETURN	___ $7.99 U.S.	___ $8.99 CAN.
32633	THE WARRIOR	___ $7.99 U.S.	___ $7.99 CAN.
31592	GOING TWICE	___ $7.99 U.S.	___ $8.99 CAN.
31548	GOING ONCE	___ $7.99 U.S.	___ $8.99 CAN.
31427	'TIL DEATH	___ $7.99 U.S.	___ $9.99 CAN.
31342	DON'T CRY FOR ME	___ $7.99 U.S.	___ $9.99 CAN.
31312	NEXT OF KIN	___ $7.99 U.S.	___ $9.99 CAN.
31264	BLOOD TIES	___ $7.99 U.S.	___ $9.99 CAN.
31241	BLOOD TRAILS	___ $7.99 U.S.	___ $9.99 CAN.

(limited quantities available)

TOTAL AMOUNT	$ _____
POSTAGE & HANDLING	$ _____
($1.00 for 1 book, 50¢ for each additional)	
APPLICABLE TAXES*	$ _____
TOTAL PAYABLE	$ _____

(check or money order—please do not send cash)

To order, complete this form and send it, along with a check or money order for the total above, payable to Harlequin MIRA, to: **In the U.S.:** 3010 Walden Avenue, P.O. Box 9077, Buffalo, NY 14269-9077; **In Canada:** P.O. Box 636, Fort Erie, Ontario, L2A 5X3.

Name: _____

Address: _____ City: _____

State/Prov.: _____ Zip/Postal Code: _____

Account Number (if applicable): _____

075 CSAS

*New York residents remit applicable sales taxes.
*Canadian residents remit applicable GST and provincial taxes.

H HARLEQUIN® MIRA®
™ www.Harlequin.com

MSS1014BL